FEB '75

APR 1992

JUL 98.

APR '92

JUL 1975

THE STRANGE CAREER
OF BISHOP STERLING

By

WALTER A. ROBERTS

(Stephen Endicott, psued.)

AMS PRESS
NEW YORK

THE STRANGE CAREER
OF BISHOP STERLING

A NOVEL BY

STEPHEN ENDICOTT

AUTHOR OF "MAYOR HARDING
OF NEW YORK"

THE METEOR PRESS

NEW YORK CITY   1932

Library of Congress Cataloging in Publication Data

Roberts, Walter, Adolphe, 1886-
    The strange career of Bishop Sterling.

I. Title.
PZ3.E5705St8 [PS3509.N367] 813'.5'2 73-18603
ISBN 0-404-11413-X

Reprinted from the edition of 1932, New York
First AMS edition published in 1974
Manufactured in the United States of America

AMS PRESS INC.
NEW YORK, N.Y. 10003

CONTENTS

THE STRANGE CAREER
OF BISHOP STERLING

1.

"HOT STUFF COMING"

Jeff Coates came out of his hotel feeling fuzzy despite a shave and massage. The nine o'clock Washington sun made him squint his eyes. He walked two blocks over to Pennsylvania Avenue, then turned on it toward the Capitol. The backs of his knees felt watery, and he knew his eyes were red-rimmed, but otherwise he was presentable. He straightened his shoulders slightly and just then caromed off a small man.

"Sorry!" he said, the jar shooting a pain up his neck into his head. "Oh, hello!"

The other stood back, opened his eyes, then put out a thin, hard hand which Jeff took. "Not in Richmond, Jeff?"

The younger man automatically fished a pack of cigarettes from his topcoat pocket, offered one, was refused, put it back after lighting up himself. "Bailey fired me last night, or afternoon."

"I'm sorry to hear that, Jeff. I really am." Congressman Shirley D. Vernon of Richmond, Virginia, assumed a compassionate expression. "Tell me what happened, son."

He reminded Jeff of an inbred collie, particularly when he smiled. His head, face and mouth were narrow, the voice resonant and the stature medium. Jeff explained:

3

"I got fired for misquoting you. I reported, 'Nullification Nothing New.' "

The Congressman looked at him steadily. " 'Nullification Nothing New.' Why, Jeff, I never said any such thing, even to a bunch of Yanks." He kept on looking.

Jeff stared back. "Why, of course not. My mistake. Anyway, when you called Bailey on it, he fired me. So here I am. I saw Veryl before I left."

"I didn't know it was you wrote that, son." Vernon used his collie smile. "I certainly—"

Jeff shrugged and threw his half-finished butt into the gutter. "All over now. No skin off my elbow. I'm goin' up the alley here to see Doc Sterling."

Before speaking again, Vernon turned, took Jeff's arm, and together they continued in Jeff's direction. "Why, that gives me my chance to do you a good turn after a bad one, son. I know Dr. Sterling right well. I'll take you up there myself."

Jeff said: "That'll be fine. Y'know, I've got a letter to him from the Bishop of my home town. Kansas City may be a hot spot, but we got a sure-enough Bishop. Pal of my old man's when the old gent was alive. So was Doc. Anyway, I thought maybe I could work for him. Richmond's not so far away 'n' I can duck down and see Veryl once in a while."

"I think that's a smart idea, son, I really do." Vernon kept the collie smile on his face. Jeff saw he was relieved. "I understand there's some hot stuff coming, what with a Catholic maybe goin' to get the Democratic nomination for President, and I know Dr. Sterling sure isn't going to like that. Hot stuff coming! You bet, Jeff!"

Jeff looked up at the building beside them. A Happiness

Candy Store took up the street front of the office building. "Here we are," he said.

They turned in, took the elevator to the fourth floor,
and were let out in the large anteroom of the Wesleyan
Board of Public Safety. Vernon advanced importantly to
face the prim, black-garbed receptionist.

"Good mornin', Miss James." The resonant voice was
in full play. "Is Doctor Sterling in?"

The spectacles looked at him. The girl rose, said, "I'll
see, Mr. Vernon," and went out. Vernon bestowed a nod
on Jeff.

The girl returned and an office door opened. She beckoned them in. There Jeff saw a very tall, very thin man.
Vernon started:

"Good morning, good morning! This is a young friend
of mine. Mr. Coates. This is the Reverend Mr. Craig.
Secretary here."

The tall, thin young man said impersonally: "You wish
to see Dr. Sterling?" He was looking at Jeff.

The ex-reporter took out of his inside jacket pocket
the letter to Dr. Sterling he had carried with him for four
months. "I have this to Dr. Sterling from Bishop Murdock of Kansas City. Perhaps if you—"

Craig reached for the letter. Jeff hoped he wouldn't
notice the trembling hand. Jeff always trembled after too
many whiskeys. Craig said, "Excuse me," and left the
office.

Vernon looked vaguely discomfited. Jeff stared out of
the window. Less than two minutes elapsed before Craig
reappeared and said, "Dr. Sterling will see you right away,
Mr. Coates. Do you mind waiting, Mr. Vernon?"

The Congressman did not hide a look of disappointment. Then he let out his smile. Turning to Jeff, "I won't wait, son. Anyway, look me up at the Willard when you have time. Good morning!" The resonant voice went away, and Jeff followed Craig into another and larger office. Behind the glass-topped desk set between and out from two windows sat a man who looked at the new-comer.

Jeff watched and heard Craig say, "Dr. Sterling, this is Mr. Coates who brings you the letter from Bishop Murdock. This is Dr. Sterling, Mr. Coates."

"Come in, Mr. Coates," said the Doctor. His voice was low and sounded tired. Craig left the unfolded letter on Sterling's desk, went to the door and said from there as an afterthought: "Oh, and Mr. Vernon was here with Mr. Coates. He—"

Sterling said, "You sent him away? All right."

Jeff advanced and said, "How do you do?"

The Doctor's face was neither fat nor thin, but had hard and deep lines on either side of thick lips that pressed together. The eyes held a hard, glassy stare through hexagonal spectacles, and the hands were clasped on the desk. Faintly purplish patches marred the mildly plump cheeks of the head of the Wesleyan Board of Public Safety.

Dr. Sterling said, "It is a great pleasure to have such a letter from my good friend Bishop Murdock. You come well announced."

"That's very nice of you. I understand you knew my father."

The Doctor's face twitched and his underlids quivered. "I knew your father well. We got our degrees at the same time. We were also young pioneers together."

Jeff knew enough of his father to know what that meant.

The Doctor added: "And I take it you want a job with us. Yes. We need young men. You have the right training." Jeff remembered his training: writing dry propaganda stories on a dry paper, though frequently too drunk to be sure of hitting the right typewriter keys. He didn't grin. The Doctor was talking, looking straight at Jeff. "We expect a very busy season, very busy indeed."

"I'm glad of that," Jeff said.

The Doctor smiled gently. "Besides, any son of Doctor Coates can work for me."

Jeff took a breath, and a chance. "I'm the only one I know of."

The Doctor stared for a second. His lips twitched, then he let out a prolonged chuckle. "Sit down, Mr. Coates. I believe we can talk business."

Jeff liked the Doctor right then. He sat down, wished he could smoke, and decided not to. "Where can I fit in here?"

"Hmmm. Not much difficulty there. Plenty of news to send out. We are a large and powerful organization, and this season—you will realize that we must oppose, as a religious body, the possible nomination of Jim White of New York?" The shrewd eyes behind the six-sided spectacles narrowed.

Jeff nodded. "Is that your plan?"

Sterling grew cautious again. "I wouldn't use that word." He smiled suddenly, genially. "The Democratic South will not support a Wet. However—" briskly—"we will talk of that another day. Suppose you see Mr. Craig now. He will arrange salary with you, and all that sort of thing. I will call you when I need you."

Jeff stood up. They shook hands, and Jeff left to seek Craig. With the tall, thin official Secretary he determined the necessary details and went out with instructions to return the next morning for regular work. A desk was assigned to him in the corner of still another office filled with clerks and files.

Jeff went back to his hotel room, wrote a short letter to Veryl Vernon in Richmond as follows:

"Honey:

Am landed with Dr. Sterling, as I told you I would maybe. Start tomorrow. At this rate the bankroll for our happy day won't be long in coming. I'll come to Richmond maybe next week-end.
                                                                        Jeff."

Then he lay down on the bed and slept until late in the afternoon. A change of clothes after a shower braced him for an early dinner, then he telephoned Vernon at the Willard.

The resonant voice floated to him over the wire. "Yes?"

"I got a job with Sterling," said Jeff. "Thanks for your help."

"I'm right glad, son. Just let me know if there's anything else I can do." Jeff thought of Craig sending the Congressman away.

"Thanks. I will. Give my love to Veryl."

"Surely I will. Good-bye, Jeff."

The next morning Jeff reported for work, went to his desk and sat down. He wanted to smoke and didn't dare.

That made him fidgety. He talked desultorily with the man next him, who was sending out circulars requesting contributions for the work of the Wesleyan Board of Public Safety. Sterling didn't call Jeff until after the lunch hour, during which the newest employe smoked eight cigarettes.

At two-thirty he went into the front office.

Now there were lots of papers on the Doctor's desk and an alert gleam animated the gray eyes behind the spectacles.

"How do you do, Mr. Coates? You're one of us now, eh?"

Jeff didn't answer, but sat down and waited.

The Doctor went right into it. "I have a very important job for you this afternoon. Very important. You musn't fail me."

"No reason why I should. What is it?"

The Doctor nodded as if answering some question to himself. Then: "You must carry a verbal message for me to Senator Blair. You will find him in Room 804 of the Willard Hotel. That clear?" A more incisive note now clipped the Doctor's words.

Jeff nodded. "Texas."

Sterling: "Senator Blair will forward the message I will give you, but that's apart from the matter in hand. This message is to request Senator Blair to tell the Texas Democratic organization not to nominate Drine in the Congressional primaries in San Antonio next month. He is not the sort of man we want."

Jeff wondered, but said, "Is he Wet?"

Sterling scowled. "He is, and as a Wet he can carry the Mexican vote in San Antonio, but that is not why the Wesleyan Board objects to him. We object to him because he is not a suitable man for the House. His personal life—why, Mr. Coates, we have learned that he has an illegitimate child in Laredo."

"Doing right by our Nell?" Jeff asked. He bit his lip to keep the grin off.

"That is not the point," snapped Sterling, looking away. "But that is enough for us to know."

"How'd he let it get out?"

The Doctor's eyes shot a look of triumph. "He didn't. We found it out. However, you must memorize this message to Senator Blair."

"Shoot."

Sterling went slowly: "Drine will not receive our support. His personal life prevents that. Suggest you give the nomination to Ranger."

Jeff repeated it slowly, stumbled, went over it twice more, then had it. Sterling opened his thick lips in a tiny smile. "Now, I will trust you to deliver that exactly. Senator Blair, Room 804. Let me know when you have finished."

Jeff went out, looking deliberately nonchalant, and found his way to Room 804 in the Willard. He knocked. A young man opened the door.

"Senator Blair?" Jeff walked in.

"Who is it?" asked the young man.

"Mr. Coates, from Bishop Sterling."

The youth became obsequious. "Go right in, Mr. Coates. Please."

Jeff walked into the next room. There he found Senator Charles Blair, Democrat, of Texas. A leviathan figure, topped by a round, rugged face and a shock of brown hair. Little eyes twinkled from among a nest of wrinkles.

"I'm from Bishop Sterling," said Jeff. "I have a message."

Blair's deep voice said, "What is it?"

Jeff grew curious for his own benefit and instead of delivering the message right away, said, "It's about the nomination of a Dry in San Antonio."

Senator Blair said, "What is the message?"

Jeff lit a cigarette. "'It's very simple. Here it is. 'Drine will not receive our support. His personal life prevents that. Suggest you give the nomination to Ranger.'"

He waited for a definite expression on the Senator's face, but nothing happened. The huge man simply nodded. Jeff grew uncomfortable, and finally said:

"It's clear to you, is it?"

"Perfectly."

"Any answer?"

The Senator considered, pursed his lips, said: "Well, yes. You may tell Dr. Sterling that his suggestion will be respected. Ranger will receive the nomination, even though a Wet Republican *could* take the district away from a Dry Democrat like Ranger. San Antonio is like that. Point that out to him."

Jeff nodded. He was enjoying himself with a feeling of being on the inside, of meriting confidence. He wondered how they had found out about Drine and his child in Laredo. Sterling had seemed proud of the feat. There was plenty of dirt here, even in this.

He got up and said, "I'll tell Dr. Sterling," and started for the door.

Senator Blair's voice boomed after him. "Tell him one more thing, Mr. Coates. Tell him you are to be trusted."

Jeff turned around, his face deliberately blank. "How do you know?"

The eyes twinkled among the wrinkles. "You gave me the message exactly as Dr. Sterling gave it to me over the phone."

The Senator boomed with laughter. Jeff went out, fast. "Confidence, hell!" he thought.

2.

SUITE 50, TASKER BUILDING

ON HIS return to the office, Jeff had to wait a few minutes before he could get in to report to Sterling. He lounged into the stock-room down the corridor from the reception clerk's desk, and watched a New England-looking spinster, thin and helplessly genial, giving a double-handful of Prohibition pamphlets to two other ladies who wore the same appearance of desperate amiability. They cooed at each other and the two went out. Jeff picked up a pamphlet called *Prohibition Change Unspeakable!* and was reading it when Craig appeared to him and croaked, "Bishop Sterling will see you now."

Jeff walked into the Bishop's office, Craig returning to his own. The gray eyes behind the hexagonal spectacles twinkled at him.

"The Senator says I'm to be trusted," Jeff declared, sitting down. "He said for me to tell you."

Sterling's eyes twinkled at him steadily. "I'm right glad, Mr. Coates. That was an important message."

Jeff made no answer, but waited. Sterling's expression sobered. The next words came from the back of his throat with a guttural rasp. He said, "I have a suggestion to make to you. I want you to study shorthand."

Jeff retorted, "I know shorthand. I went to business col-

13

lege once. I'm still good at it, but I'd rather not do that for a living. I took all my reporting notes in shorthand."

Sterling stared at him, considering. Jeff stared back. The Bishop leaned forward suddenly, and the guttural rasp was stronger. "I think you're to be trusted. But if you're not. . . ."

Jeff asked sharply, "What is this?"

"I expect loyalty."

"All right. Anyway, it would have to be a powerful reason to make me disloyal." Jeff kept his eyes widely open.

Sterling sat upright, seemingly relieved. "Tonight I am attending a meeting. Unofficial. I want notes, but I won't use any of the secretaries here. That's where you come in." The Bishop hesitated, his expression changing. "I perhaps should explain that in my work—which has so much to do with the secular world outside the Church—I need a . . . let us say right-hand man. The previous incumbent was Dr. Lamb—Templeton Lamb, but he has recently been made a Bishop. Besides, I never quite liked him. He would think that secular matters must be handled like Church matters. Now, I have thought this over carefully—you have come to me from two of my oldest friends, your father and Bishop Murdock. I hope that we will be able to work together." He gazed upon Jeff.

"I hope so. You can count on me."

"Very well. Be at the Tasker Building, Suite 50, at eight-thirty. Bring a notebook of some kind."

"Anything else?"

Sterling shook his head. Jeff started out, and heard the Bishop say, "Don't tell folks."

Jeff grinned back at him and went to his own desk. After

a few minutes of peering through the window at the graying
sky, he took his hat and coat and went out. He turned
toward the Capitol, walking slowly. He climbed the gentle
slope of Capitol Hill, crossed the parking space on that
side of the huge whitish structure, and dropped down toward the Tasker Building. Next to the latter was a ten-
story family hotel, The Dempsey, and to the right an empty
lot. He stopped where he was to look at the old redstone
pile, its lower story windows bearing the gilt-lettered firm
names of respectable law offices. Sterling had said Suite 50,
fifth floor, and there were only five. He'd see tonight.

Jeff went back to his hotel, stopping on the way for an
early dinner. Inside his room door, he found a phone message. Mr. Vernon wanted him to phone. He stuffed it in his
pocket.

At eight-ten he started, notebook in his pocket. At eight-
twenty-five he was ascending to the fifth floor of the Tasker
Building in a rickety metal open-work elevator, operated
by an undersized Negress. Left from the elevator shaft,
in a blind corridor, he found a wooden door, with a frosted
glass panel like all the rest, bearing in black digits the
number 50. He knocked. Bishop Sterling opened and let
him in.

"Good evening, Jeff." Jeff noticed the use of the first
name.

He dropped his hat and coat on a worn, black-leather,
backless divan immediately to the right of the door. He
followed Sterling out of the bare outer room, containing
only a series of half-empty book-shelves against the left-
hand wall into the next room. This was furnished with a
four-fringed imitation Persian rug, several old-style easy

chairs, each with a metal bar across the rear-arms to regulate the angle of the back cushion, a battered roll-top desk and two small tables covered with ash-trays, books, pencils, yesterday's newspapers and other small items. Through a farther door, Jeff saw, in a room of about the same size, one end of a cot-like bed and the edge of a bureau.

Sterling introduced him to the other men present. He nodded and sat down in an upright chair beside the desk. So far, he knew the names only. Prince, a middle-sized man with puffy cheeks and a garnet ring on the middle finger of each hand; Hillary, tall, spare, high-cheeked like an Indian, with protuberant brown eyes; and then three men whom Jeff grouped together. They sat in a row opposite him. They were plainly dressed, rusty as crows, with high black shoes, unpressed trousers and starched white collars. They had in common one thing—thin, compressed lips.

The middle one spoke now. "Can we begin?" Nobody answered. Sterling stood leaning against the door jamb. The middle crow crossed and re-crossed his legs impatiently. Sterling left the room in answer to a knock on the outer door. In ten seconds he returned with another visitor, who left his hat and coat with Jeff's on the outer divan.

Sterling introduced him. "Senator Seed."

Jeff sat up straight. He knew Seed's reputation for a pious but sharp-tongued politician from Arkansas. The Senator nodded around briskly, and placed himself gingerly on the last unoccupied easy chair. He said, "Let's begin. I hope I didn't hold you up." His eyes roved over the room, then settled on Jeff. Of Sterling he asked, "Who's this?"

The Bishop placed a straight-backed chair by the door for himself and sat down. "This is my own confidential secretary, Senator. He's all right."

Seed's eyes switched to the Bishop. "Meaning he's all right for you. Well, let's go ahead."

Sterling said to Jeff: "I'll tell you when to take notes. Now, Hillary, outline the situation to the Senator."

Hillary, the tall, spare man, cleared his throat. "We've come here, Senator, to get some advice. I hope you can help us."

Seed inclined his head ironically. "My fellow Senators are not always so polite. Go ahead."

Hillary went on. "Bishop Sterling thinks we got to try and prevent the nomination of Governor Jim White of New York by threatenin' to break up party regularity in the delegations to the conventions. That's what we're tryin' to do in Mississippi. On'y we ran head-on into a snag. We got a leader there we can't bring into line."

Sterling's voice, containing the guttural rasp Jeff had heard earlier that day, cut in. "Here's the point, Senator. It isn't everywhere we can get folks to revolt on religious grounds. I think we can in Mississippi. Now, it's up to these boys to whip the obstructionist into line—no matter how!"

Hillary continued. "We talked ourselves hoarse to him. But he won't listen. He says he's the leader of the Democratic Party in his county, and that he ain't goin' to go back on freedom of conscience and free speech. That's all he says."

"He's a Catholic, isn't he?" Sterling asked confidently.

The middle crow snapped, "French mother. She's dead, but he keeps it up."

Seed grinned suddenly and said to Sterling: "You

brought Prince and Hillary here. I don't see what you need me for."

The Bishop did not grin in reply. "We need your political advice, Senator."

Seed snorted wrathfully. "The deuce you do! This is no question of politics. It's religion. What's the idea of wasting my time?" He stood up.

Sterling said smoothly: "Don't go, Senator. We really need you. The moral forces in your State would approve of your helping us. I wouldn't go if I were you."

Seed looked at him, hard, then sat down. He blinked. "All right. Get on with it."

Sterling began. "Smeath, do you think the voters will follow that county leader?"

Smeath, the third crow, spoke for the first time. "He's right strong in the district! But they won't follow him if *we* come out against him. We can, too!" His eyes blazed suddenly. The other two nodded.

Hillary said, "I reckon we cu'd raise the countryside against him."

Prince volunteered: "We could make a special distribution of our paper in that district whenever you say." Jeff spotted him for the managing director of *The American People,* the anti-Catholic, anti-Jew, anti-alien paper published weekly in Washington.

Sterling: "You-all talk like mealy-mouthed schoolboys! I want action. Raise the country!" Sterling's gray eyes blinked rapidly. "You bet I'm going to make you tear things wide open!"

Hillary asked respectfully, "What d'you want us to do?"

"Several things. First of all, make sure how many people will stay with us before you take real action. Then declare war on the rest—get 'em good! Isn't that right, Senator?"

Seed gibed, "God help me if I ever get on your bad books!"

Sterling ignored that, and continued, "Now, you— Smeath, Cobbett, Harmsworth—you tell the Mississippi Wesleyan Conference I want all the brethren out against Jim White. And at next month's meeting. Then you ministers denounce White from your pulpits. The Wesleyan Church, little by little, is coming out against White. Is that clear?"

Smeath said, "I wouldn't make it so official. They's people who don't like politics in the pulpit."

Sterling waved a hand. "They'll like it. You do as I tell you. Now, Prince, can you put twenty thousand copies down in Mississippi?"

Prince clasped his pudgy hands. "Give us the money."

Sterling grunted.

Prince added, "I can't give you an exact quotation. You'll want the papers for several months. Between three and four thousand dollars."

Hillary figured briefly on the back of an envelope. "If it don't go over four thousand, I reckon we can do it. We got near that in the treasury now, and we can collect more."

"That takes care of that." To Prince, Sterling added: "Be sure you get some strong stuff about this man in the issues you send down there. It won't be wasted on the rest of your readers anyway."

He continued, after a momentary silence. "Now, the most important thing of all. What can you *do* to this man?"

Nobody answered. Their faces remained blankly inquiring. The Bishop spoke impatiently. "Hillary, you! What can you do? You must frighten him."

Smeath said calmly, "I should think we *will* frighten him."

"Not that way. I mean by using your Klan people. Does he own property?"

Hillary, Mississippi Klan leader, answered: "Sure he does. He's right rich, I reckon. Has a plantation."

"Then you'll have to stage a demonstration against him in the nearest town. You know how to do that."

Seed protested. "I don't think you'll have to go that far."

Nobody paid any attention. The Bishop continued: "Find some reason for a demonstration. If you can't find one, invent it. Burn his fields, or march to his house. Put him in fear of his life. He's a rich Catholic. That ought to be enough for you. And you preachers, attack him every Sunday in your churches. It won't take long for something to happen. He'll probably come back with some line of talk that will give you an excuse for attacking him with the Klan."

Cobbett challenged gruffly: "Suppose all this don't have an effect! His county is right on the Louisiana line, where there's other Catholics."

The Bishop gestured toward Prince. "His paper will keep it up, anyway. And you've got a lot of time before election, even if White is nominated. Nothing must stop you!"

The Senator from Arkansas cleared his throat. "You may be doing all this for nothing. This will be waste effort if somebody else is nominated. White is by no means sure to get it."

"We will have prevented his nomination, then. A Dry Democrat is certainly acceptable."

"Here's hoping! I'd like to see you free to work with your old friend Taitt, in Virginia," Seed grinned.

Sterling frowned. "Senator Taitt and I—well, we'll see!"

Hillary stood up. "I reckon we're through, gentlemen."

"Just so. My political advice was very valuable to you. You couldn't possibly have reached a decision without it, could you?" said Seed.

"Let's say that your mere presence served the cause," the Bishop replied, glancing sideways at the waspish Senator. "Wait a minute. Jeff, take this down—" He summarized the decisions made. "Let me have that in the morning."

"Okay."

"There's to be no copy for yourself, young man," Seed told him.

"Of course not."

Sterling glowered at Seed, then said to Jeff, "There's a typewriter and paper in this desk. Suppose you use it now."

Jeff said nothing, but as the others left—Hillary and the three parsons together, Prince and then Seed—he typewrote what Sterling had dictated to him. Inside of ten minutes, he had bade the Bishop goodnight and was walking through Capitol Park on the way to his hotel. He wished that Sterling had not insisted on his tearing out of his notebook the pages of shorthand notes he had just typed.

It was just ten-thirty when he entered the lobby of the Lathrop Hotel and, in a chair opposite the newspaper and cigar stand, found Representative Vernon sitting. The latter rose quickly when he saw Jeff and said:

"Son, I've been waitin' for you since nine o'clock. Didn't you get my message?"

Jeff recalled the phone slip in his pocket. "I didn't have time to call you, sir. Veryl sick, or something?"

"Veryl?" Vernon was surprised. "No, no, she's all right. It's something else. Will you walk out with me?"

They went out into the street and turned past the White House. Vernon said hurriedly, "I've been thinking, son, about you and Doctor Sterling ever since I got you that job up there yesterday, and—"

"I like it up there," Jeff drawled. "Only you can't smoke. That gets on my nerves."

Vernon laughed without humor. "Well, I was thinking. After all, you're goin' to marry Veryl some day, and it seems to me. . . ." He stopped.

Jeff suggested: "You don't want too close a connection with Sterling in Richmond? That it?"

The Virginia representative protested. "No, no, son. Not that. Bishop Sterling's Board of Public Safety in Richmond is a great help to me politically. But I thought maybe I could get you a better job."

"That all?" asked Jeff.

Vernon said, "Yes," without looking at him.

"Where are we going?" Jeff inquired, as Vernon steered him around a corner.

"You'll see. Now, a better job for you, I thought, would be, perhaps, with Senator Randolph Taitt of Virginia. I think you would be valuable to him."

"You're not taking me to see him at eleven P. M. just because you *think* so."

Vernon cackled and produced the collie grin. "That's right, Jeff. I talked to him, and he wants to meet you."

Jeff made no comment. After two more blocks they entered the lobby of a four-story apartment house. Vernon

led him to an apartment on the second floor. A Negro
butler admitted them to a small but very luxuriously furnished suite of rooms. The study featured a large Colonial
desk, behind which sat a small, sandy-haired man with a
pugnacious jaw and an upper lip curled back curiously
against his teeth. He came around the desk, shaking hands
with Vernon, who said:

"Senator, this is Mr. Coates."

Taitt barked genially: "I'm right glad Mr. Vernon could
bring you up tonight. Make yourself at home here. Will
you have a drink?"

"Please."

The Negro brought them Scotch highballs. Taitt passed
cigars.

"Mr. Vernon tells me you're with Bishop Sterling."

"Just started," replied Jeff.

"That's very interesting," Taitt remarked. He took a
long swallow of highball. "After Vernon mentioned you to
me this afternoon, I asked him to bring you because I
thought you might be interested in coming with me."

"As what?"

Taitt smiled slowly: "You understand, of course, that I
have many political activities here and in Virginia, and
there is always room for a smart young man. Campaigns,
and so forth."

Jeff drank and smoked in silence. He looked at Vernon
and at the tiny Taitt, who had a peppery reputation. Good
man to work for, probably. Jeff said finally:

"I like the job I've got, anyway for the time being."

"I can pay—" began Taitt energetically.

Jeff shook his head. "The Wesleyans pay pretty well,
too. Point is, I don't think I'd be much use to you—now."

Vernon protested. "That's foolish, son. You'd be very useful to Senator Taitt. Why—"

But the toy bulldog of a Taitt rubbed his palms together. "Smart boy! I think he's right." He lit a fresh cigar. Looking straight at Jeff, he said, "We might have another talk in the future, when you think the right time has come."

"You bet, Senator."

A few minutes later, Jeff and Vernon were walking back the way they had come. After a while Jeff remarked. "I'm going to ask you a question, and I'd like a straight answer."

"You know that anything you ask—"

"This is it. Is Bishop Sterling a trustful feller?"

Vernon walked several paces in silence. "I'll tell you. Your predecessor, so to speak, was made a Bishop. And Sterling never quite liked him. Lamb—his name was— really wasn't the right sort. Besides that, Sterling never took to anybody the way he has to you." Pause. "That's what interests people."

"Interests me, too."

3.

A SENATOR'S BROTHER
ENTERTAINS

THE FOLLOWING morning Jeff spent wandering through the Wesleyan Building. In the waiting room on the second floor he came across Craig reading proofs of a new pamphlet.

"Morning. Anything I can do to help?"

Craig glanced up, without expression. "No, thanks."

Pause.

Jeff: "I'm not very busy."

Craig gave him a routine smile. "I don't believe there's anything you can do. Hasn't Bishop Sterling given you any more confidential work to do?" The dour face retained the empty smile.

Jeff said: "No." Then: "Sorry I can't help," and walked away.

He loafed in the room where literature was given out, he conversed about the weather with the reception clerk, he went to the men's room to smoke secretly; then, in desperation, he spent an hour and a half over luncheon and a copy of the Washington *Post* in a cafeteria two blocks away. At two-fifteen he was back at his desk where he found a memo:

"Please come to my office when you return. T. H. S."

Jeff went directly to the Bishop's door, knocked and walked in.

The gray eyes behind the hexagonal glasses looked at him briefly and the gray head nodded him to a seat. "Got a little job for you."

"Fine. I haven't anything to do."

Sterling flicked a narrow look at him. "Senator Seed called—"

Jeff cut in. "Before we get to that, let me ask something. Why is Craig sore at me?"

"Craig?" Sterling faced him, eyes open. "Angry at you?"

"Barked at me this morning—out of a blue sky. Is he worried about last night?"

"What do you care if he is?"

Jeff shrugged. "I don't. If you don't."

Sterling smiled pleasantly. "I don't."

Jeff said, "Senator Seed called and . . .?"

Sterling took up again doubtfully. "He wants a transcript of a certain part of last night's proceedings." The full, tight lips pursed up. "I don't know."

Jeff said nothing.

The full lips opened again. "You take down on the machine there what I dictate to you. Then take it over to his office across the way."

Jeff moved to the chair before a secretarial desk, removed the cover from the typewriter, inserted one sheet of paper and looked at Sterling. The Bishop took from his pocket the sheet Jeff had typed out the night before, scanned it, then said:

"All right. Here we are. 'We are to attempt, by means of the proper political pressure, to influence the convention delegates of the Thirteenth Congressional District of Mississippi to pledge themselves not to vote for Jim White. Hillary, Prince, Cobbett, Smeath, Harmsworth, will co-operate.' "

Jeff typed quickly. He heard Sterling say, "I reckon he wants those names."

"That the only paragraph that has 'em?" Jeff gave the newly typed sheet to the Bishop, who answered:

"Yes," and, folding the paper twice, inserted it in a plain, long, unaddressed envelope and gave it to the younger man. "You'll find his office over there," jerking his head toward the left-hand window, through which could be seen the long, whitish, sprawling bulk of the Senate Office Building.

Jeff put the envelope in his pocket, collected his hat and coat from the outer office, and, once outside, walked swiftly across the avenue and up the gradual slope to the front entrance of the building. A directory told him the Senator's office number, second floor. He found the wide, winding staircase and started up. Half-way, on the curve, he stopped, looked above and below. There was no one. He drew from his pocket the unaddressed envelope, whisked out the sheet, and on an envelope of his own jotted in shorthand the paragraph he had just typed. Then he re-placed the typed sheet in the plain envelope and continued on his way.

On a tall mahogany door, he found a tiny brass plate:

MR. SEED

He turned the ponderous doorknob and went in. He found himself facing a large mahogany secretarial desk with a hand and an upright phone, a stack of magazines, a litter of miscellaneous papers, but no one seated there. A black leather divan blocked the double window at the other end of the room, a bookcase stood at the left, beside a row of three wooden arm chairs for visitors. Opposite the bookcase was another door, closed, leading into the inner office. Jeff sat down and looked around the room.

On the mantel was a bust of Thomas Jefferson, and on the wall near the window hung a large framed collection of Jefferson engravings. There was no sound. Then the main door opened and a young man walked in. He wore a topcoat with the collar turned up, a battered gray felt hat, and a meditative smile. He sauntered up to the secretarial desk, shuffled the papers, then turned to Jeff.

"Waitin' to see the Senator?"

"Is he in?" asked Jeff.

The young man smiled more amiably, sauntering over to face Jeff. "No. I b'lieve the Whip called him over to the Senate. Some special vote, I guess. I'm the Senator's brother."

Jeff waited.

"I don't b'long here, I s'pose, but maybe I can help you, seein' as the Senator ain't here himself."

"Maybe you can," Jeff said. Then he took out his cigarettes, offering Seed one, lighting one himself. Seed sat down beside him.

"Anything special you wanted to see him about?"

"Yes. How long will I have to wait?"

Seed rambled: "Oh, I wouldn't advise you to wait. Are you the feller he expected from the Wesleyan Building? Said you'd have a paper for him, or something like that." He paused. "Say, you can trust me, all right. The Senator told me all about it."

Jeff looked at him sidewise. "Looks as if he did. Well, here's the envelope. What will you do with it?"

The Senator's brother took the plain envelope gingerly between thumb and forefinger, and grinned. "Oh, he told me just what to do with it! You watch." He went to the secretarial desk, took from it another long envelope and crammed the first one into it. He sealed the outer one, running a large and very red tongue along its flap, pasted it down, and wrote on it. He came back and held it under Jeff's nose. "There. That's just what he told me to do."

"That's fine. Now what?"

"Now I take it over to the Senate and send it in to him."

Jeff looked at him. "Going over now?"

Seed grimaced. "Say, I don't think you trust me, do you?"

Jeff stood up and smiled. "Sure I trust you. I only asked because I'm going that way myself and I thought we could walk on over together. That's all."

Young Seed's face broke into a relieved smile. "Oh, I see. Gosh, I thought you maybe was scared I would steal it or something! Shoot, I wouldn't do that!"

"Of course not. Let's go."

They left the office, tramped the long marble corridors, and strolled toward the Capitol.

Seed said, "Don't mind my askin' you if you work for the Wesleyan Board, do yuh?"

"No, I don't mind. I work for Bishop Sterling."

Seed whistled a low note. "Yuh do, eh?" Then he shot a new kind of glance at Jeff. "You don't look like that kind of feller to me. I always thought they was sort of sour-lookin' old guys."

"Maybe I'll get that way," said Jeff. "I feel pretty spry now, though."

Another idea struck Seed. "Say, you must be a big shot up there. Judgin' from what my brother the Senator said, this paper is mighty important. They wouldn't be sendin' just an office boy with it."

"I'm not an office boy, if that'll help you any." Jeff lit another cigarette.

"No, I s'pose not." Seed walked in silence. Jeff saw he was thinking heavily. Then: "Say, why don't you drop around to my place tonight? I'm givin' a little party. You know, end of the session and all."

"I might do that. What's the address?"

"43 K Street, first floor. I got a little apartment there. It's gonna be just a few friends, and a few drinks. Very friendly."

"That's nice of you. I'll try and get there."

They reached the Senate entrance. Jeff started on with a "See you later," when Seed held him.

"I'd sure like to have yuh come, all right. Any time after eight." His amiable face was serious.

Jeff said, "Sure. I'll do my best." He walked on, turned a few feet on to smile back and saw young Seed going purposefully up the steps. Jeff turned, cut a little down the hill, then went back to the Senate Office Building. Inside the front entrance he found an aged man in attendant's uniform.

Jeff asked him, "Have you seen Senator Seed's brother this afternoon?"

Aged gray lips puckered thoughtfully. "No, I ain't seen him, sir. Might try the Senator's office."

"Thanks. That man's so hard to find, you'd think Senator Seed didn't have a brother," Jeff smiled.

The old white head wagged. "Oh, the Senator's got a brother all right! Yes, sir. That way, sir, to his office."

"Thanks a lot." Jeff walked down the corridor and out the wing entrance. In three more minutes he was back at his desk.

It was nearly nine when Jeff found the white numerals 43 on the door of a three-story remodeled private home on K Street. The shades of the first-floor window were down, but the windows themselves had been put up. The babble of voices and radio music floated out. Jeff went in, found the apartment door open and walked in.

A shout greeted him. "Hi, there!" Young Seed was on him, one arm around his shoulders in comradely fashion. "Glad you could come, old fella. Let me take your hat and coat."

Jeff said, "Thanks," gave him his things which Seed hastily threw on an already overloaded hat rack just inside the door. Then he took Jeff's arm. "Let me introduce you . . . say, I don't even know your name!" The amiable brother of the Senator giggled.

"Jeff Coates."

"Jeff Coates. Okay, Jeff. My name is Ben—Ben Seed. Ben."

Jeff smiled, lighting a cigarette. Ben Seed introduced him to men and women hastily, jovially, so that Jeff caught only names. Voorhees—he guessed that was George Voorhees, correspondent of the New York *Express;* Dixie Siegel—but he couldn't remember to which of several young girls that belonged; Vegas—Berry—Whitton—he'd identify them later.

"Just a second—I'll get you a drink." Ben vanished into a rear room.

Conversation, laughter, picked up again. Jeff looked around for a place to settle. He saw a dark, pretty girl looking at him from a corner. She was alone. Jeff walked over to her.

"Mind if I find myself a place to sit—even if it's here?" He sat down on the small backless divan beside her.

"Not at all. Got a cigarette? I always run out at the beginnings of parties."

She lit up. "Help me identify some of these people. I hate not knowing who belongs to what name. Who's Voorhees?" Jeff said to her.

The girl switched her veiled black gaze to other persons in the smoke-filled room. "Voorhees is the Washington man for the *Express*. There he is talking to that little fat man." Jeff saw a medium-sized man in a double-breasted brown suit, with a strong European air about him.

"Who's the little fat man?"

The low clear voice of the girl said, "Nobody at all. Who are you?"

"Jeff Coates is the name. Like it?" He smiled at her. Her lips were dark red, only slightly rouged, he judged.

She smiled slowly and nodded as if it didn't mean much one way or another. "Joe Whitton, over there by the hatrack, that's Senator Crookes' secretary."

Jeff singled out an ill-put-together individual leaning against the door jamb with a glass in his hand. Angular shoulders, a knobby bald head, bony hands. "And the man with him is Bill Vegas, Congressional secretary of Tom Herron."

"From Tidewater, Virginia?"

The girl nodded.

"Is he as poisonous as his boss?"

"What's the matter? Don't you like Herron?"

Jeff said: "I ran into him a couple of times, and he and I don't get along."

The dark girl said amusedly: "Sounds as if he stole your girl."

Jeff grinned at her behind a cloud of tobacco smoke. "Not him. He makes passes at her, though."

Ben Seed's voice sounded from the other end of the room. "Dixie! C'mere a minnit!"

The girl by Jeff's side got up and answered the call. Jeff placed her as Dixie Siegel. He got up and strolled over to Voorhees, whom he now found seated alone by the window.

"Need air?" Jeff asked.

Voorhees nodded without expression. "Nice girl, that."

"Helpful, anyway. Where'd she get the crazy name?"

The newspaperman smiled thinly under his close-clipped brown moustache. "Claims she's descended from General Siegel of Missouri."

"It could happen," said Jeff. He liked the smart way Voorhees dressed, even though an ochre tie against a blue shirt was better for morning wear.

"Ben tells me you work for Doc Sterling."

"Didn't he also tell you I am free, white, over twenty-one, have a mole in the middle of my back and am intermittently nice to my aged grandmother?"

Voorhees smiled again, sympathetically. "He chatters, all right. But you meet people here."

A burst of voices at the door distracted them. The room was getting crowded. Ben greeted them, dashed over to give Jeff his drink, dashed away again. The dark girl returned to her former seat, another man with her.

Voorhees asked. "You new around here?"

Jeff nodded. "Three-four days."

"Then you're just in time for the excitement. Wait'll the convention. H'lo, Joe!" Voorhees extended a well-kept hand to the rawboned man, Joe Whitton, Senatorial secretary to Senator Crookes. "This is Mr. Coates."

The angular face split in a friendly smile. "Ben was telling me you'd be here. I hear Bishop Sterling is going out for blood this summer."

Jeff said, "Blood?"

Voorhees laughed. "Blood is right! The old coot will nail Taitt and Tom Herron to the mast some time."

"I didn't know Sterling had it in for Herron."

Whitton guffawed. "Hasn't got it in! Oh, boy!"

"Well, it suits me. I—" He felt his arm taken by a soft hand. Dixie Siegel was joining them.

"Pardon me, gentlemen, but I'm getting left alone in the corner. Can I spoil your fun?"

"Let me get you another drink," said Whitton eagerly. He left them. Voorhees stood up, his face faintly reddened by the two drinks he had had and the stuffiness of the room. "I'm going out for a breath," he said. That left Jeff again with the descendant of General Siegel. They reoccupied the divan.

"You know all these people?"

She was sitting up, leaning on one straight arm, her cheek against her shoulder. She smiled, very friendly. "Oh,

I know a lot of people here in Washington. But I never knew a Wesleyan insider before."

Jeff took out an envelope from his inside pocket, holding it on his knee. His right hand groped for a pencil. Her eyes were downcast. "Let me put down your phone number." He followed her gaze, saw she was looking at the envelope. He had brought out the one having on its back the shorthand notes he had made that afternoon in the Senate Office Building. He turned the envelope over, wrote "Dixie Siegel," and then, at her dictation: "District 4607." He put that down and restored the envelope to its place.

"I'll get some fresh drinks."

He went to the back room, pushed his way past increasing groups of people and mixed two highballs. He had some trouble finding ice, gave it up, and when he returned to Dixie, found Ben there. Whitton had disappeared. Dixie smiled at him, secretly. Ben was saying, "Gosh, Dixie, I gotta keep these people entertained—H'lo, Jeff." Ben looked at him with vague sourness.

"You go right ahead, Ben. I'll be happy," Dixie said, looking straight at Jeff.

Ben hesitated, then went away. Jeff sat down. Dixie's arm brushed his. He lit a match for her, and her hand held his a fractional second.

"It's very close in here," said Jeff.

She took a deep draw on her cigarette. Then she stood up. "Wait a minute. I'll get my things. We can break away." She left him before he could answer. He sought out Voorhees, back from his airing.

"I'm ducking along. I'll drop in your office some day."

The cosmopolitan-looking man nodded. "Be glad to see you. We could have dinner together."

Jeff plucked his hat and coat from the heap and slipped out. In another minute, Dixie joined him on the stoop. She took his arm, squeezed it and said, "This is better," taking a deep breath of cooler air.

A cab took them to a large apartment building not far from Executive Avenue and the State Department Building. She led him to a door on the street. "I use a doctor's apartment."

"Good idea. More freedom." He noticed that the main entrance to the building was around the corner.

She led him into a large front room, lowered the shades. "I'll mix a drink in a minute." She disappeared into the bedroom, where she stayed about five minutes. Jeff lit a cigarette, inspected the room, which was well, but not luxuriously, furnished. Facing a mock fireplace was a divan, and against the left hand wall was a cretonne-covered day bed. When Dixie returned, she had changed her dress for a heavy silk wrapper of black silk with small Chinese golden dragons climbing sparsely over it. Black silk mules on her feet completed the outfit. The very white skin of her face and neck made the dark red lips stand out. She smiled cozily at him, and mixed drinks at a liquor cabinet. Then she joined him on the divan.

"What do you do around here? In Washington, I mean." Jeff drank deeply, refreshed. He tasted the whiskey strongly.

She stretched luxuriously. "Oh, different things. Mainly I specialize in knowing people."

"No job?"

"Now and then." She took his already empty glass and refilled it. Then she fixed another for herself. "Right now I'm not doing anything. Going to be in Washington long?"

Jeff felt in himself a great feeling of friendliness. He took her white hand and kissed it. "Long enough," he said, gently beaming. Ben's gin and this Scotch were giving him a quick glow.

"How do you like your work?"

"I like it all right. It's fine. Doc Sterling is a great old guy, and for some reason or other he's taken a fancy to me. Well, why not? I'm bright and deceptively disreputable looking. Ideal for the Wesleyan Board. I sh'd think you'd be swell for them too. Wiggle your way into all kinds of places, I bet."

"Oh, I do that without working for your Doc Sterling!" She stood up. "Ready for another?"

"I bet you do. Let's wait a minute. You're makin' 'em pretty potent." He liked her looks: her short blue-black hair, the way her eyelids drooped. He said: "Do your eyelids droop naturally, or do you do that?"

She returned from the cabinet with refilled glasses and sat down. She handed him one. "They're that way of their own accord, thank you. Like 'em?"

Without saying anything, Jeff leaned over and kissed her on the lips. Then he took her glass, giving her his own in exchange: "You're not makin' yours as strong as mine and I'm only a young feller."

"Jeff!"

"What?"

"We'll be good friends, won't we? I want to know what funny things you have to do."

He grinned. "Sure we'll be good friends." He noticed they were both getting a little drunk. "Come on, bottoms up."

"No, I can't."

"Come on!" They drank. She coughed, spluttered. "There, there!" He rocked her in his arms. On the release, her lips brushed his cheek.

He got up and went to the cabinet. "Come on, here's another."

"No more, Jeff, please!"

He poured out a half-finger for himself, and half the tumbler for her, filling up both glasses with ginger ale. He rejoined her.

"This is first edge I've had in Washington. You're an angel."

"Ben Seed'll be sore as hell." She giggled.

Jeff waved an arm. "A drink to Ben Seed, my pal."

She was drunk and so was he. Again she coughed and spluttered. "You made that too strong, Jeff." She giggled again.

"No stronger than mine, sweetheart." He took her in his arms again, her head fell back on his shoulder, her lips slightly parted. He kissed her hard. She stood up, breathing heavily. "I want a drink of water." She walked uncertainly toward the kitchen, then turned to the divan. "Oh, boy, am I—"

She lay down. Jeff stood up, walked toward her. She smiled very slowly, very vaguely, her lips now pale red. Then suddenly she was sleeping peacefully. He picked up her hand, dropped it. It fell like dead flesh. He lit a cigarette and stuck his head out an open window for several lungfuls of fresh air. Then he extinguished the cigarette, went into the bedroom and opened her bed, first taking two extra blankets from the foot into the other room. These he threw over Dixie, then he put out the light. Inside of five minutes he was fast asleep in her bed.

He awoke at eleven-fifteen in the morning at the sound of a nearby church bell. He remembered it was Sunday. He felt woolly. He got up, found the bathroom and took an icy shower, then dressed. Dixie still slept in the other room. In the kitchen he made strong black coffee and some toast which he put on a tray. This he placed on the center table and shook the girl. She stirred and opened her eyes, staring at him in surprise.

"How do you feel, sweetheart?"

She looked at him. "What did you feed me in that drink?"

"Nothing but Scotch, but plenty of that." Jeff grinned down at her. "Have some coffee."

She sighed, and sat up on the edge of the divan. "That was a bum trick." She lit a cigarette.

Jeff munched a piece of toast. "Where'd you learn to read shorthand? And why are you so interested in the Wesleyan Board?"

"Bright boy. Ever since—well, I've known it a long time. Show me that envelope." She poured coffee for herself.

He sat her on his knee before she picked up the cup, and said, "I'll show you nothing, but we'll be good friends."

She stared at him somberly, then kissed him.

4.

HERRON'S SILENT WITNESS

"MISS BLANTON is supposed to have reserved a room for me," Jeff told the desk clerk.

"Yes, Mr. Coates. Just a moment, please." The clerk ducked behind a partition, giving Jeff a chance to survey the lobby of Murphy's Hotel, Richmond headquarters of Virginia politicians. Large, musty portraits of Confederate Generals—Fightin' Joe Johnston, Jeb Stuart, Marse Robert—hung under the high gilt ceiling. A bus line desk, a telegraph station, both bedecked with tourist posters, cluttered the space.

"Boy! Room 932. The boy will take you to your room, sir."

Jeff followed the bellhop into the aged elevator and to Room 932, which contained a brass double bed sagging slightly amidships, a tapestry-covered armchair with hassock, a bed-table with lamp, an imitation mahogany bureau, and one window looking out on Broad Street. Jeff tipped the boy and was left alone. He unpacked, cleaned up and then made a telephone call.

"Hello, Miss Blanton? This is Jeff Coates. Bishop Sterling said you expected me." He listened and then said, "Two o'clock is fine," hung up and went downstairs for lunch. At two o'clock he knocked at the door of a room on the second floor. A voice said, "Come in."

After he had shut the door behind him, he faced a woman of about forty-five, though spinsterhood may have added five years to her appearance. A soft round face was the indeterminate background for blue-gray eyes behind pince-nez. Graying brown hair was drawn fairly tight toward the back, and there was no ornament of any kind decorating the front of the dark brown dress.

"So glad to meet you, Mr. Coates. The Bishop has written me so much about you in the last week or so."

"That's very nice," Jeff said.

Clara Blanton sat down; so did Jeff.

The very sweet, soft voice continued: "I am glad Dr. Sterling suggested you come down here now, because there is a great deal to do, Mr. Coates, a great deal."

Jeff smiled dutifully. "I'm ready for lots of work. Have you anything you want me to start on right away?"

The full, colorless lips made as if to kiss. Then: "Why, there are several things—we are temporarily working under the name of the Virginia Board of Public Safety. There is a little money, Mr. Coates. Not much, for we must fight our fight without a great deal of assistance." She inclined her head at him, and he nodded.

She continued, "Do smoke if you wish. There's an ash tray . . . yes . . . now my duties here—" she gestured around the room fitted as an office—"—consist almost entirely, Mr. Coates, of pure administration. Records, receipts, and that sort of thing. I know the Bishop doesn't want you to spend your time on that, now, does he?" Her blue-gray eyes were steady on him.

"I don't believe so."

Sweetly she continued, "Yes, I thought so. Your activities will center mainly on our differences with Representative Tom Herron. Do you know Mr. Herron?"

Jeff nodded. "Slightly. I gather I'm to see what I can do to defeat him in the primaries in June. Maybe I can do something."

Clara Blanton smiled approvingly. "I'm sure you can, Mr. Coates, I'm sure you can. Mr. Herron must not be renominated!" She was unexpectedly vehement. Then, calmly, "Now I have learned that there may be some startling information to be obtained about Mr. Herron in Tidewater. His home is there, and—"

Jeff smoked and looked out of the window. "Mind answering me a question, Miss Blanton? Just what kind of information do we want about him? His voting record in Congress? His connections in Tidewater—"

Clara Blanton leaned toward him, hands clasped in her lap. "No! We want stronger information than that, Mr. Coates, stronger information! We know he has left his wife, is trying to get a quiet divorce from her; we believe he makes her live in Chicago, somewhere in the North. Now—" she stopped, watching Jeff.

He stared at her, and made no answer. She nodded vigorously. "That is what we want, Mr. Coates. Do you understand?"

"What about Randolph Taitt?"

She relaxed and leaned back. "There is nothing immediate we can do about Senator Taitt. The Bishop has told you . . . ?"

"He said we could weaken him a little bit, maybe."

"Yes. Well, Dr. Sterling will be here tomorrow, or the day after. We shall see then. Meanwhile . . ."

Jeff stood up. "I'll go to Tidewater tomorrow. Can I draw expense money from you?"

Clara Blanton stood up. "Yes. I'll leave a check at the desk for you. Oh—and will you stop at this address and pay this bill?" She handed him a printer's bill, and the exact amount of cash, thirty-two dollars and sixty-four cents. "Some pamphlets," she smiled.

Jeff went out, found the address and left the cash, collecting the receipted bill which bore the initialed okay of Thomas H. Sterling, Chairman, then sought a public phone.

"Hello, Veryl, this is Jeff. I'll drop in tonight after dinner. . . .Be glad to see you, honey. . . . Yeah. . . . Murphy's Hotel, 932 . . . yeah. All right, honey, by-by."

He spent the next two hours loafing around the office of the *Globe-Bulletin*.

Bailey, who had fired him three weeks before, was cordial. "How ya doin', Jeff?"

On being informed of the Wesleyan Board connection, the city desk man raised pale eyebrows. "We'll be seein' right much of you round here, then?"

"Reckon so. Vernon wasn't as sore at me as you figured."

Bailey's emaciated face flushed. "I'm right sorry about that, Jeff. He acted mad as hell."

Jeff grinned: "Forget it. He got me my new job, after a manner of speakin'. He was *with* me when I got it, anyway."

Bailey laughed outright, relieved. "Good enough. See you later."

Jeff gossiped with his ex-colleagues, and at five drifted back to Murphy's Hotel. In his box he found an envelope containing a check for his expense money—thirty dollars —signed by Clara L. Blanton, Treasurer, Virginia Board of Public Safety. There was also a memo: "See J. T. Flager, 42 Langhorne St., Tidewater, C. L. B." He cashed the check at the desk, caught an hour's sleep in his room, had dinner by himself at Kirsh's, and then decided to walk part of the way to see Veryl.

He walked up Grace Street, later cutting over to Monument Avenue, out along that highway as far as the Lee statue, then turning left toward the home of Representative Shirley D. Vernon.

The walk had taken a long time and it was nearly nine when he rang the bell and was admitted by Veryl.

Her smooth voice said joyfully, "Jeff!" He had her in his arms and kissed her several times. Her hands clung to his shoulders. "I'm right glad to see you, Jeff."

He stroked her cheek. "Me too, honey."

She hung his hat and coat in a hall closet and led him into the living room. The narrow face of Shirley Vernon emerged from the shadow of a wing-backed easy chair. The collie smile appeared.

"Why, son, this is fine to have you back in Richmond so soon."

Jeff dropped on a divan opposite the fireplace. "Only few days. Glad to see you-all lookin' so well. Especially the baby here." He chucked Veryl, beside him, under the chin. She smiled, her amber eyes on him, their yellowness looking more yellow because of the snug-fitting ochre dress she wore.

The doorbell rang, a servant answered it. A man's voice was heard, and Vernon jumped up and went out to the foyer. Jeff shot a look of inquiry at Veryl.

"Tom Herron," she said quietly.

"Damn! Why didn't you tell me?"

Her hand wriggled its way inside his. "I didn't know till after you phoned. He just came down from Washington."

A voice boomed, "Hello, Veryl! My, doesn't she look wonderful?" Jeff stood up. Herron was a big man, but not fat. His face, with large nose and massive chin, was made for a wide-brimmed black hat, even if he didn't affect one. The eyes that stared glassily out of this expanse of face were hazel. One lock of blond hair fell toward his forehead, not over it.

Herron held Veryl's small hand between his two huge ones, then said to Jeff, "How are ya?"

"Haven't seen you for a while," Jeff said, and went to the fireplace to throw away a match.

The booming voice went on: "I certainly missed this cozy little room while I was in Washington. What do you say, Shirley D.?" His laugh rumbled.

Jeff said to Veryl, "Pardon me, can I go in the kitchen and get myself a glass of water?" Herron's smile stopped, then started again.

Veryl jumped up. "You come with me. I'll get it for you." She took his hand and led him into the dark kitchen. He snapped on the light. She got a glass, ran the water, and he said:

"I don't want a glass of water. Come on out here."

They went into the darkened garden. He threw away his cigarette. "I can't stand that guy. Don't see how anybody can."

"Oh, Jeff! What of it?"

"Hell with him! He comes round here to see *you*, even if he and your old man are bosom pals."

She went into his arms, and in the dusk he could see her

eyes wide. "Forget him, Jeff. I'm glad to see you." Her body pressed against his; their lips came together. Jeff felt her soft body under his hands.

"I got a fairly good spot now, honey. We can be married pretty soon," he said.

Pause. "Yes, Jeff."

He looked at her, then kissed her again, hard.

They went inside. Herron and Vernon had begun to fill the room with cigar smoke, and Jeff noticed Vernon was fidgeting. He felt uneasy himself. His eyes wandered from Herron's large face to Veryl, whose amber eyes watched him strangely. He thought of her pause in the garden before she had said, "Yes, Jeff."

"I'll have to be ducking along soon. Early riser." Jeff said.

Herron looked at him, sidewise. Jeff added, "My easy days don't come just because a Congress stops sitting."

Herron said. "Not in your work, I could bet."

Jeff began to speak, Vernon stood up. "Before you go, Jeff, could you step in the other room a moment?"

They went into the dining room, Vernon closing the door. "There's something I wanted to say. Er—did you see Taitt again?"

"No point to it."

"No. No, there isn't. But that wasn't what I wanted to ask." Vernon's eyes shifted away from Jeff, then back again, but wavered. "I wanted to know, in a way, you understand, what Sterling is going to do about Tom." He jerked his head toward the living room.

"Do about him? Why do anything about him?"

Vernon shuffled his feet and blew a great puff of cigar smoke. "Oh, well—it's hard, Jeff, this Virginia politics, and

I thought that if Herron was pretty sure to be beaten, I'd—"

"It won't make any difference if you do ditch him."

Vernon protested poutingly: "You know I mean a lot politically here in Richmond."

Jeff watched him a moment. "I don't know what will happen."

Vernon looked back at him. Then started out, saying, "Oh, if you won't tell me—"

Jeff arranged to phone Veryl early the next morning and took a bus back to the hotel.

Jeff phoned from a booth in the station at eight-forty-five the next morning. "Listen, honey, I'll be busy around town all day and maybe tonight. I better call you in the morning. Let's figure on getting together tomorrow night . . . yeah . . . that's right . . . bye-bye."

He boarded the train for Tidewater, and about noon reached his destination. After lunch he sought out J. T. Flager, 42 Langhorne Street, as per the message from Clara Blanton. The address turned out to be a small apartment above a furniture store. A dirty white card tacked to the inside of the jamb announced that one Flager lived there. Jeff climbed a flight of worn steps and found a door to the right of the first landing. Another dirty white card indicated that this was Mr. Flager's residence. Jeff knocked once, then twice, louder. A shuffling footstep sounded and the door came open, revealing a small bent man with perfectly white hair, a prominent hawk's nose surmounted by a pair of steel-rimmed glasses. The man merely looked at Jeff, who said:

"Mr. Flager? Miss Clara Blanton said I should see you."

The man stood aside, without saying anything. Jeff

walked into the combination living room and bedroom overlooking Langhorne Street. The furniture was old and decrepit, and two steel engravings hung lopsided on the wall opposite the door. A deal table blocked the left hand of two windows, and its surface was buried beneath a great disorderly heap of papers, letters and books of clippings. Jeff turned to face his host, who sat down on the bed, and began to fill and light an old curved stem pipe.

"What do you want?" The white-haired man's voice was very low, and he didn't look at Jeff.

"I don't know what you've got. Clara Blanton gave me a note to see you."

"Well, you know why you came here."

"I'm after a lead or two on Tom Herron."

The eyes on either side of the hawk's beak twinkled. "For Miss Blanton?"

Jeff nodded. "I reckon that's where you fit in. What can you tell me?"

The old man chuckled. "When you go back, tell Doc. Sterling for me that he's an old fool. Wasting his time with Herron!" The keen eyes inspected Jeff. Then the narrow shoulders shrugged. "Herron keeps a girl two blocks from here. That help you?"

"It might. Have to think about it. What's her name and address?"

"Viola Stane, 13 Kinney Street. Second floor, I think."

"Anything else?"

The man sighed and stood up. "No. But give the Bishop another message for me. Tell him that if he's going to spend campaign money, I want some for the paper."

Jeff raised his eyebrows in inquiry.

"For the paper, the paper," Flager said petulantly. "I

work on the *Gleaner* here. I want something for this favor."

Jeff stood up. "All right, I'll tell him. He took care of you all right, before, I reckon."

The man nodded and watched Jeff go out.

It was now nearly three—hardly the time to go calling on a young lady. Jeff went to a movie that let him out about five, then walked back to Kinney Street. Number 13 was one of a row of wooden houses separated from each other by about five feet. Tiny lawns set each house back from the sidewalk, and deep porches shaded the entrances. He rang and a Negro maid answered.

"I'd like to see Miss Stane, please."

"Ah'll see if she's in, suh. Come in."

Jeff entered and stood in a small front room evidently serving as waiting space for visitors. The place seemed to be a high class boarding establishment. He heard the Negress shout: "Miss Stane! Miss Stane!" Then a faint voice, "Yes?" "A gemmun to see you!"

Jeff waited nearly ten minutes, and then a girl came. She came in quickly and smiling, but on seeing Jeff, stopped short and the smile vanished.

"Oh! . . . You wanted to see me?"

Jeff talked quietly. "Yes, Miss Stane. I'm afraid I dropped in unexpectedly—won't you sit down?"

The girl's very large brown eyes watched him as she seated herself. She was small-boned, with a pale small face, featuring a thin-lipped mouth with delicately curved lips. Jeff smelled a faint perfume. He continued:

"I'm right sorry to bother you this way. I'm a friend of Tom Herron's."

She said nothing.

He sweated. "I think you ought to know what I'm going to tell you. He—"

"You're from his wife!" the girl burst out.

"I never saw his wife. How's Tom treat you?"

The girl stood up. "You impertinent—"

Jeff said, "Oh, hell! Listen, I don't like this any more than you do. What do you waste your time on him for?"

The underlids of the brown eyes suddenly brimmed. "Oh, what do you want?" Her hands wrung stealthily.

"Let's get this over with. I'm no friend of Herron's, and neither are you if I figure you right."

"I am!" She tossed her head.

Jeff struck quickly. "Then why do you stick to him when he's makin' passes at a girl in Richmond?"

She gasped. This was news to her. Jeff lit a cigarette and saw his hands were trembling. She said, in a choked voice, "He wouldn't. Not after. . . ."

Jeff waited to see if she would continue. She didn't. He said, "Not after what he promised you?" Her eyes held a fear of him. He went on, "Well, forget about him. How long have you known him?"

"T-two years." Her manner suddenly changed. "Who are you, anyway?"

"I'll tell you in a minute. Damn this business anyway! Listen, are you really gone on him?"

"You go to hell!" The girl turned venomous. "I love him, but if the dirty—" Her hand covered her mouth suddenly.

"Now you're talkin'! You forget about Tom Herron and come to Washington. Jeff Coates, Lathrop Hotel. Can you remember that?"

The girl nodded, and now her eyes were narrowed. "What do you want?" she said slowly.

Jeff laughed, relieved. "You dig me up in Washington, two weeks from now. I can do you some good."

Her eyes were still narrowed. "He'd never take me there!"

"All right, Viola Stane. Lathrop Hotel. I'll tell you a few things then. What are you doing for dinner?"

Unexpectedly the girl sat down again, hunched over and hid her face in her hands. Jeff waited, astonished. No sound came, until he heard a horribly agonized sob.

He crossed to her, took one of her hands. It was wet with tears and nervous perspiration. "What the hell!" he said.

She gulped. "Why did you have to come and tell me . . . tell me I'm gettin' thrown over? Why? Like a pr-prostitute. . . ." Then her head was suddenly up and her voice savage. "What chance has a girl got in this rotten town? She can be a whore for a thief like Tom Herron, or get kicked around by any man that walks in. God-damn you!" Her voice rose.

Jeff sweated some more. He clapped a hand over her mouth. Her teeth dug in his finger. He grabbed her by the shoulders and hauled her to her feet. Then he took her in his arms, and she began to cry, copiously and silently.

It took him half an hour to calm her down, and then she became hard and cold. "Forget the fireworks," he said when she was finally quiet. "Let's get some dinner before I go back to Richmond. We can talk."

She stared at him, nodded quickly and went out, "Wait till I get a hat."

The lateness of their talk kept Jeff from getting an early train, so that it was nearly four A. M. when he landed at the Union Station in Richmond. He went to the hotel, left a note for Clara Blanton, and went to bed.

At nine-fifteen his phone rang.

It was Sterling. "Mornin', Jeff. Sorry to get you up, but can you come to my room in half an hour?"

"Let me get some breakfast. What room?"

Sterling told him. Jeff hung up, shaved, showered and breakfasted, and then went to the Bishop's room. Clara Blanton was there ahead of him. He and the Bishop shook hands.

"Well?" asked Clara Blanton.

Jeff said: "I made out pretty well. I dug up Herron's girl friend. I got her mad and she told me plenty about him. He gets a cut on a public utilities set-up they've got in Tidewater, among other things. I was right sorry for the girl."

Sterling said: "What can we use against Herron?" The gray eyes glittered.

"I don't know what you can use publicly. Shame to use that business of the girl. She came through fine. But you can scare him on the public utilities set-up—I'll bring you the notes I made later. Also he's hooked up pretty close with some mills there. As far as I can make out, they helped his last campaign on a tariff deal, and he fell heir to a lot of their stock. How you can prove all this—"

"We don't have to!" Sterling was excited. "All we need is to know these things, and for him to know we have learned about the girl. Was she pretty?"

"Girls like that should be put away," Clara Blanton said.

Jeff lit a cigarette and yawned. "I didn't get in till four. What's next?"

Sterling pursed his lips and turned to stare out of the window. Then he spun round to face Jeff again. "Here's what. Herron's here in the hotel. You go see him and—"

Jeff squawked, "I just got through the rottenest job I ever did."

Sterling said, "You're working for me. You tell Herron that unless he feels he can agree with my policies—he'll know what that means—we'll use this stuff on him."

Jeff leaned forward. "Tell him right out like that?"

Sterling nodded vigorously. "Straight. There'll be no witnesses."

Jeff couldn't stifle a yawn. He stood up to go. "All right. I'll call you later in the day." He went to the desk to learn Herron's room number. Then he re-ascended in the elevator.

He stopped in his tracks half-way down the hall and stared at the carpet, his eyes glassy with thought. Then he said, "The bastard!" and walked on again, faster. He knocked at Herron's door, and the Congressman himself opened to him.

Jeff said, "Like to talk to you a minute."

Herron stood aside, then shut the door. "Sit down."

Jeff lit a cigarette, looking around the room, which differed from others in the hotel in having a large writing desk against the wall. "I've got a message for you."

The bulky man said, without expression: "Who from?"

"Bishop Sterling. He says that unless—"

Herron said, "Wait a minute," went over to the desk and sat down on it. "Bishop Sterling sent you to me?"

"Yes. He said for me to tell you that unless you can see

your way to agreeing with his policies—you know what that means—he's prepared to fight you good and hard."

Herron stared at him, cocking his head sideways like a bird. He said slowly, "Bishop Sterling says that unless I knuckle under to him he'll fight me. This is a threat, isn't it?"

"Call it a hint. What's your answer?"

Herron considered. "How will you fight me, as you put it?"

Jeff grinned: "Why should I tell you? You're a good public utilities man in Tidewater. That freshen up your memory?"

Herron's eyes darted away from Jeff's face, then back. "You're sure that Bishop Sterling sent you?"

Jeff snarled. "Of course I'm sure. What's the matter with you?" He watched for Herron's anger, hoping for a chance to hit him. Then Herron's irritating voice started:

"You can tell Bishop Sterling for me that his threats fall on deaf ears. I am interested and consecrated to representing my constituents in the halls of Congress, not to obeying the dictates of fanatical clergymen. And let me add—" Herron stood up and pointed oratorically at Jeff "—that this is the most insulting, the most humiliating, proposition that has ever been advanced to a duly elected representative of the people."

Jeff had to yawn. He felt uneasy at this burst of political highbinding, as if they were on a platform. "Too bad you haven't got an audience," he said.

Herron ranted on strangely. "I am not intimidated by the hints of dirty work by Bishop Thomas Sterling. Those cannot frighten me. I am devoted to—"

Jeff's eyes wandered around the desk before which

Herron was declaiming. An upright phone stood at one end and its wires ran off behind the bed. Then he saw another double wire running out from behind the desk and then around the door jamb by the floor into the other room. He looked twice, then jumped forward, placing both hands against the desk and giving it a powerful shove. It slid aside.

Herron barked, "Hey, you—"

Jeff saw the small flat black box of a dictograph. He brought his foot back to kick it, when Herron's right arm swept against his chest. He staggered back.

"Get the hell out of here, you lousy—"

Jeff stood still, panting. "Makin' speeches for a record, you lowdown punk!"

Herron's nostrils dilated. "Go on, get out! Go back and tell your Bishop I've got the goods on him now. You'n your 'hints.' "

Jeff doubled a fist, relaxed it again. Then he walked out swiftly.

He went downstairs and out into the street. He walked fast, aimlessly, smoking one cigarette after another. When he stopped at a street corner to wait for traffic to pass, he felt sweat running down the side of his face. He wiped it off.

In the middle of the block, he turned about face suddenly and walked as rapidly in the other direction. He entered the first telegraph office he found and sent a wire to Dixie Siegel, in Washington:

"CAN YOU COME DOWN TO RICHMOND TODAY STOP I'M ANXIOUS TO SEE YOU STOP IMPORTANT. JEFF."

5.

THE BISHOP PASSES THE HAT

JEFF had an answer to his wire during dinner, saying that Dixie would arrive later that night. She finished with, "Love, Dixie." He met her at the Union Station, and she put up her face to be kissed. After a dutiful peck, he escorted her to the Hotel John Marshall, and waited in the lobby while she went to her room to clean up. Inside of half-an-hour she was down again, and they went into the Coffee Shop for a bite and a chat.

After they had ordered light sandwiches and coffee, and before Jeff could begin, she put her hand on his. "I'm awfully glad to see you, Jeff."

"Swell. Good thing you were able to get down here. I've got a job for you."

Her eyebrows drew together. "Is that the first thing you have to say? Can't you say you're glad to see me?"

"Sure, I'm glad to see you, honey. I missed you a little bit, especially that coffee you make for breakfast." He grinned. "That keep you happy?"

She smiled. "That's better. Now what's on your mind?"

"There's a feller here—Tom Herron, Congressman from Tidewater—and I want you to get after him."

She started to say something, hesitated, and finally said, "You're not exactly mad about me, are you, Jeff?"

"What's that got to do with it?" He flicked his cigarette.

She stared, emitted a small sigh. "Nothing much, I suppose." Pause. "Anyway, I'm glad to be with you. I know Herron, slightly."

"That's great. I thought you probably would. What he's got is a dictograph record of me telling him a few things. Point is we're sunk if he uses that against us in the primaries in June. Have to get it back. I'm in a hell of a spot."

She bit into her sandwich, and patted his hand. "Leave it to Dixie. Poor little Jeff."

"It's not funny. I made a horse's neck out of myself. You have to get me out of it."

She shrugged, then smiled at him. "I don't have to, sweetheart, but I will. Tom Herron's awfully small time, though."

Jeff considered her. "I'll make that end of it worth your while."

She put her hand in his quickly: "Oh, Jeff, I didn't mean it that way! I am running low, but I like you. That's a good reason."

"I suppose. Anyway, we'll fight that out later. Herron's staying at Murphy's, where I am. You can ring him casually, say—"

"Leave that part of it to me. I'm sleepy now. When do you and I see each other again?" He was paying the check.

"I'll call you, baby. Noon, about."

He left her at the elevator and went back to his own hotel.

He had lunch the next day with Sterling, to whom he

had reported the evening before, though he had said nothing about the dictograph. The Bishop had been pleased. He smiled at his helper across the table.

"Want to run up to Washington tonight with me?"

Jeff ate for a moment before answering. "I don't know. I'm low on cash."

The Bishop looked at him, surprised.

Jeff went on, "Y' know, I need a little money now and then, and Miss Blanton must think I'm a camel, the size of the Tidewater check she gave me."

Sterling stiffened. "We haven't much money in the treasury as yet, Jeff. It seems to me—"

Jeff protested. "Don't get me wrong, Doctor. I mean this: if I'm goin' to go off on little side trips like Tidewater, or other places, I have to have a little more liberal purse. Suppose I have to entertain, buy liquor, things like that." Sterling was listening carefully. "You know as well as I do that I'm goin' to have to buy plenty of liquor from time to time."

Then the Bishop smiled. "Sure, I understand." But he was a trifle worried. He added: "I suppose you could use extra money, eh?"

Jeff thought of Dixie at the Marshall Hotel. "Well, a few extra dollars never get in the way."

"Hmmm! You come to Washington with me. We'll start this afternoon, be there for dinner, and go on to New York in the morning."

"New York?"

Sterling was looking straight at him. "I have a friend up there—I'll introduce you—if you need a little money, I think it can be arranged."

Jeff said noncommittally, "That'll be nice."

"He has helped me in the market. Very liberal, indeed."

Jeff was silent. He ate steadily, watching his plate, and after a long silence, said, "I'll meet you at the station. Two-thirty?"

An hour and a half later Jeff was in a phone booth in the station.

"Hello, Dixie. Jeff. Yeah. I'm goin' to Washington . . yeah. No, no, I'll be back in about three or four days. Stick at it . . . yeah. . . . . Any news? . . . . Okay. 'Bye."

When he came out the Bishop was walking toward him, bag in hand. Under his arm was a brown paper parcel. They nodded to each other, Jeff picked up his bag, and they sought the train. Instead of heading for the chair car, the Bishop climbed into the first day coach. Jeff followed. Side by side they sat, their bags under their feet. The rest of the car was not crowded. When the Bishop removed his lightweight coat, Jeff noticed the pockets were full of clippings. From the news butcher they bought reading matter, the Bishop taking both Richmond and Washington papers, while en route he bought Baltimore papers. The brown paper parcel turned out to be a cold lunch.

Their stay in Washington overnight was routine, consisting of a few telephone calls by the Bishop, the nature of which he did not tell Jeff. In the morning they caught the early train for New York, and arrived at the Pennsylvania Station for a late lunch.

Over the table the Bishop said, "We'll go to the O'Gilpin, where I usually go. Is that all right?"

"Expensive, isn't it?" asked Jeff.

The Bishop laughed, more freely 'than Jeff had ever heard him. "Oh, don't worry about that! I've got a little scheme that'll relieve us of worry by tomorrow. How much money did you bring?"

"Hundred and some."

"We'll double that by morning."

Entering the hotel, the Bishop said, "Don't make any comments." They registered, and the Bishop's remark was clear to Jeff when he saw the old gentleman write the name "Sidney Brent" in the book. Jeff wrote his own name under it. The bellhop gave them connecting rooms.

Hurriedly the Bishop cleaned up; then, in Jeff's hearing, called a number and asked for a man named Silverman. He told him to wait until they arrived at the office. The Bishop chuckled when he hung up.

A taxi took them to an office building not far from Trinity Church, and an elevator let them off at the eleventh floor. Sterling led him to a double glass door, bearing in gilt letters the firm name Gunter and Company, Securities. A small man of pronounced Jewish cast of features greeted the Bishop at once.

"Oh, this is your friend! How do you do?" He guided them into a tiny office apart from the main, where the click of the ticker and the hubbub of voices was subsiding as the market closed. Silverman shut the door, turned and blinked his brown eyes at Sterling.

"I hope you've been well, Bishop?"

The gray face brightened. "I'm feeling marvelous, son. Now, I and my young friend here want to pick up a few dollars by tomorrow. Can you do it for us? You've been pretty good to me before."

The young Jewish broker's face remained blank. "Well, I may be able to single out something for you. How much had you planned to use?"

"Six hundred, altogether. Will that be enough?" Jeff saw the Bishop sitting forward in his seat. The eyes were eager.

Silverman nodded briskly, seized a memo pad from the desk, made a note. "All right, phone me about this time tomorrow. Still be here then?"

Sterling stood up. "Yes, yes, indeed, we'll be here. Be sure and get us something good. We need that cash, don't forget."

Silverman ushered them out. He smiled for the first time. "I'll do my best. You phone me tomorrow. G'bye."

Walking down the corridor, flanked by gilt-lettered doors, the Bishop chuckled again, then slapped Jeff on the back. "Tomorrow you'll see."

That night, after a quiet dinner in a chop house in the West Forties, Sterling took Jeff to a cabaret on Broadway and Forty-seventh Street. On the way, as they walked, the Bishop took Jeff's arm and let out a small laugh. "We'll have a little fun tonight. They have beautiful girls over here where I'm taking you."

"Not much fun just looking at 'em."

Again the small laugh. "Well, we better take it easy."

The head waiter gave them a table against the wall, from which they had a clear view of the floor. A ten-piece orchestra was crowded under a gaily-colored awning in one corner, whence came its subdued croonings and rhythms. A few couples—it was early—swayed on the floor. Waiters dodged between the close packed tables, and people began drifting in to fill up the place. Jeff saw, at a table to the right of the orchestra, a group of girls in evening gowns.

The waiter came to take their order. Jeff said, "Ginger

ale," and, when the waiter stared at him, added, "What have you got?"

The waiter shrugged. "We don't keep anything here. I can get you something. Scotch, rye, champagne, martini, bronx—"

"Two Scotch."

"Yes, sir. Are you alone, sir?"

"Yes."

"Very well, sir." The dark-browed Italian ducked his head and bustled away. Jeff lit a cigarette and looked sideways at Sterling. The older man was leaning his elbows on the table, and apparently he had not heard Jeff's few words with the waiter. The gray eyes behind the hexagonal spectacles darted from spot to spot in the stuffy room. He seemed to Jeff to be breathing fast in a sort of childish excitement. The waiter returned with a tray, on which there was two half-filled whiskey glasses, two ginger ale bottles, and water tumblers. Sterling looked at the whiskey before him.

"I never drink, son."

"Keep it in front of you anyway. I'll take it. Don't mind if I have one, do you?"

Sterling shook his head. "Go right ahead, son."

A girl stopped by the table and said to Sterling, "Mind if I join you?"

"Eh?" The old man was startled.

Jeff said to her, "Sit down, unless you've got millionaires somewhere."

The girl smiled impersonally and sat down next to the Bishop. "Got a cigarette?" She was black-haired, wide-eyed, button-mouthed, and her gaze kept wandering all over the room. Jeff gave her a smoke, and she said to him, "Want company for yourself?"

He nodded. The girl turned and stared across the room at the table full of girls Jeff had noticed before. Then she nodded vigorously to one, who rose and crossed the room to join them, She was blonde, tall and thin, wearing a pale-blue low-cut dress. Her voice, when she said, "Good evening," was husky.

The black-haired one asked, "New Yorkers?"

"Listen to me talk," said Jeff, grinning at her.

Huskily the blonde laughed. "No kiddin,' I get a big giggle outa you Dixie boys. Ah sho' dew!" she mimicked.

Sterling said, "Think we're a funny lot, eh?" He had the black-haired girl's hand and was massaging it gently.

"Funny—but nice."

The Bishop laughed his little laugh, picked up his Scotch and swallowed some, reaching immediately for his ice water glass.

"How about some for us?" said the blonde, and without waiting for an answer told a passing waiter, "Hey, Joe, two on the Scotch."

The orchestra suddenly blared, all lights but those illuminating the floor dimmed down. A young man in dress clothes bounded out and in lilting tones announced the beginning of the floor show. Sterling hunched forward in his chair.

Again the orchestra blatted forth at a speedy rhythm. A line of twelve girls, in brief rhinestone panties and similar bandeaux, marched out and around the floor. Forming a circle facing the ringside tables, they sang nasally, making routine gestures without particular facial expression.

"Good lookin' kids, 'ncha think?" said the husky blonde.

Jeff nodded, watching them. Slim bodies covered more with whiting than with clothing pranced about, then suddenly they were off and the lilting master of ceremonies was back. He bawled a few lines, the orchestra plunged into a slow, hot number, and a parade of semi-nudes began, while a prima donna with a brassy throat sang indistinguishable words. Tall blondes with protuberant busts barely covered with gauze, willowy red heads with very white skin, sturdy brunettes with bulging buttocks and thighs marched and exhibited themselves at close range to the ringside customers.

The dark-haired girl at their table leaned across to the blonde. "Look at Mary. She's cock-eyed."

"Which one?" Jeff asked.

"That one by the orchestra now. With the gold pants." Jeff saw a large, heavy-lipped face wearing a vague smile. He switched his gaze to his companion.

Sterling sat forward, his nostrils dilated, his hands absently holding the fingers of the black-haired girl. His eyes roved, wide open, keenly inspecting everything exposed to view on the floor. His lips were parted loosely. As Jeff watched, the older man picked up the whiskey glass, emptied it quickly, choked slightly, then went on watching.

Jeff grinned at the black-haired girl.

For half-an-hour more the show went on: the lilting announcer, the brassy soprano, the semi-naked girls, dancers, singers, parade of breasts and thighs and navels, until it wound up in a blast of nasal singing and a brandishing of well-curved bare legs and arms. The room lights came up again and the orchestra reverted to a quiet dance rhythm.

Sterling leaned back. "How 'bout another snort, laddie?" the blonde asked.

Jeff said, "Sure."

Sterling wagged his head. "I think we better be going. We have to be up early, Jeff."

The black-haired girl said, "All right. Excuse me, please."

She stood up to leave them. The blonde put her hand on Jeff's shoulder. "Look me up if you drop in again."

"Yeah."

He and the Bishop paid, went out and back to the O'Gilpin.

They exchanged no words until in the corridor outside their rooms.

"In the morning," said Sterling, "we're going to see an important man. I'll meet you in the dining room at nine."

After breakfast the next morning, Sterling took him in a taxi to a lawyer's office in a thirty-story building on Madison Avenue near Forty-sixth Street. Sterling announced himself to the girl.

"Will you tell Mr. Wint that Bishop Sterling is here?"

"Have a seat, please." The girl talked into her phone, then said, "Will you go in, please? Second door on your right."

Jeff followed the Bishop into a large leather-furniture equipped office. A tall, Roman-featured, rather severe man got up leisurely and shook hands with Sterling.

"How are you, Mr. Wint? This is my assistant, Mr. Coates."

Wint said: "Right glad to see you. Sit down. We have this office for a few minutes. I had your letter, Doctor."

Jeff sat a few feet away; Sterling and K. Cuthbert Wint, formerly Secretary to Republican President Dollo- way' and now Virginia Republican State Chairman and a big figure in the Republican National Committee, sat nearer together.

Sterling began quickly. "I'll outline my situation to you, Mr. Wint, and then we'll see if there's any way we can work together."

Wint nodded gravely.

"You know that I am leading the opposition in Virginia to .the nomination of Jim White of New York. He must not be President, Mr. Wint! He is wet, he is associated with the worst element in the national Democratic Party, and we in Virginia believe that his nomination will be fatal to the Democrats. However, he will probably be nominated."

"Of course. I don't see how you can stop it."

Sterling continued: "But I am going to make that nomination as difficult for him as possible. I shall attend the Houston Convention, and work for a dry plank in the platform. If Jim White is nominated, there is only one course for Southern Democrats in general, and Virginia Democrats in particular, to take. We will then have to work for the election of Gilbert Molleson, or whoever makes the race on your ticket."

Wint raised bushy eyebrows. "You mean you'll come over to us?"

Sterling shook his head vigorously. "Not at all. We will continue to be Democrats, merely for this election bolting the ticket. I tell you, Mr. Wint, if Jim White is nominated for the Presidency by the Democratic Party, I am going to break the solid South. You know what that means!" The gray eyes were glittering and the guttural rasp was in the voice. "We have worked hard for years to maintain Prohibition, and I am not going to stand by quietly while a Papist Wet tries to nullify our labors!"

"That will, of course, be welcome to us," Wint said cautiously.

Sterling almost leaped out of his chair. He pointed a finger at the ex-Presidential Secretary. "Exactly! That is why I come to you. For our work we need money—more than I can raise by individual cont. ʰbutions, even stimulated by the Wesleyan Church. I cannot raise enough in Virginia, because I am going to be working against the State Democratic organization. You can see that, for you're a Virginian yourself, sir.

"But our work will help you. The Republicans will likely nominate Molleson, whose election will be too close for your comfort unless you help me break the South. Will you do it?"

Wint took a long time to clip a cigar, light it and get it drawing properly. Then he said, with renewed caution: "I know a man—possibly more than one man—who might be induced to contribute to your fund."

"When can I meet him?"

Wint smiled. "Oh, you don't want to meet him until White is nominated. That will be time enough." The stoutish man spoke more slowly now. "Yes, the more I think of it, the more I am sure that I can help you in a rather large way. I have a particular man in mind, and some time after the Houston Convention, if White is nominated as you expect, I will arrange a meeting."

Sterling said, "I know I can depend on that. This will be good news to my helpers."

"Oh, I wouldn't say anything about this for some time yet," Wint retorted hastily. "It—er—it might be embarrassing."

Sterling rose, Jeff likewise. The Bishop said, as he shook hands, "Fine. Then you'll hear from me during the summer. This little talk has been a great pleasure."

"All mine," murmured Wint. He saw them both out.

In the street, Sterling took Jeff in another cab to the office of Gunter and Company again, where they found Silverman. The broker said, with customarily blank face: "I thought you were going to phone me." Without waiting for an answer, he led them into the same little side office they had used before. "Sit down. I'll be right back."

He returned in less than a minute with a check in each hand. "I guess you want to take the sugar along with you, Doctor. I tripled for you. The checks are less commission of course."

Jeff looked at his check, then put it away. Sterling cackled and told Silverman: "I'm very appreciative of this."

"Yeah, that's all right," Silverman answered. "But you ought to be able to sink a little more dough in here. You know, a few grand. Then we can really do something."

Sterling cocked his head at him. "What would you say, Silverman, if I told you I'd have a lot of money for you some time during the summer?"

Silverman jerked his head briskly. "Swell. Let me know."

They left the office, had lunch and caught the first possible train for Washington.

6.

FIRST BLOOD

JUNE days in Richmond are warm, and this one was no exception. Jeff sat in a tilted upright chair by his open window in Murphy's Hotel. He looked down on sparse traffic on Broad Street, and was glad he wasn't in Washington, where it was hotter. He looked at his wrist-watch; it said ten-fifteen. He got up and went to the phone.

"Get me the John Marshall, will you, sweetheart?" He lit a fresh cigarette and kicked another chair around in place for him to sit. "Hello, Marshall? Has Miss Siegel arrived yet? No? Ask her to call Mr. Coates the minute she gets in, will you? Thanks . . . G'bye."

He hung up and went back to his chair by the window. He picked up the paper, re-read the front page and let his eyes rest a moment on a two-column head which proclaimed:

HERRON-DELLENBAUGH PRIMARY FIGHT ENLIVENS TIDEWATER
Bishop Sterling Says Dellenbaugh Will Win

Jeff threw the paper down. The phone rang and he jumped up and answered it.

"Hello? Oh, good morning, Miss Blanton . . . Yeah . . . the two-ten. . . . I'll phone you in the morning and let

69

you know . . . 'Bye." He replaced the receiver with exaggerated gentleness, made a face at the instrument and resumed his position. The phone rang again, he answered it leisurely.

"Hel-lo? . . . Yeah, Dixie! Where the hell have you been? I can't meet you this afternoon—I have to go to Tidewater. Be back tonight or in the morning. . . . Well, did you get the damn' thing? . . . What? . . . I say have you got it . . . Jesus, tomorrow's the primaries. . . . You'll call me back? . . . When? . . . Why can't you tell me now? . . . All right. G'bye."

He slammed the receiver down, put on his jacket and went downstairs. "I'm in the drugstore if there's a phone call," he said to the desk-clerk. "Be sure and tell me."

Then he sat at the counter and drank a cup of black coffee. Back to his room he went, and by phone told the operator, "I'm up here now, sweetheart. Okay."

Then he took up his seat by the window. Time crawled by, and he grew more and more fidgety. Eleven o'clock came and went, and he lay down and tried to sleep. Ten minutes of tossing drove him up, and he stripped for a shower. Twelve had arrived by the time he was dressed again. He called room service and had sandwiches and coffee sent up. Savagely he ate. Twelve-thirty, one—now he stood up steadily, glaring down at passers-by on Broad Street below him. At last he jammed his hat on his head, put on his jacket again, felt all his pockets to make sure that he had wallet, handkerchief, pencil and pen, keys, change, address book—and went downstairs. Dropping his key at the desk he walked the three blocks to the John Marshall Hotel and picked up a house phone.

"Miss Siegel does not answer," the operator told him sweetly.

He sat down at a writing desk and wrote a note:

"Baby:—
I couldn't wait for your call. Back from Tidewater to-
night. If H has that record and uses it, you better beat it
for Washington quick. J.C."

He left the train at Tidewater in mid-afternoon. He first made his way to the headquarters of Thompson Dellenbaugh, Wesleyan-backed candidate against Tom Herron in the primaries for the Tidewater Democratic nomination for Representative in Congress. There he found J. T. Flager, who crinkled his eyes at him and stuck out a dry, bony hand.

"Hello, young man. You like Tidewater?"

"The hell with Tidewater. You running this shebang?"

The snow-white-haired man nodded and sucked at his empty pipe. "Running it, after a fashion. Thanks for giving the Doctor that message."

"You mean about spending some dough in your paper? Don't mention it."

"What do you want this time?"

Jeff lit a cigarette. "What I'm goin' to ask you is not what I want by a damn' sight. The Bishop wants me to speechify for Dellenbaugh."

Flager smiled. "We can use you. Are you any good?"

"How do I know? Give me a spot where all I have to do is yell. Don't give me any bunch of women, or anything like that."

"You'll get one of the district clubs. Everybody yells at those. Will that suit you?"

Jeff nodded. "Where, what time?"

Flager made a loud sucking noise in his pipe. "Meet me here about six-thirty. We'll eat, and then I'll take you where you have to go."

"All right. See you later." Jeff drifted into the street. He found himself hungry, and stopped in a lunch room for a sandwich, a piece of pie and a glass of milk. He lit a cigarette and lounged into the street again. Suddenly he picked up speed, and walked at a moderate pace until he found Kinney Street, then No. 13. He rang the bell.

The same Negress answered the door. "Yas, suh?"

"Miss Stane here?"

The servant wagged her head ponderously. "Oh, no, suh! She gone to Washington, suh."

"How long ago?"

"Oh, Ah reckon 'bout two month' ago, suh! Wasn't you heah befo', suh? Ah seem to reckernize—"

"Yeah, I was here." Jeff licked his lips.

The broad brown face broke in a smile. "Well, suh, it was probly er couple days after you was heah, suh, that she went to Washington. Ah remember now, suh."

Jeff went down the stoop steps. "All right. Thanks."

"Yo're welcome, suh." The door shut.

Jeff walked back toward the center of town. He frowned for a long time; then shrugged, and walked a little faster.

A movie killed time for him until six-thirty, when he met and had dinner with Flager. This citizen, newspaperman and firm friend of Sterling, said little during their meal. He asked Jeff a few questions about the main Wesleyan headquarters in Washington, which Jeff answered generally.

Then Flager asked, "How's Clara L.?"

"Blanton? Know her?"

The white-haired man nodded calmly. "Right well. Look out for her."

"What'll she do to me except glare?" Jeff was interested.

Flager ate steadily for almost a minute before replying. "I gather you're pretty much on the inside—"

"Not so much."

"I gather you're pretty much on the inside, and Clara's idea is that there shouldn't be anybody except her on the inside. That's not hard to figger. Besides—"

"How come you know so much? Mind if I ask?"

Flager smiled his slow smile. "I don't mind a bit. Sterling 'n' I used to work together on the *Protestant Ecclesiast*. Clara was around then, only just a beginner in the Wesleyan outfit."

Jeff was thoughtful for a moment, and then: "What do you know about Mrs. Sterling?"

"Sick, ain't she?"

Jeff nodded. "Stays in a sanitarium some place in Maryland. I never saw her."

"Yeah, I reckon she's not long for this world. The Doc used to be right fond of her, but lately—I dunno. O' course, I don't know much about her."

"Good-lookin'? Ever?"

"Terrible."

They finished their meal in silence, paid off, and went out. Flager took him to one club, the front room of which was jammed with campaign workers, each wearing a badge. A very fat man was bellowing at them. Others gabbled among themselves, paying no attention to the fat man. People came and went steadily, their hands clutching lists and pencils, their faces red with sweat and excitement.

"I'm not goin' to speech here," said Jeff.

Flager wagged his head without opening his lips. Then he led Jeff out. They walked several blocks to another club. Flager said: "Herron 'n Dellenbaugh are outside town now, catchin' the country folk before they go to bed. They'll be around here soon."

Bannered automobiles dashed by with loud tooting of horns and blaring of bugles. On one corner a loud-speaker over the pavement bellowed the virtues of Tom Herron, from an opposite corner the accomplishments of Dellenbaugh poured forth, and nobody could understand anything. Flager led him into the front room of the second club, also filled with noisy campaigners. Flager seized by the arm a tall man in the act of dashing past them. He joined them.

Flager said, "Here's a feller from Richmond, works with Sterling and he wants to talk." Jeff felt an unfamiliar empty pit in his stomach.

"Fine. Now?"

Jeff swallowed, and nodded.

"Name?"

Jeff told him. The tall man dragged him by the arm to a low platform at the head of the room, and from there yelled:

"Hey, listen! Silence, please!" The chatter subsided a little, but not much. "I've got a man here from Richmond—he brings us a message from Bishop Sterling."

Quiet was had in two seconds, and strained faces turned attentively. The tall man's voice dropped to a more subdued pitch. "This is Mr. Coates, from Richmond. Let's

greet Mr. Coates!" A salvo of handclapping crackled,
then subsided. Jeff stepped to the edge of the platform,
imbued with a sudden idea.

"Folks, I just want to say a few words. I represent the
greatest man in Virginia politics, who in turn represents
the greatest force in American politics, the public conscience." His stomach felt all right again. He raised his
voice. "Bishop Sterling is allied with the forces of right,
and of progressive action within the Democratic Party
of the Commonwealth of Virginia! And I have come here
to tell you that Thompson Dellenbaugh is also allied with
those forces. Therefore, Bishop Sterling and Thompson
Dellenbaugh are natural allies. I am going back to Richmond tonight to tell Bishop Sterling that you have worked
hard, no matter what the outcome, so let's put Dellenbaugh over!"

Cheers and catcalls answered him. He was grinning and
sweating. The tall man had vanished, and Jeff rejoined
Flager, who smiled sympathetically. They took chairs
against the wall, and watched and listened. A stream of
speakers now began rotating between the various headquarters. Flager was kept busy greeting acquaintances,
to many of whom he introduced Jeff as "an associate of
Bishop Sterling's." They were all respectful.

When it was nearing ten o'clock, Flager plucked Jeff's
sleeve and nodded to him to come. They went two blocks
across town to an assembly hall.

"Herron's due here in a few minutes." They found
chairs at the rear, while the rest of the space was taken up
by increasing numbers of campaigners, observers, newspapermen, groups carrying banners, and numbers of

small boys. A heavy-set man was orating from the platform when Jeff and Flager came in.

"That's your candidate," said Flager.

"Dellenbaugh?" Jeff inspected the pompous man whose sonorous voice was barely audible. He caught phrases only: " . . . the right wing of the party . . . public conscience demands . . . the principles of Thomas Jefferson . . . the people of this Congressional District . . . ."

Jeff said, "Even Tom Herron makes a better Congressman."

Dellenbaugh finished amid solid and determined applause. The babble of voices broke out, when the tall man from the room where Jeff had talked appeared on the platform. Then he jumped down and another man came. He raised a hand and quiet ensued.

"Ladies and gentlemen, I have a great privilege for you. The opponent of Mr. Dellenbaugh is here—the man who is contesting for the support of the Tidewater Democracy —Representative Tom Herron!"

A burst of applause, and Herron's bulk appeared before the gathering. The other man jumped down to join the spectators. Herron gazed over the assemblage with the poise of an experienced orator. Then he began slowly, carefully:

"Ladies and gentlemen of the Democratic Party—I'm not going to argue with my worthy opponent. We have our differences of opinion that will be settled tomorrow at the polls. He has his record as a public-spirited citizen of many years' standing; I have mine as a Representative of the people of my district. Both those records speak for themselves. Now—I'm going to talk about something else."

Herron's manner changed from one of confiding gentleness to ferocious attack.

"I'm going to talk about fanatics and their influence in politics. I'm going to talk about the revival of the Spanish Inquisition in a new form—and, worst of all—in the Democratic Party of the Commonwealth of Virginia. The day has come, my friends, when you hear before you a candidate who has been threatened by men who are little less than priestly tyrants. Why don't they turn their Wesleyan pulpits into voting booths?"

Jeff found himself sweating. He sensed tenseness in the audience. Herron went on, pounding his right clenched hand into his left palm:

"Think of it, my friends! And it is not only I who have been threatened, but the voters. Dominated from the pulpit—the results of a free primary jeopardized by the bulldozing tactics of men who believe they can bring God into politics! That's what I'm telling you about!

"In short, the Wesleyan Board of Public Safety have told me that if I didn't take orders from them—as other politicians do, alas!—they would use their influence to defeat me. I tell you—"

In the middle of the hall a man jumped to his feet. "That's a damned lie!" Other voices burst out, short and sharp like explosions: "Sit down!" "Shut up!" "Liar!" One man with a bull voice yelled repeatedly: "Can you prove it, Tom Herron? Can you prove it!" His voice dominated and Herron had to answer.

"Prove it? Do I have to prove it? You know it as well as I do!"

The battle of angry voices broke out again; several groups broke into repeated cheers, others stood up and yelled, red-faced. Herron's lame failure to back up his statement broke the tension.

Jeff shouted to Flager, "Let's git!" They rose and pushed their way out. Jeff was breathing hard. The roar and voices followed them.

"He started something," Flager grinned. "Here, let's go through this way." He led Jeff down an alley past the side of the building they had just left. Ahead of them, an unshaded electric bulb blazed over a doorway, like the stage entrance of a small-town theatre. They walked slowly, lighting cigarettes.

"Think he'll win?" Jeff said.

"Dellenbaugh's got a lot of strength. Don't make much difference."

"No."

The door under the single bulb burst open; two men came out and started toward them. Herron was one; Jeff didn't recognize the other. Herron saw him at the same time.

"Well!" he said.

Jeff grinned. "Why didn't you spring the big—"

Herron snarled! "You God-damned bastard!"

"Mustn't say nasty words. And don't yell so loud. You'll lose votes."

"Yeah," Herron's mouth twisted with rage. "Of all the dirty tricks—steal and lie—only way your God-damned Bishop—"

"Now, now." Jeff ducked to avoid a swinging fist. He doubled his own hands, and his left grated along Herron's chin. The big man lunged forward and Jeff's right caught him full on the chest. The Congressman staggered back against the wall, gasping.

Jeff started toward him, breathing hard, when Flager's surprisingly strong hands hauled him sideways. "Cut it, you damn' fool!" Jeff stood upright; Herron had out a handkerchief and was mopping his streaming face.

Jeff said, "Dark-haired women are poison to you. I know of two."

Herron said nothing for several seconds, then stood up straight. His voice was husky but controlled. "This is the first round for you, but I'm not through. Take that message back to your pious psalm-singin' son of a—"

A group of people, all talking loudly, turned into the far end of the alley. The man with Herron said, "Can it, Tom. Let's beat it."

Herron braced, waved a hand at Jeff, as if leaving a friend, and the two pairs walked in opposite directions. Jeff suddenly realized pain in his left hand, where it had come in contact with the other's chin. He wound a handkerchief around it.

"Better come up, sleep in my place," Flager said. "I think you missed the best train."

Jeff looked at his watch. "That heel! . . . Can I get an early train? There's good news for me in Richmond."

"Seven-thirty."

"All right. Let's eat."

The seven-thirty train left Jeff, in wrinkled clothes, unshaven, but otherwise calm, in the Richmond station at about ten-thirty. He taxied to the John Marshall Hotel in about ten minutes. At the desk he asked for Miss Siegel.

"Why, she just checked out," the clerk said. "Said she was catching the eleven o'clock for Washington."

Jeff said nothing, but turned and ran from the lobby.

Another cab whirled him right back to the station, where he dismounted at three minutes to eleven. He paid the driver and ran inside. Of a passenger porter he asked, "Where's the eleven for Washington leave?"

"Track Fo'teen, suh."

Jeff tore down the ramp, and caught the train just as the conductor shouted his, "All aboard!"

Into the one parlor car he went, and in the third seat found Dixie. The only other people in the car were a group of four at the other end. He sat down in the next chair and said:

"What are you trying to pull on me?"

She stared at him, surprised. Her eyes then showed an amused gleam. "Jeff, darling! I'm glad to see you." Her hand went out to his.

"The hell with that! Why didn't you call me yesterday?"

Her red lips pursed, and he moved uneasily under her eager expression. She said softly, "Jeff, don't snarl at me." She glanced up hurriedly at the conductor, and proffered her ticket.

Jeff said to him, "I'll take one to Fredericksburg." He paid, and the attendant passed down the car. "Well, come on. I gather you got the dictograph record."

She smiled at him. "You're a darling. Did you worry? Of course I got it."

Jeff rubbed a hand irritably across his mouth. "You'll drive me nuts. Why in the name of hell and Mary didn't you let me know? I sweat all day yesterday, I get in a fight last night, all on account of—"

Dixie's expression sobered. "Listen, Jeff. I didn't like

this job one bit. But I'm real fond of you. I am, Jeff. But I'm not going to give you the dictograph."

He stared at her. "What is this, anyway? . . ." Then he shot at her, "You double-cross me with that yahoo Herron?"

She flushed. "No! I had to be nice to him—you knew that." Her voice went panicky. "Jeff, you knew I had to go that far—" Her hand went out to his again.

Jeff's lips tightened. He leaned back and looked at her. "Let me straighten this out in my own man's brain. I pay you to steal that record. You steal it. Now you won't give it to me, and you're in a sweat cause maybe I'm sore you stayed with the bastard. What the hell!"

Her black eyes glistened momentarily; then they cleared and she said, "Jeff, I'm crazy about you, and besides that, we can work together, I'll tell you how. If you won't do it of your own accord—if you don't care enough for me—"

"Oh, for God's sake!"

"Jeff! I'm going to Houston with you."

"To the Convention? Like hell you are!"

Her hands were tight-clasped in her lap. "Jeff, I've got that record. If that's the only way I can be with you— anyway, I've got it!" She smiled triumphantly.

"Fredericksburg . . . Fredericksburg!" The porter shouted at one end of the car.

Jeff stood up and said savagely: "All right, come to Houston. We'll work together, if that's what you want!"

"I almost love you," she whispered.

He stamped out to the platform to catch the next train back to Richmond.

The evening editions of the afternoon papers told of Herron's victory by a narrow margin over Dellenbaugh in the Tidewater primaries.

"We can get him later," Sterling said to Jeff.

7.

THE HAPPY WARRIOR

IT WAS the evening of June twenty-fifth. Texas heat made everybody keep windows open, and the courtyard of the Rice Hotel, Houston, echoed and re-echoed to shouts in all tones of voice, from anger to drunken joyousness. The corridors likewise were the stamping grounds for single men and groups, with females of secretarial aspect intermingled, who maintained a constant coming and going. From his chair in the living room of Bishop Sterling's suite Jeff watched the passage of people in the corridor. The open door was an invitation for those who were expected. In the other room Clara Blanton was tapping at a typewriter, dispatching a load of the Doctor's dictation.

A man came in and asked Jeff, "Bishop Sterling here?"

"Have a seat. He'll be back from dinner in a minute."

The short round man sat down, and began looking quizzically at Jeff. At length he said, "We met some place, didn't we?"

Jeff nodded. "Sorry I don't remember exactly. Oh, yes, in the Bishop's office in Washington—the night Senator Seed was there."

The man's face broke in a smile. "Oh, yes. You're the Doctor's young man! My name's Prince."

Jeff nodded cordially. "Glad to see you. Just get in?"

"Yes. Though I can't see where—Hello, Doctor!"

Sterling came in, threw a newspaper in the wastebasket, and shook hands. "How are you, Prince? Come inside . . . Oh, Jeff, let me know who comes, will you?" The Bishop and the managing director of *The American People* went into the room where Clara Blanton was working. The phone in the outer room rang sharply, Jeff rose slowly to answer, but Clara Blanton was quicker. She was in the room and answering the phone. Jeff stood up lazily. She turned and said:

"A *lady* for you, Mr. Coates," and without looking at him a second time, she reentered the inner room.

Jeff picked up the instrument. "Hello? . . . Harya, baby? . . ." His words and tone were cordial, but his face was blank. "I got Room 710 in this joint. . . . You go to another hotel, 'n I'll call ya later. . . . Go to the Rio. . . . Yeah . . . Bye-bye, sweet."

He hung up, and turned to greet a group of three men, as Prince came out, said, "Good evening," and vanished into the corridor. The three men nodded casually to Jeff, who followed them in. Sterling was resting in an easy chair.

"Good evening, gentlemen. Take what chairs there are." Two took straightbacks, the third perched on the bed. "Well?"

The man on the bed said dourly, "I don't see how Jim White can fail to get it."

One of the other two—who chirped like a bird—said, "We've just come from his rooms upstairs. Every State leader has been in there today."

Sterling sighed and looked at them with a tired smile.

"Houston isn't the place for us to do our fighting. I have another plan."

The man on the bed asked eagerly, "For afterwards?"

"Not for now, of course!" Clara Blanton snapped.

"Clara," said the Bishop.

The three men got up. "We'll see you tomorrow. Coming to hear the keynote speech? Salton will be good."

"Yes, we'll be there. If you see any of my friends, tell them to drop in."

The three men left. Jeff stood where he was for a moment. "Need me?"

Clara Blanton said, "I don't believe so."

"If you want to go anywhere, Jeff, go ahead. Phone me in an hour or so. There might be something," the Bishop told him.

"Right." Jeff drifted out. As he left, four other men came in to see Sterling. Jeff went down to the lobby, then walked the four blocks to press headquarters in the newly built Convention Hall. In the long room lined with typewriter tables and telegraph instruments and operators, he found Voorhees, his coat off, sweating out a story.

The newspaperman stood up and put out his hand. "Many's the day, stranger. How do like this racket?"

"I like it fine," said Jeff, "only it's hotter'n hell. What do you know?"

"White's in the bag," said Voorhees, grinning.

"Tell me something," Jeff mocked. "Who's in line for Vice-President?"

Voorhees made a face of exaggerated mystery. "And you'd run and tell your Bishop, and—"

"Oh, hell! Listen, what time you through tonight?

Come on over to my room, and we'll have a couple snifters."

"Okay. Say eleven."

"Rice Hotel, Room 710. Bring a wench if you have one."

Bands paraded in the streets, sweating men with State badges walked busily in all directions. Workmen toiled on the few unfinished portions of the Convention Hall, and across the main thoroughfares hung large-lettered banners:

WELCOME TO THE NATIONAL DEMOCRATIC PARTY— HOUSTON MEANS VICTORY.

Jeff walked back to the Rice, and went up to the floor on which Jim White, Governor of New York State, had his rooms. Next to them were the lobbying headquarters of a favorite-son candidate, doomed to defeat on the first ballot, but holding on to his delegation in order to bargain for future favors with the victorious candidate.

A special press room had been set aside for newspapermen here also, by courtesy of the New York State Committee. Jeff went in, and found Bailey, of the Richmond *Globe-Bulletin*, Flager, from Tidewater, both of whom greeted him casually. They were intent on jotting down a statement which had just dropped from the lips of Judge Andrew Jackson Walters, leader of the Hall, New York City's Democratic organization, and one-hundred-percent backer of White. Walters' impressive bulk dominated the room, and his faintly sulky voice, when he handed cigars to the correspondents, sounded absurd by contrast. Then he padded out and across the hall to White's rooms.

"How you boys doin'?" asked Jeff.

Flager said, "White's all right—maybe. But the platform! . . ." He shrugged, and went on typing.

A burst of cheering came in from across the way. A man stuck his head in the door, "There's liquor in Room 608. Go to it."

Bailey grabbed Jeff's arm. "Come on. That's all tonight."

From Room 608, jammed with men, cigar smoke, bottles of all kinds of liquor, Jeff 'phoned Voorhees. "Room 608, big doin's."

Then he called Sterling, who said he had no need for him until the morning. They would meet in the spectators' gallery in the hall.

The phone woke Jeff. "Yeah . . . aw, honey, don't scream at me that way. I called you. . . . Tha's right, I forgot. . . . Well, we got drunk. . . . That's the way it is at Conventions. . . . Yeah, we'll have lunch. . . . No, I won't forget."

He hung up, consulted his watch, then leaped out of bed. Inside of fifteen minutes, with an empty stomach, he was entering Convention Hall. In the gallery he found Sterling, Clara Blanton, and a group of observers, most of whom Jeff had seen in and out of the Bishop's rooms. On the floor below them a sea of heads was broken by colored blotches which were bands, one to almost each State delegation. New York, for some reason, had no band. Banners floated, boxes flaunted their slogans, groups broke into spontaneous cheering. It rang and throbbed in Jeff's liquorish head.

The hullabaloo continued, until the Chairman brought silence only after repeated banging of the gavel. Then his voice, introducing Victor Salton, came through the amplifiers with a metallic tone. Salton, a slim, gray-headed man with a thin, sardonic face, began the address which was to set the keynote of the Convention—to hint at policies and planks, to voice, if possible, the dominating sentiment of the National Democratic Party with a view to hooking a few votes. This choice as keynoter was thereafter to raise Victor Salton, a newspaperman, to considerable renown as a political historian and commentator. He talked for three-quarters of an hour while the restless delegates sweated and shuffled and squirmed. But the speech was not for them. At a table in the press box beside the platform, Jeff saw Voorhees fast asleep, a flimsy of the speech clutched in one hand.

Jeff's mind wandered. Sterling brought him to with a whispered request to get back to the hotel and prepare a statement for the press. From outside the hall, Jeff sent a messenger boy in to Voorhees.

"The Bishop has a statement on the speech. Come over to the Rice."

At the room, he got out sheets of flimsy, inserted carbon paper and waited. Soon Sterling arrived. On a typewriter Clara Blanton took down his statement.

"It will be suicide for the Democratic Party to include an outright Wet plank in its platform. Leaders of the Southern Democracy realize with sinking feelings that the domination of the party by the liquor interests and the Roman Catholic Church will disrupt the Democratic South, and revive race hatreds that have not existed for fifty years. Insistence on an anti-Prohibition attitude by these leaders means disaster—nothing more—nothing less.

As a member of the Headquarters Committee of the Anti-Liquor League, I feel this keenly."

Jeff's head ached. He excused himself, welcomed incoming reporters with, "Sit down, boys. You'll get yours soon," and went over to the Rio Hotel. The clerk told him Miss Siegel had Room 444.

He went up and knocked. Dixie answered, let him in, and closed the door behind him. He took her in his arms and kissed her. "Oh, you *were* drunk," she said.

He lit a cigarette. "Was I! Let's eat."

"Having a good time?"

"No. This business is a lot of nonsense. A bunch of crazy guys running around, yelling and screaming; nobody knows what anybody else says—"

"I wish now I'd stayed in Washington. It's hot enough there, but you can go to a beach—"

"Be back there soon, honey. Tomorrow they nominate, and the day after they vote. Everybody thinks White is in the bag, and that means few ballots, perhaps only one."

"Aren't you glad I came down to keep you company?"

"You invited yourself. Got that record?"

She sat down beside him on the bed. "No, darling, I haven't got it. I left it in Washington. Let's not talk about it."

"Humph!"

The next day Van Brunt Adams made the speech that took four years to impress the American public. Four years before, he had risen at the National Convention of the Democratic Party in Madison Square Garden to place in nomination the name of James White, Governor of the Empire State. He had soared then to heights of slogan-

making and had dubbed the East Sider "The Happy
Warrior." But four years before, Jim White, apart from
the matter of local color, had not captured the national
imagination. This time Van Brunt Adams, speaking in
his gentlemanly voice, supporting his paralyzed leg by
leaning heavily on the rostrum, made The Happy Warrior
ring the bell.

Van Brunt Adams was getting to be a landmark at
Democratic Conventions. Eight years earlier, he had been
the nominee for the Vice-Presidency with Saxe of Ohio.
And here he was again, putting Jim White in the running
where he could not be put out of it, as he had been before,
by a deadlock and recourse to a dark horse. This time
Adams would collect a debt of gratitude, and that could
be anything from a Cabinet seat to the Governorship of
New York, or even some day the Presidency.

Delirious cheers from the Eastern delegations met the
name of The Happy Warrior. At least fifteen bands
played at once, and flagstaffs rocked like the masts of
sinking ships. Van Brunt Adams limped from the platform, to receive the handshake of Judge Walters, of
State leaders from everywhere.

Nobody, unfortunately, paid any attention to other men
who nominated candidates. A Representative from
Tennessee was put forward, a banker from California
coasted on favorite-son backing for a while, and the
belligerent Senator Bede of Missouri went into action
with the support of his State.

The afternoon was given over to seconding speeches,
drawing more thundrous cheers. By evening Jeff's head
throbbed from the heat and noise. Dixie, sitting at the far
end of the gallery, left in the middle of the session.

The next day saw the balloting—a scene that eclipsed everything that had gone before. By this time delegates were hoarse from two days of official yelling and unofficial drinking

As the chairman called for the *viva voce* votes, delegation leaders rose and tore their lungs in the effort to be heard emphatically.

"Louisiana casts twenty votes for White."

"Massachusetts says thirty-six votes for White—Massachusetts!"

Governor Montrose of Maryland, wringing wet Southern aristocrat, had released his loyal followers, and after passing the first call they now threw their votes to White. The entire Convention indulged in a delirium of cheering. The ornate State flag of Maryland went reeling around the hall above the heads of the roaring, parading delegation of the Free State.

But there had been a few recalcitrants. Alabama, which four years before had been for her own Senator Underwood for one hundred and two ballots, now sullenly split her vote among three candidates. Georgia and Florida recorded themselves hopelessly for the Tennessee Congressman.

A burst of band music delayed the balloting for a minute. Then in rapid succession, punctuated by further and even more deafening explosions of musical and vocal sound, the States spun off their votes. It needed the barest attention only to understand that Jim White was coasting in, leaving the favorite sons wallowing in the ruck. "Virginia casts twenty-four votes for White!" and it was all over. The Happy Warrior became the Democratic nominee for President on a delegation landslide.

Jeff looked sidewise at the Bishop. The thickish lips were slightly drawn back from the teeth in the beginning of a snarl, and the hands were clenched together. Suddenly one of the hands clutched Jeff's arm, and the rage-contorted face was close to the younger man's.

"I tell you, he'll never be President!"

The gray eyes returned to the spectacle below.

Further ballots only confirmed what was already in the bag: the nomination of Senator Bob Jackson of Arkansas for Vice-President. Sterling sneered to Jeff:

"If they expect Jackson to keep the South in line. . . . A Wet President with Bob Jackson—one of our staunchest allies!"

Band music burst out again, cheers resounded, wearied delegates trudged out, clapping each other on the back, planning the gay evening ahead.

Outside, a victory parade by the New York and other Eastern delegations was forming. At least seven bands were spaced out, their blares mutually confusing:

East Side, West Side. . . .

We'll dance the light fantastic on the Sidewalks of New York.

Surrounded by his advisers, Jim White came out, doffing his straw hat to all sides, lighting a cigar and grinning widely. With him were Van Brunt Adams, limping haltingly to a car, Judge Walters, Mayor Billy Harding of New York and minor aides. The parade followed The Happy Warrior's car around the town.

All the way back to the hotel, Sterling said nothing, but tramped dourly between the grim Clara Blanton and Jeff with his buzzing head. In the lobby Jeff excused himself and went upstairs to sleep. Dixie phoned him before he could slip under.

"H'lo, honey! Jim White got it . . . like rollin' off a log . . . I feel lousy . . . I'll come over after I chow. . . . 'Bye."

He stared at the ceiling for half an hour until his throbbing head subsided, then went to the restaurant below for a solitary dinner. Between mouthfuls he watched the tables, filled with whooping delegates, their racket filling the marbled room with clattering echoes. A bellboy paged him just as he was halfway through a piece of lemon meringue pie.

"Mistuh Coates! Mistuh Coates!"

"Here y'are!"

"Bishop Sterling says come up!"

"Okay, sonny!" Jeff finished his coffee, and went to the Bishop's room. There he found the man standing by the window. Sterling turned.

"Where were you?"

"Eating."

"Oh!" Side glances inspected him, but not suspiciously. "I want to send about fifty telegrams. All the Wesleyan Bishops and lay leaders of importance, understand?"

Jeff sat down. "All I understand is you're goin' to send fifty telegrams. What will they say? Want me to send 'em?"

"Yes. Listen, wire this:

"WHITE NOMINATION MEANS DISASTER FOR CLEAN GOVERNMENT AND PROHIBITION IF ELECTION FOLLOWS STOP I PLAN CONFERENCE TO ORGANIZE WESLEYAN OPPOSITION.

"How's that? Make any sense?"

Jeff read it over from the sheet of hotel stationery he had scribbled on. "It makes a little sense, but not much. Better add something like ' Letter follows.' "

Sterling snapped his fingers. "Of course. I'll send those tomorrow. We'll change it. Make it like this:

"WHITE IF ELECTED MEANS DISASTER TO CLEAN GOVERN-MENT AND PROHIBITION STOP WESLEYAN CHURCH MUST LEAD OPPOSITION BY CONFERENCE OF WESLEYAN LEADERS STOP DETAILS FOLLOW IN LETTER.

"There, that'll do it. You have the official list. Send it to all of them."

"Okay. That all?"

Sterling sighed. "This has been a sad day for us. I'm tired."

Jeff left him, found a telegraph office near the hotel, and sent the messages, noting the cost thereof for future reimbursement. Then he walked to the Rio Hotel. In the lobby he found George Voorhees, who hailed him.

"Defeat for the forces of righteousness and temperance! Staggering blow dealt to clean government, et cetera, et cetera. Where are you going?"

Jeff thought a moment, then said, "Visit a friend up-stairs. Come on."

The dapper newspaperman held back. "I can get my own women. I don't want to butt in."

"Nuts. Come on. I'm not that grabby. We'll gas a while." He dragged Voorhees with him into the elevator, and led him to Dixie's room. She opened the door.

"So it's you," said Voorhees. He walked into the room, kissing her in a fatherly way. Jeff saw him look quizzically at Dixie when her back turned to him. Then he added, "Got any liquor?"

Dixie laughed. "Scotch'll suit you, won't it? I'm thoughtful, I am. Here's ginger ale and ice, too. Mix your own." Jeff fixed three drinks, and then stretched himself across the bed, leaning against the wall. Dixie sat first on the edge of the bed, and Voorhees tilted a chair against the wall.

"I should have thought of doing something like this." He sighed.

"Like what, Uncle George?"

"Like having a charming young lady in Houston simultaneously with myself. I would then be spared the necessity of witnessing your contentment."

Jeff said, "You haven't got a Bishop either, though. Nor Clara L. Blanton. It works out."

Dixie turned on him. "Implying my presence is nullified?"

"Baby!" Jeff sat up, kissed her solemnly, and leaned back again.

"Speaking of Bishops, how is the old coot?" Voorhees asked.

"He's healthy."

"I know that, you ape. I mean what kind of a citizen is he?"

Jeff drank and said, "My God-damn' head aches. He's not a bad guy. But that Blanton is a pain where it hurts most."

"You should've had that Scotch straight if you have a headache. Why didn't you say something?" Dixie placed her hand on his forehead.

"All right, next drink is straight. Take your hand away. It makes me feel like an invalid. Boy, take it from me, Clara and I care for each other in a large way."

Voorhees was grinning. "Doc Sterling go for her, or what is it?"

"Damned if I know. Maybe she's got a yen for him. To me it seems mostly as if she was nuts on all this Board of Public Safety hooey. Nuts about him like you admire Greta Garbo."

"I don't."

"Otherwise the Bish isn't a bad egg. Except he travels in coaches and takes food in a paper bag. That's hot."

Dixie snuggled up to him. He put an arm around her, stroking a shoulder as he talked and listened.

"But the Bish is a right powerful lad, isn't he?" he asked.

"You know that better than I do," Voorhees said, looking at him steadily. Then he added, "All right, little boy, if you won't talk—I won't wheedle you."

"Oh, hell!" Then Dixie jumped up and mixed fresh drinks. After she had distributed them, Voorhees without preamble went into a speech.

"Let me inform you of something. You're a newspaperman but you don't have the right slant on your racket. Did you ever think of becoming a Washington correspondent? Do you know how to be a good one? I'll tell you, and you, sweetheart, make your boy friend take heed.

"What you want to do is accumulate inside information. I mean by that, make it your business to know the events that really happen behind the doors. Make that your business, and then you can begin to understand what's going on. You're enough of a newspaperman to know that only about one percent of the real news ever gets into print."

He stood up, lit a cigarette, and faced Jeff seriously.

"I don't mean that papers are afraid to print that stuff, though that's part of it. What I mean is, one piece of real good inside dirt is worth more unpublished than it is published. Get the idea?"

Jeff said, "Of course. But what's that got to do with me? I've got a pretty good job now."

"Want to be office boy for a Bishop?"

"No, he doesn't," said Dixie suddenly.

"You pipe down," said Jeff. To Voorhees: "What're you feeding me this for?"

Voorhees stared at him, then laughed and sat down again. "I'm trying to give you a slant on what you can do for yourself. You're the first guy the old coot ever took such a fancy to. You can make that mean a lot to yourself. Get me?"

Jeff looked at him. "It's an idea. Let's talk some more, some time."

Voorhees glanced at his watch. "All right with me. I'm sick of looking at you two now, and I'm taking myself off. When do you go back to Washington?"

"Tomorrow some time."

"See you on the train, or in Washington, or some place. Goo'-bye." The dapper man went out.

Dixie said, "He talks real sense. That's what you'll do."

Jeff grinned lazily. "So you can get all the inside, too?"

Her black eyes flashed angrily. "No. Because I'm crazy about you!"

He went "Tse-tse!" with his tongue, then said: "Mix your lord and master another drink."

8.

POLITICS IN A PROTESTANT CHURCH

THE FIFTY-ODD telegrams sent by Bishop Sterling from Houston late in June brought concrete results in the shape of the Corinth, North Carolina, Conference, just after the middle of July. After the telegram, had gone a letter to clerical and lay leaders of the Dry Southern sentiment, as follows:

"Dear friend and fellow-worker:

"We are faced with the task of averting a national calamity—the possible election to the Presidency of a man who stands for repeal of the liquor laws for which we have all so valiantly fought. His influence will weaken the foundations of our nation. While political leaders regard this possibility with indifference, we, the spiritual leaders of millions, must be alive to the danger—and to our duty.

"Therefore I call upon you to attend the Corinth Conference, July 18th and 19th, where we shall decide upon a course of action calculated to martial against the forces of corruption the mighty army of morally indignant citizens. This Conference will be non-political, for its aims are above the sordid aims of paid politicians, and are

rather identified with the maintenance of a higher and purer form of government.

"I look forward eagerly to greeting you at Corinth, and shaking you by the hand.

> *I remain, yours,*
> THOMAS HENDERSON STERLING,
> *Bishop, Wesleyan Church, South."*

Richmond, Va.

The Bishop and his entourage—Clara Planton and Jeff —went to Corinth, North Carolina, on the seventeenth. The next day began the gathering of the brethren: Wesleyan Bishops, ministers and laity; and even a strong Immersionist delegation, headed by one Dr. Evans J. Bruce. A short meeting the morning of the seventeenth between Dr. Bruce and Sterling produced between them a feeling of amity and cooperation.

The same morning there arrived in Corinth the delegation from Alabama, headed by Bishop Calkins Blake.

Reporters set up press headquarters in a suite of rooms given them by the hotel on the ground floor, and to them, Bishop Sterling said, among other things:

"The Corinth Conference does not want politicians. It is not interested in politics, but in the preservation of national probity and the sanctity of the Constitution. This is no place for the cynical bargainings of committeemen."

This was duly published in the national press.

The Conference opened in the Corinth Auditorium, the only public hall in the North Carolina town. The first speech was by Sterling. His gray eyes roved the determined faces of the spiritual leaders of the South. He said:

"Fellow workers: we are met here for a solemn purpose. We still feel the sting, the outrageous affront, offered us by the Democratic Convention in nominating for the Presidency a man who has behind him an evil record. He is honest, yes. He may even be sincere, but we are not here to pass on his personal attributes. We are here to find a way to combat his campaign with the forces of morality and righteousness. We have no interest in politics as such, though we may be forced to use political methods as a weapon. Nothing must stand in the way of our defeating Governor Jim White of New York in his attempt to foist on the United States the principles and aims of a policy nurtured in the shadow of a brewery and carried into partial execution in a State where reverence for truly American ideals is a thing of mockery and jest.

"This is our task, my friends: to humble the brazenry of a man whose very nomination means disaster for the Jeffersonian principles of the self-determination of States, though he prates of States' Rights with parrot-like amiability. But does he know our problems—does he care? He does not!

"He stands for repeal of the Eighteenth Amendment and of the Volstead Act, though his party platform says otherwise. But let us not be deceived. Let us not sink into the indifferent state of mind that characterizes the rest of this nation. Let the South, that has never hesitated to fight for what it considered its rights, fight again for its honor and for the integrity of its existence. Let it defy a representative of New York's Hall—the most corrupt of boss-run political entities—and refuse to give support to him. We may even find it necessary to throw our support to Gilbert Molleson!"

Applause broke out, mingled with a murmur of voices. This was the first time any had even played with the idea, not of refusing to vote for Jim White, but of going so far as to vote for a Republican. This was heresy. Sterling stormed at them before they could realize all its implications:

"This is why we have met! On every hand we encounter the apathy of Democratic leaders who are more interested in political control itself than in the forces by which they retain it. It is our sacred task to visit defeat on these men. And to do that we must cast out our fears!"

He sat down amid a rattle of applause. broken by sharp vocal outbursts. A Bishop from Maryland took the platform next.

"I want to endorse the stand taken by my worthy colleague, Bishop Sterling. He advocates support of Gilbert Molleson, and I think we should realize a few facts about this statesman. During the war he fed the starving people of Poland, but that is merely the best known feature of his long and splendid record. As Secretary of Commerce he helped bring prosperity to our country. His earlier years were spent in building up his well-earned reputation as a great engineer. I feel that if ever we should break party lines, Molleson is the man we should do it for."

A Tennessee Bishop spoke along the same lines, emphasizing unctuously that Molleson had been an aide of the Democratic War President, Jastrow Judson.

Then Bishop Calkins Blake of Alabama made his way to the platform. Jeff watched this man with special interest, for he knew that all the opposition to Sterling policies centered in Alabama. Blake was a medium-sized man, looking more like an insurance salesman than a highly-placed cleric. He wore a black suit, and carried his apparent fifty years easily. He had wide, innocent eyes, and a nasal cracker voice.

He said: "It may be premature for me to speak at this time, but I feel that I must. My worthy colleagues strongly, and with some show of reason, advocate active aggression against the Wet forces in the Dry South. As much as any of you, I am an ardent supporter of the Prohibition laws of this country, but perhaps there are other things to be considered. They call Gilbert Molleson a great engineer, yet I have recently talked with a Birmingham banker returned from England. He referred in passing to Molleson's early career. It seems that he was only nominally an engineer. From his London office, he promoted oil wells, mines—almost anything, in fact, that would return large profits. Molleson today is a millionaire, and he did not make his fortune in American industry. For the greater part of his life, he was an expatriate."

Shocked ejaculations went up from the pious delegates. A lantern-jawed preacher from Arkansas yapped, "Shame!" but his outstretched finger was pointed at Bishop Blake and not at the record of Molleson.

"The stock promoter selected by the Republicans as their candidate is not the man to hold the affection of the American people, or to maintain American prosperity upon a sound basis," continued Blake stubbornly. "On the other hand, though Governor White is a Wet, perhaps he has other recommendations. In New York they think very well of him, for he has been, they say, a brilliant director of the large-scale finances of New York State. His budget system has been widely praised. Perhaps that is what his country needs, rather than a stock-exchange engineer!"

Critical exclamations mingled with some applause interrupted him.

"This is all food for serious thought," insisted Blake.
"We have met to take counsel. And there is still another
point to be considered. I do not believe—and I will find
many to support me in this assertion—that politics has
any place in the program of the Wesleyan Church, South.
I do not believe that we should, no matter what happens,
pledge ourselves to any other policy than passive resistance to the Wet forces of the North!"

Blake sat down quietly, his wide-open eyes staring at
Sterling, who rose at once. His thickish lips worked nervously; when he spoke, Jeff heard the guttural rasp he had
already noticed on several previous occasions. Sterling
announced in an obviously controlled voice:

"It is useless to conduct our deliberations so publicly.
We shall end only by weakening our strength. I move
that a committee be formed to draft a program and a platform, on which the Conference as a whole may vote tomorrow."

Viva voce seconding followed, together with the forma-
tion of the committee, including, among many others, the
Immersionist Bruce, and Blake and Sterling. They agreed
to meet at two-thirty that afternoon, and the meeting
broke up.

Jeff spent the afternoon, while the committee was in
session, in inspecting the quiet town. Its tree-shaded
streets offered little in the way of interest, its main street
held small promise of diversion. Depending on the nearby
mill towns for trade, Corinth was a slightly glorified
county seat, little more. Its hotels were taxed to the

limit in providing accommodations for those attending the Conference.

Later in the afternoon Jeff entered into conversation with the desk clerk. "What can you do here for amusement, liquor, and so forth?"

"Corn's right easy to get. You might go out to Tommy's, two miles south of here. It's a sort of roadhouse, and it might be interestin' to you. I can hire a car for you."

"We'll see. Thanks, anyway." Jeff went to his own room, cleaned up, then went to the Bishop's suite, the front room of which, as usual, was employed as an office. There he found Clara Blanton waiting.

"Warm, isn't it?" he said.

"Yes, isn't it?"

Jeff let the conversation die there. He lit a cigarette and waited for the Bishop to return, which he did inside of ten minutes. Again the thickish lips wore their snarling expression. He shut the door behind him vigorously. The phone rang.

Jeff answered. "No, the Doctor won't talk just now. Right after dinner there'll be something." He hung up. "Reporters."

Sterling sat down and said, "Right after dinner is correct. I'm not going to let Blake get in my way. He's impudent!"

"That man has always been annoying," Clara Blanton said. "What did he do?"

Sterling stood up again, angry. "Curse him! He sits there with his baby eyes and says that all we have to do is not vote for White, and then Molleson will win. He doesn't know what he's talking about, and yet he influences some of those other fools." He turned on Jeff.

"Call that Tennessee fellow here, and tell him to bring Stone, from Kentucky, with him!"

Jeff called Bishop Bingham of Tennessee, gave him the message. In a few minutes he and Stone arrived.

They were both plump, round-faced men, with the set lips of fanatics. Sterling began on them right away.

"Gentlemen, it's necessary for us to have a serious talk. Otherwise this Conference is doomed to failure."

Stone said, "I don't think I can agree with you, sir. Mind you, I don't know much about politics, but—"

"You don't have to know!" Sterling ripped out. "Look here, I'm trying to prevent a downright Wet from getting into the White House, and you sit around and think that passive resistance is enough. Pah!"

Bingham objected. "I don't believe, Tom, that you have the right to take that attitude. We are every bit as interested—"

"Then listen to me. I've come here to tell you that there's only one way to keep Jim White out of the White House—one sure way. That is to break the Solid South. Can you understand that, or will you take my word for it?"

"That's clear enough, but we don't agree with you as to the best way to break the South. That's our point."

Clara Blanton said, "Surely you gentlemen realize that Bishop Sterling has a very fine understanding of politics?"

Bingham grinned. "Too fine, to hear Blake tell it."

Sterling snarled at him: "If you think Calkins Blake is going to lick me on this proposition, you're out of your mind. Get that straight."

The two Bishops seemed startled at his tone. Sterling

realized it. "This gets me pretty excited, so don't mind how I talk."

"That's all right," said Stone. "But I think we'll stick with Blake."

Sterling sat down. "All right. Then I'll see you to-morrow."

Silence hung in the room as the Bishops tramped solemnly out.

Sterling said to Clara Blanton: "After dinner, tell the reporters that—"

A knock on the door interrupted. Jeff answered. There were four reporters, one of whom said, "We've got a question to ask the Bishop."

"Okay. Come in."

The four came in, and the spokesman said, "Sorry to bust in this way, Doctor. Bishop Blake says the Wesleyan Church, South, will not meddle in politics. We'd like to know if you have any comment to make, so we can send it out with the same story?"

Sterling jumped from his chair. "You're right I've got a comment. Here it is. The Wesleyan Church, South, it is true, will not meddle in politics for their own sake. But when a moral issue arises, like the sanctity and protection of the Constitution, the Wesleyan Church, South, will take an active part in the defense."

The four men went out respectfully. "We have to get Blake," Sterling said.

Clara Blanton said, "Oh, I'm sure you will, Doctor."

Before he went out to dinner, Jeff read over the rough draft of the resolutions made by the committee that afternoon.

"WHEREAS, the Corinth Conference has met and agreed that the anti-Prohibition principles animating the political career of Governor White of New York are not acceptable to the people of the Southern States; and

"Whereas, the Corinth Conference considers that there are four major reasons why Governor White is not acceptable to the body politic of the Southern States, these four reasons being: his repudiation of the Dry platform adopted at Houston; his Wet record; his choice of a dripping Wet big business man as National Chairman; his affiliation with the Hall, political machine of New York City; therefore be it

"Resolved: that the Corinth Conference urges non-support of Governor White in his campaign for President by the voters of the Southern States."

Sterling tapped a trembling finger on the last paragraph. "That's Blake's doing. Non-support! The fool!"

"Have to change it somehow," said Jeff.

Sterling stared at him bleakly. "Yes. But how?"

After dinner Jeff went to a movie, but that killed the evening only up to ten-fifteen. And he was far from sleepy. He went back to the hotel, hired a car and had himself driven to Tommy's, the roadhouse mentioned by the clerk that afternoon. It turned out to be a modern, Florida-style house, set back about fifty feet from the main road toward Asheville. Its windows betrayed only the slightest threads of light seeping around drawn blinds. The chauffeur of the car got Jeff in, then waited outside.

In the rear room Jeff found a small bar doling out all kinds of drinks. Jeff ordered corn, and looked around. Next to himself, he found the reporter who had acted as spokesman for the four just before dinner. The man nodded.

"H'lo!"

Jeff asked, "What goes on here?"

The man shrugged. "Not a hell of a lot. Some girls usually blow in around eleven. Factory girls from Asheville, if you go in for that." The man looked at him curiously.

"Tryin' to figure what I'm doin' here?"

"I know why you're here," the man grinned. "On'y a Bishop's Secretary—I've seen funnier things at that."

"Have to do something. Hello!" Jeff had been idly watching the door.

"Whatsa matter?"

"There's a funnier one for you. Bishop Blake of Alabama. There, at that table in the corner."

The reporter looked, then chuckled. "Innocent-lookin', ain't he?"

He and Jeff drank again, when some girls arrived, in pairs. A radio was turned on, and the girls began dancing with each other on the tiny floor in the front room. Men cut in on them, and friendships were established. Jeff saw Bishop Blake dance several times.

After the reporter and Jeff had had several snorts, Jeff went over to talk to the Bishop, who was momentarily alone. The baby eyes stared resentfully.

"Excuse me, Bishop, I don't think you know me. Coates is my name. I'm a sort of assistant to Doctor Sterling."

Blake merely looked at him. "Are you surprised to find me here?" he asked.

"Yes."

"Well, nobody will believe you."

Jeff grinned to cover his surprise. "Maybe nobody will have to," he said. "See you later." He rejoined the reporter, who had his arm around a short dumpy girl who talked with a thick tarheel accent. They drank some more.

It was nearly twelve when the sound of several automobiles pulling up sharply on the gravel roadway beside the house was clearly audible. The bartender yelled: "Cops!" and ducked out of sight. A trapdoor top slammed down after him.

The reporter said, "Let's git. Sometimes these raiders get tough."

The lights stayed on, while for several seconds the customers remained staring at each other in astonishment. Then the sound of crashing wood came from the front of the house. Somebody knocked over the radio, and its voice said loudly, "We take pleasure in presentingeeeee-uuuuurf!" A girl gave a little scream. A man said: "Damnation!" and put his foot through a window. The splintering of wood continued. A shot sounded outside.

Jeff leaped across to the table where Bishop Blake sat, his innocent blue eyes unblinking in horrified amazement. Jeff grabbed him by the arm and hustled him to the side of the reporter standing by a rear door. The reporter said:

"I think this goes to the cellar."

A man charged into them; Jeff's right clipped him on the jaw. The man said, "Ow!" and spun away. A girl started a high-pitched sobbing in one corner.

Loud cursing voices burst out in the front room. The reporter said, "Jesus, here they come!" He tore open the door, and the three men tumbled down dark steps, colliding with a rough brick wall at the bottom. A shaft of dirty moonlight came in a basement window; that was enough for them to see the under part of a cellar door leading outside. Cautiously the reporter shoved it open. Meanwhile Jeff kept a tight hold on Bishop Blake's arm, while the Bishop made no sound whatever. They crept out into the open, keeping in the shadow of the building. Once at the corner, the reporter whispered:

"There's a road back yonder. We'll run!"

Together, running as lightly as they could, they charged across the open ground back of the house. A man's voice shouted from the house; the crash of breaking glass followed. Then the three gained the cover of a swale. In the dark they caught their clothes on brambles, stumbled over rocks, until, breathless, they reached a dirt road running parallel to the main highway on which the roadhouse stood.

"We're safe here." The reporter stopped and lit a cigarette.

Jeff said, "I suppose we'll have to walk to town. I had a car, but that guy must have beat it by now."

"Yeah. Well, it's only two-three miles. Take us an hour."

The Bishop said, "If we must walk, we must walk. It was very kind of you to help us out that way."

"Hell!" said the reporter, and they started the long walk.

It was close to two o'clock when Jeff inserted his key in his room door and let himself in. His clothes were torn somewhat, and his whole body ached from the unusual exertion of tramping a country road. But his first move was to telephone Sterling's room. A sleepily hoarse voice answered him.

Jeff said: "I've got something hot to tell you. Can I come down?" He hung up when answered and went downstairs. He found the Bishop attired in an old-fashioned felt bathrobe, with leather slippers on. The gray eyes were bleary and wore the startled look of a man without his glasses.

"What's the matter?" he said.

Jeff told him what had happened, finishing up with: "Point is that at first, when I talked to him, he wasn't scared just because I saw him there. Said nobody would believe me. But after the raid, he was in a real sweat. Thanked me very heartily for helping him when I left him at his hotel down the street."

Sterling was more awake now. "Nobody will believe *him* now," he said. "You had that reporter right with you?"

"That's correct."

Sterling went to the phone, called the hotel down the street, and got Blake on the wire. Sterling said politely:

"I'm sorry to keep you up this way, Bishop, but Mr. Coates has just told me of your little adventure this evening. I'm right glad you got out of it safely. . . . Yes, indeed. . . . It must have been very exciting. . . . Yes. . . . Good night, I'll see you in the morning."

Sterling turned away from the phone and looked at Jeff, gnawing his lips.

In the morning the Committee on Resolutions met as per schedule. At two-thirty the Conference met as a whole and approved the resolution drawn by the committee. It was identical with the one Jeff had read in the Bishop's room the night before, except that the last paragraph was changed. The phrase "non-support of Governor White" had been changed to "active opposition."

"That means defeat for White. We'll break the Solid South!" Sterling said triumphantly.

Clara Blanton said: "I think it was fine of Bishop Blake to change his mind."

9.

MEET WINT, OBERWASSER AND JOHNSBURY

The evening of September seventeenth, Bishop Sterling returned from a three weeks' trip to Madrid, whither he had gone to confer with authorities of Spanish Morocco concerning missionary work in Northern Africa. Jeff felt a mild amusement at the Bishop's titular activities as Bishop of Peru and Morocco.

It was late in the Richmond afternoon when Sterling came to the suite of rooms in Murphy's Hotel that now served as headquarters for the Anti-White Democrats. Clara Blanton greeted the gray-haired man effusively, but Sterling was more interested in getting reports of what had happened.

"What have you done?" the Bishop asked Jeff.

As Jeff answered he saw Clara Blanton catch her lower lip under her upper teeth. "To give it to you in a paragraph, we've kept up the ads in the small-town papers, and I've kept Prince well supplied with stories attacking White on the Roman Catholic angle. Miss Blanton has been more active than I have in keeping up the spirits of the State groups, though personally I think our best allies are in North Carolina and Texas. Blake has been peaceful in Alabama, but not what you might call cooperative. That's about all."

Sterling asked, "How's the financial situation?"

Clara Blanton said, "I must talk to you about that, seriously, Doctor. I'm worried."

The Bishop's gray eyes traveled back and forth rapidly between Jeff and the secretary. "Yes, yes. All right, we'll have a talk. In the morning, say. I'm tired now."

Jeff was glad Sterling had returned. The past three weeks in Richmond had been dull, for Vernon had taken Veryl North for the summer. Dixie had come down from Washington only once; he had week-ended in the Capital twice with her, but the flats of the Potomac were even hotter than Broad Street at noon.

Jeff did his bit of publicity-story writing in the early morning, and it was just before luncheon that he had a chat with Sterling.

"I think we'll take another trip soon, probably today. Will you be ready?"

"Of course. Where to?"

Sterling watched him. "I suppose you know that the Anti-White Democrats haven't much money."

"So Miss Blanton has been saying. An awful lot of small contributions came in—you know, a dollar from an old lady in Crewe, twenty-five from a parish in Tidewater, a hundred from a guy in New York, but that doesn't add up fast enough, according to her."

"Exactly. We need a lot of money right away. You remember Wint?"

"K. Cuthbert Wint? I'll never forget a man with that name. He promised you money."

Sterling got up and paced back and forth. "Well, now

we're going to get it. I spoke to him on the phone this morning, and I found he's going to New York this afternoon. We'll go tonight, on the eight o'clock."

"Fine," Jeff said. "Mind my asking why I have to go?"

"Not a bit." The Bishop looked at him with the first glimmer of kindness in the old eyes Jeff had yet seen there. "I like to have you along." The kindness was replaced by craftiness. "Besides, we can stop in and see our mutual friend Silverman."

"My pal Silverman."

The next morning saw them in the Pennsylvania Station, whence Sterling phoned Wint at the Ambassador Hotel. Coming out of the booth, the Doctor said, "We're to meet him in Room 1414, the Mutual Assurance Building, Newark. Will you remember that?"

Jeff repeated it to fix it in his mind. Then they checked their bags and started for Newark. An hour later saw them entering Room 1414. No one was in the anteroom until a tall, fat man came in, also from outside. He carried a heavy knobbly cane, and wore a wide-brimmed taupe felt hat. He started to pass them, then stopped.

His voice rumbled puffily: "This is Bishop Sterling, isn't it? Come on in."

Sterling said, "I—I'm waiting here for Mr. Wint."

The big man shook his head. "That's all right. So am I. I'm Senator Oberwasser. Come in." He led them into a private office and placed chairs for them. "Wint should be here any moment. He told me you were in town. I've heard a lot about you, sir, and I'm mighty glad to meet you at last."

"The pleasure is all mine, Senator. I hope we're **not**

taking up your time." Oberwasser really was an ex-Senator, but everyone knew that he clung tenaciously to the courtesy title.

The beady eyes in the vast face eyed Jeff. Sterling caught the look and said hastily, "Oh, I'm sorry, Senator. This is Mr. Coates, my most valuable assistant."

Jeff placed his hand in the Senator's big one. They sat down again. Then Wint arrived, the imposing neat man. He came in fast and shook hands with everybody.

"Sorry to have held you up. How do you like Newark, Doctor?"

Sterling said: "Busy enough. I didn't know you made your headquarters here, Senator."

The big voice rumbled. "I keep this private office for myself. I have another at the insurance company's main place in New York—I'm in insurance, you know." The vast face creased in a smile.

"Senator, I feel we ought to get right down to business," Wint broke in. "Shall I give you the story?"

All settled in their seats. Wint continued: "The Bishop here, as you know, is leading the Anti-White fight among the Democrats of the South. He has built up a great organization which, I can tell you, is going to mean greater Southern strength for Gilbert Molleson on November 3rd. But the Doctor finds now that he is in dire need of campaign contributions. He tells me that he needs—and right soon—a considerable sum. He came to me for reasons that are obvious—he thought that perhaps I could help him, my work giving me a natural interest not only in getting votes for Molleson, but in pulling them away from Jim White. Now, today, we both found ourselves at once in New York, and I suggested this little meeting. I thought, Senator, that you would know of someone able to make a sizeable contribution to the Anti-White Democrats of Virginia and other States."

Wint stopped. Oberwasser inspected him ponderously. "It's pretty interesting to you to see that the Bishop gets this money?"

Wint smiled easily, too easily, Jeff thought. "Why, of course, just as every campaign contribution is of interest to me."

Oberwasser: "Why don't you make a contribution direct from your funds?"

Wint shot back: "You can see yourself that wouldn't be wise. We're Republicans, and against White. They're against White also, but they're Democrats. It would look funny—"

Sterling said: "I believe you'll understand, Senator, that we are not only opposing White, but working actively for Molleson. And to sow the seeds of Republicanism in the South, sir, is a right hard job."

Wint: "I thought your friend Johnsbury would be the man. He is a Republican, too."

Oberwasser smiled faintly. "I agree with you. Point is, just how interested are you Southern Republicans in seeing this money go down there?" The beady eyes shifted from Sterling to Wint. They were worried eyes.

Wint smiled again his easy smile. "We want to see Gilbert Molleson elected. Naturally we will be sensible of anything done to further that end."

Oberwasser said "Hmmm!" then picked up the phone. "Mr. Johnsbury free? . . . Fine. Tell him Senator Oberwasser will be right down to see him with some friends."

They went to the eighth floor, and were passed into the

office of Henry L. Johnsbury. As they went in Wint said
to Sterling and Jeff, "He's president of this company.
Rich as . . ."

They were introduced to a man who looked like a
popular magazine's conception of a successful business
man. Six feet, broad shouldered, iron-gray hair, a little-
lined face, and straightforward gaze. He looked like a
man who played handball or squash regularly at his club,
golf on Sundays, bridge every night. He passed around
good cigars.

Oberwasser began. "Henry, these gentlemen have come
to me with a very interesting little proposition. Suppose
you go over it, Wint."

"It's like this, Henry," the Republican campaign leader
said. "I'm here, first of all, as an intermediary only. I
want that understood. Now—" And he outlined again,
only in more detail, what he had told the ex-Senator upstairs. Johnsbury listened with the business man's poker
face, but at the finish he said, without hesitation:

"It sounds very good, indeed. I think that I would like
to help Bishop Sterling. Would ten thousand be a good
starter?"

Jeff watched Sterling, whose lips twitched. "I—I think
it would."

Johnsbury smiled broadly. "I'm glad to do anything
that will help the Republican cause."

Wint did not say anything.

Johnsbury pushed a buzzer. A male secretary answered.
"Make out a check to cash—personal check—for ten
thousand dollars, even. Right away, please."

Oberwasser said, "I think, Bishop, you can count on me
for something a little later on, though I expect to have my

hands full." He turned to Wint. "Dammit all, did you hear that Bradford Day is going to run against me in the next primaries?"

Wint looked alarmed. "Did he resign his ambassadorship to Cuba?"

"He's going to. He's got a great reputation. . . ."

They were interrupted by the entrance of the male secretary with the check. Johnsbury said, "Now, George, you go to the bank with the Bishop and help him get this cashed."

"Yes, sir." He went outside to wait.

Wint said to the ex-Senator, "You and I will have to talk about Day some time soon. That's certainly a hot piece of information. Oh—and might I make a suggestion about this talk we have had?" Wint looked at the circle of faces with a bright air. "I would like to suggest that my part in this be kept quiet, for very obvious reasons. Further, I would like to create the impression—"

Oberwasser said with solemn haste, "Look here, Wint, nobody's going to—"

Wint smiled patronizingly. "I know. But if . . . What I would like is for the Bishop to write to Mr. Johnsbury, say tomorrow, referring to this meeting, and voicing the hope that Mr. Johnsbury will see his way to making a contribution. Is my point clear?"

Silence. Then Sterling said, "Perfectly. I'll do it."

Oberwasser said nothing; Johnsbury merely smiled, his gaze vague.

An hour later, ten thousand dollars in cash in his wallet, Bishop Sterling was talking to Silverman in the office of Gunter and Company.

Silverman was saying: "I really think you should have more working capital in here. Of course you realize that the biggest profits are not to be made in odd lots, but in larger transactions. Now, five thousand—"

Sterling bit his lip. "That's a large amount for me, Silverman."

The young Jewish broker smiled professionally. "With this bull market I can run it up to ten, fifteen. Of course, I've made a little for you, but big profits are what you want before the bottom drops out of this."

Sterling laughed quaveringly, suggesting to Jeff that the laugh hid thoughts of something else. "Oh, this market won't fall!" Pause. "I—I wish I had five thousand dollars to give you—Tell you what, Silverman, I'll get five thousand for you within a month!"

The broker smiled. "Fine! I know I can depend on you."

The morning after their return to Washington, Jeff went deliberately to see Voorhees, the Bishop going on to Richmond at once.

The newspaperman pushed a chair forward for Jeff. "So! We meet again."

Jeff sat and both lit cigarettes. He frowned at Voorhees, and said, "I'm just back from New York, and I've got a feeling I'm in something maybe a little deeper than I figured on. I need advice."

"Uncle George is glad to see his nephew Jeffie."

"Listen, I'm serious. You know how you wanted dope from me on the Bish. Well, here's some and if you can figure all of it, you're a better Wesleyan than I am."

"Which is a hell of a Wesleyan."

"Get this," Jeff urged. "Two-three days ago the Bish and I leap to New York and meet Wint there—" Voorhees' eyebrows went up. "And K. Cuthbert takes us to see old Oberwasser."

"Republicans! I thought you fellows were Democrats." Voorhees was paying serious attention now.

Jeff nodded sarcastically. "Yeah. Wait. Angle is that old Obie is perhaps going to dig up dough for our anti-White campaign in Virginia and North Carolina, see? And Obie comes through. He takes us to his buddy Johnsbury, who is the great gazook of an insurance company in Newark. This Johnsbury practically apologizes for not giving us more than ten grand. Cash. And promises more. Oberwasser says he'll give till it hurts."

"Jesus!"

Jeff leaned forward. "Before we get ahead of ourselves, did you know that Bradford Day is going to run against Oberwasser in the next primaries and try to get that Jersey Senate seat?"

Voorhees sat upright with a jerk. "Day running for the Senate? Why in God's name didn't you tell me when you came in? Holy mackerel!" He stood up in his excitement. "Are you giving me that tip to use?"

"I didn't know it was as hot as all that, even if Oberwasser was sore as hell over it. He just heard that Day was about to resign his Cuba ambassadorship, and—"

"Let me use it. I'll beat every God-damn' paper in the country. Okay?"

Jeff grinned. "Sure, go ahead. But don't even hint where you got it."

Voorhees did not answer, but strode into another office. Jeff heard him typewriting furiously, then instructing the

secretary to wire the story to New York. In ten minutes
Voorhees was back, more controlled. "Boy, you're my pal
for life. What can I do for you?"

"Sit down. I didn't get through telling you. Here's the
situation. Wint, Republican leader, takes us to a Republican ex-Senator, who shunts a lot of money our way. For
what? To elect Molleson? To defeat White in the South?
I would figure that—"

Voorhees wagged his head. "That's not so hard. Not if
you know that Oberwasser is trying to get solid with this
Administration and with Molleson. He'll take any means
to do it."

"Yeah, sure, that's easy, but—"

The correspondent blew a great cloud of smoke. "Here's
the way it works. Molleson'll probably be elected. He's
Dry as hell, isn't he? All right. Oberwasser is personally
Wet as a rainstorm, but he's voted Dry. But he knows that
Molleson will hold that wetness against him. So he works
every angle to obligate the party to him. That way he'll
get their support in the primaries and get his seat back
in the Senate. That's clear."

Jeff nodded, looking not much wiser. "All right. But
why does Wint shove him off on us? Who the hell is Sterling up North?"

Voorhees smoked thoughtfully. "Wint probably has a
reason. Maybe it's like this. Oberwasser is bothering him,
and Wint and the rest of his National Committee boy
friends don't want to be bothered. At the same time Wint
would like to help Sterling dent the South. Obie is the
answer to his prayer. That way he helps himself without obligating himself. If Molleson wins and Obie wants
a reward, Wint shrugs and says that Obie helped the Dem-

ocrats. I think that's probably what animates K. Cuthbert Wint."

"That sounds like lots of sense. In that case I think my Bishop is going for a sleigh ride. They're too smart for him."

Voorhees scoffed. "The hell they are!"

"How about Johnsbury?" Jeff suggested. "With your line of reasoning, Johnsbury then wants something from the Republicans too."

"Sure. A job in the cabinet."

"Not that guy!"

"I know a little about him. He'd like a Cabinet post. Only you can bet Wint isn't going to be bothered with him. Nor Oberwasser either. Looks as if Wint shunted Oberwasser, who in turn shunted his boy friend. Very neat, I would call it."

"Yeah, isn't it?" Jeff looked at the other without enthusiasm. "That's what I'm in."

The newspaperman nodded slowly, staring shrewdly at Jeff. At length he said, "Listen, you brought me a hot tip today. Day coming into a senatorial campaign is damned interesting. I bet you Molleson will support him against Oberwasser, because he's afraid of him as a possible rival within the party. If they get him into the Senate, that takes care of him for six years, or two Presidential terms. Get it?"

Jeff nodded. Voorhees went on. "I want to make you a proposition. I think that you and I can exchange inside dope to good advantage for both of us. If you're in a big thing, as you think, I can help to steer you, like today for instance. On the other hand, you'll pick up a lot of stuff, like this Bradford Day piece, that'll help me a lot. How about it?"

Jeff smiled. "I'll be needing lots of help."

Voorhees stood up and thrust out a hand. "Okay, it's a deal." They shook hands.

"Think I'd be better off workin' for Randolph Taitt? He wants me."

Voorhees glanced at him quickly. "You can be more valuable to yourself and to Taitt later on. I'll give you a piece of real advice. You stick to Bishop Sterling right through the campaign, and get as much dirt on him as you can!"

10.

THAT JOB WITH TAITT

ON THE twentieth of September, Jeff joined the Bishop in Richmond. He found the old man staring out of the window of the room-office in Murphy's Hotel. He faced Jeff blankly.

"What's the matter?" Jeff asked hurriedly.

Very gently the Bishop said: "Caroline—my wife—died—yesterday."

"Oh! Suddenly?"

"No. She has been very ill—years." The Bishop turned again to stare out of the window. His voice came to Jeff almost inaudibly. "We were very happy together when we were young. I haven't even been allowed to see her for months. Poor woman."

Jeff said nothing.

"Her sufferings have ended now, I thank God." The black-clad shoulders lifted in an enormous sigh. Then the weary voice came with renewed strength: "But I must go on. Sorrow has no place in my life."

Jeff found no comment to make on that flat statement. The next day he sat again with the old man in the same room, but he never heard another mention of Mrs. Sterling. The Bishop behaved as if he had never borne the sufferings of a permanent invalid. The gray eyes were

shifting from one set of clippings to a heap of letters—
from a bunch of bills to the carbon copy of a letter in his
hand. He showed this to Jeff. It was a letter to Johnsbury in Newark:

"My dear Mr. Johnsbury,

It was with great pleasure that I learned, during our
short chat the other day, that you are interested in the
national political campaign now going on. The paragraphs
below will provide you with a clear picture of our work
here in the South, through the Anti-White Democrat
organization, to defeat the New Yorker in his absurd at-
tempt to gain the White House. I hope that you can see
your way to swelling our lamentably slim coffers. Etc.,
etc."

As Jeff read, he heard the Bishop chuckling. "Good idea
of Wint's, wasn't it? To write him as if he hadn't yet given
a dime?" Without waiting for Jeff's answer, he added,
"And I think Mr. Johnsbury will be even more liberal
later on in the campaign. I'm going to see him on my return."

The younger man looked up. "Return? Where are you
going?"

Sterling grimaced. "My work for the Church takes me
to Texas for a few days. A conference. I will have to leave
several very important matters in your hands."

Jeff waited.

The Bishop answered his thought when he said, "Miss
Blanton will of course be in charge of the office here, in
its routine. What really concerns me now is—" He
stopped, apparently embarrassed.

Jeff remained silent. After a few seconds' pause the

Bishop went on, "The organization here finds itself suddenly in possession of considerable money. Johnsbury's money and an equal amount, approximately, of minor contributions. I don't want those all in one bank." The thickish lips moved uncertainly; the fingers of both hands interlocked. Then he cleared his throat very loudly and plunged on, staring straight at Jeff, who maintained a perfectly blank countenance. "I want you to take this money—" he uncovered a thick package of bills under a letter— "to Lewes, Virginia, and open two bank accounts in the bank there for me. Can you go in the morning?"

"Of course. Better give me details and written instructions."

Sterling nodded hastily, and cleared his throat again. "Yes, yes, of course. Here is everything. You will notice one account is to be in my own name, the other for the organization. Here are my instructions to the bank, with my signature and further conditions for the cashier." He handed Jeff a long envelope, thick with folded papers. "And here is the money." He handed over the package of bills. "Eight thousand dollars," he said in a low voice.

Jeff pocketed both, lowering his eyes. When he looked up the Bishop had a check in his hand. "Now here is one other little job I must ask you to do tomorrow, or perhaps today if there is time." Jeff had never seen the old man so diffident, superficially. "This is my personal check on the Virginia Trust for three thousand. Send it by money order to Silverman, and enclose this letter." He folded check and a letter together and gave them to Jeff, who placed them in his inner pocket with the other envelope and cash.

There was silence.

"Is that all?" Jeff asked.

"Unless you wish to add something of your own to the money order—"

Jeff stood up. "I'm strapped right now."

The Bishop nodded absent-mindedly. "Yes. I suppose so."

Jeff left him and went to the Post Office to send the money order. The letter contained instructions to Silverman to use the money as he saw fit.

In the morning, Jeff entrained for Lewes, a town of some ten thousand inhabitants in the southern part of the State. Without difficulty he opened the two accounts, receiving in return not only the necessary passbooks, but also a letter to the Bishop from the Vice-President of the institution, thanking Sterling in dignifiedly effusive terms for singling out the Lewes National Bank in which to deposit eight thousand dollars. An unusual occurrence, Jeff judged.

From there Jeff went to Lynchburg, where he had to lose an hour in changing trains. He went to the biggest hotel for lunch, and at a table a few feet away saw Randolph Taitt with another man. Jeff jerked his head toward the lobby. Taitt stared at him.

Jeff ate rapidly, then walked past the Senator's table into the lobby, where he sat down. In five minutes the cocky little man came out, alone. He joined Jeff, and said, "I wasn't sure it was you. How are you?"

"Fine. How's campaigning in this part of the State?"

The Senator's pugnacious jaw stuck out. "The organization will win. I got here this morning, and I'm leaving at four. I never had such a campaign in my life. Mind you,

I'm speaking confidentially. An extension of our first talk."

Jeff smoked leisurely. "Of course."

Taitt looked at him appraisingly. "Still with the Bishop, eh?"

"Naturally."

The Senator's thin-lipped mouth twitched. "I don't know about 'naturally.' You don't look like his kind of man."

"Well."

Taitt lit a cigar and smoked a moment in silence. Then said, "I'm very anxious to have you work for me, young man."

"You know as well as I do that I wouldn't be much use to you—now. We went over that."

The little man chewed his cigar. "I suppose you're right." He smiled with sudden grimness. "I never thought I'd be as friendly as this with one of Sterling's men. Never."

Jeff looked at his watch. "Excuse me. I'm just worrying about time. Let me make a suggestion, Senator. We've both talked too frankly not to go further. Isn't that so?"

Taitt looked at him, startled. "Why—why, yes, I reckon you're right."

"Then let's go further. Just what do you want me to work with you for?"

Taitt looked at the tip of his cigar. "I'll tell you. First off, you're the only man I ever knew of who had that old fox's confidence. Let me tell you that lots of people in Washington have been watching you." He cocked an eye at Jeff, who nodded as if he knew all about it.

Taitt went on, cautiously. "I believe that you have

enough of an inside knowledge of the workings of the Wesleyan lobby, and of Sterling himself, to provide us with ammunition against him."

"But what do you want to do—beat him in this campaign, or get him later?"

Taitt's quiet voice exploded. "Damn it, man, I've been trying to get him for years!"

Jeff breathed deep. "I don't see how I can help you."

Taitt's lips worked exasperatedly around the cigar. Then he removed it from between his lips and snapped, "Why, that hoot-owl is apt to put the Democratic Party out of commission in Virginia!"

Jeff said gently: "Even then, what use would I be *now?* I'm identified with his present campaign, and I should think you'd find it better to get him after the campaign is over."

Randolph Taitt thought for a full minute, gazing, vacant-eyed, across the lobby. "Wallace of Massachusetts would like to get him too. Know Wallace?"

"The wild-animal-hunting Boston Congressman with a beard. Isn't that the feller?"

Virginia's junior Senator nodded. "He's the man for us." He clapped Jeff on the knee. "You've given me an idea, young man. I'll talk to Wallace when I get back to Washington"—He made a wry face. "Wallace is Republican, Wet, and he doesn't have to toady to these Sterlings, and others. Now—I'm going to ask you a question."

"Yes, sir."

"Let's suppose that Jim White is defeated, and consequently that Molleson is elected. I gather from your remarks that you will know more after November third.

We can then begin a campaign to get Bishop Sterling
out of the way. Will you come with me then?"

Jeff looked away. "I'd have to have a reason for wanting to get him."

Taitt waited silently.

Jeff said finally: "A promise like that mightn't be wise
to make now. Couldn't we talk about it later?"

They stood up, and Jeff judged from Taitt's conclusive
manner that the little man felt satisfied.

"You let me know," said the Senator, and strode away,
bantam-like.

Jeff went and got his train back to Richmond.

11.

NIGHTSHIRT JUSTICE

OCTOBER FIFTEENTH—about a month after Jeff's chat
with Senator Taitt in Lynchburg and two weeks after
Bishop Sterling's return from Texas—the old gray gentleman announced that he was going to New York. When
he uttered the words, Jeff's back was to him.

Clara Blanton asked, "Will you be gone long, Doctor?"

"No." Jeff waited for instructions for him to accom-
pany, as usual, but instead the Bishop said, "Before I
go I'll want to give you some special orders. You, Jeff."

The younger man spun round in his chair. "Sorry.
Whenever you say." He saw Clara Blanton looking at him.

The Bishop fidgeted, then added: "Er—after lunch
will be all right. Say in my own room upstairs."

Jeff nodded and went back to his typing of campaign
letters.

After lunch he met Sterling in the room upstairs. They
both sat down. Sterling began right away, "I'm going up
to see Mr. Johnsbury again. I find that we need more
money—for the campaign." Jeff kept his face empty of
expression. "I hope to induce him to give us perhaps as
much as twenty-five thousand this time."

"That'll be very nice."

"Yes." Bishop Sterling's lips drew together. His voice

emerged guttural. "Now, I'll be gone three or four days, depending on just what happens. Meanwhile you must go to the Great Smokies."

"North Carolina? To do what?"

"This." The old man sat up straighter. "In a little town called Iron Springs we are encountering strong opposition from the county leader. He lives there, even though he dominates the entire tier of counties that run along the outskirts of the Smoky Range. Your job is to bring that man into line."

Jeff thought a moment.

"How?"

The Bishop nodded decisively. "First of all, his name is Ely John Bagby, and let me warn you that he's a very stubborn man. But I—"

"Why can't Senator Tibbetts take care of North Carolina? I've got more than enough to do as it is right here."

"Tibbetts isn't the man to do this job. He's tried, and failed. The people stick to this Ely John Bagby, but I have arranged for that. Now, I know that he has a girl— a Roman Catholic girl—that he has near him. He had her made school teacher in Iron Springs, and she lives there."

"I don't like these jobs, with girls mixed up in them. Herron's girl—"

The old man snarled. "Forget it! You're not working for a Sunday school. Now, listen. The townspeople who follow Bagby in politics don't know that the girl teaching their children is a Roman Catholic—she poses as an Episcopalian—nor that Bagby is particularly friendly with her. But he is. And they will take orders from me!" The thickish lips twitched. "Now, you are to go down there, and see the leader of the Klan. His name is—better

write these down—Jeremiah Baker. Tell him that Bagby
is supporting this girl—using his power to keep a girl right
there in town—and that she is Roman Catholic. Now, I
want the Klan to attack her—giving this story as the pre-
text. That will break Bagby—"

"I think that's going too far. What's the girl got to do
with it?"

The Bishop made a gesture with his right hand. "Who
cares about the girl? The point is that unless—"

Jeff cut in. "Why wouldn't it be just as good to threaten
Bagby with that instead of pulling a real brutal stunt?"

"Don't be a fool! This is the only way. Bagby's a stubborn man. And unless this is done publicly—"

Jeff sneered: "Publicly? In nightshirts?"

"I said unless this is done publicly, it will do no good.
As it is now, Bagby is able to order the people to stay in
line with the organization Democrats, instead of joining
the bolters under Tibbetts. But Bagby won't take orders.
So we have to get him this way. You tell—you give Baker
my *orders*—that the girl is to be taken from her home,
stripped, beaten, tarred and feathered and driven out.
But give as a reason the fact that she is Bagby's Roman
Catholic mistress!" The gray eyes stared glassily.

"I'm damned if I'll be mixed up in a deal—"

"What are you talking about? Nobody's going to kill
the girl? Nobody cares about her. I want Bagby broken!"

"Get somebody else to go down there!"

The eyes behind the hexagonal spectacles narrowed.
"Are you afraid you'll get hurt, or are you soft about
some girl you never saw?"

"It's a cowardly way to—"

The Bishop laughed shortly. "Listen to who talks! If

you don't do it, somebody else will. Does that make you feel differently?" He stared.

Jeff thought a moment. Then he said, "All right. I'll do it."

On an old enevelope he wrote the names: Iron Springs, Ely John Bagby, Jeremiah Baker. "What's the girl's name?"

"Mary Porter."

Jeff wrote down "Mary Porter." Then he asked, "What else?"

"Tell Baker the girl is to be driven out unmercifully. You'll have no trouble getting them started. But be sure it's done for the reason I gave you. The whole point is to weaken Bagby with those mountain people."

"I get you. When shall I go? And does anybody down there know I'm coming?"

"Get there tomorrow, say late afternoon, however the trains run. You'll find you're expected. Better leave to-night some time. Miss Blanton'll give you expense money. But don't spend too much."

Jeff grinned sourly. "In the Great Smokies?"

"I'll be back in three-four days. I'll expect to see you about the same time."

Jeff nodded, and left without shaking hands.

It was nearly four on the next afternoon when Jeff, his battered brown suitcase in hand, climbed out of the creaking wooden train at Iron Springs. He stared up the street from the platform that boasted only a tiny station. At the left, beside a rocky stream, was a dilapidated mill of some kind. In its yard lay a heap of rusty farm tools, while over the remnants of a concrete dam the water broke whitely. On his right was the bare front of a hay, grain and feed supply establishment, and beyond that stretched a dismal row of frame houses. More than a block up Jeff caught sight of a dirty hanging sign: Hotel Iron Springs.

He started walking. Men in overalls passed him, stared curiously, whispered to each other. A woman in a gingham dress, bulged with pregnancy, went by, her eyes vacant. A horse and gig rattled up the street. In the hotel Jeff found a man sitting behind an ancient roll-top desk. He stared lazily, without special interest, at the newcomer, who said:

"Can you let me have a room?"

The man nodded, rose lazily, led Jeff up a flight of steps carpeted with faded material of an elaborate floral design, to a room overlooking the main street. A bowl and pitcher stood on a wooden stand. "How much?"

"Three dollars a day."

"I'll pay you two."

The man lazed out without answering. After cleaning up, Jeff went downstairs. The man was again lolling behind the ancient desk, gaping at the ceiling.

"Where'll I find Jeremiah Baker?"

"Second house tuh ther right. Ther one with ther vine climbin' up hit."

"Thanks." Jeff went out. A few more people moved to and fro, the majority of men seeming to come from beyond the Hotel, at the opposite end of the town from the railroad station. Two houses to the right, Jeff found a vine-covered house that was little more than a shack. Lights showed in its side windows.

Jeff knocked at the door. A very bony woman opened to

him, but said nothing at first. He asked: "Is Mr. Baker in? I'd like to see him for a few minutes."

The woman's eyes glowed in the dimness. She asked in a low tone, "Who is hit wants ter see him?"

"Coates is my name, but you'd better say I come from Bishop Sterling."

That name moved her. She said hastily, "Just er minnit," and, leaving the door open, she vanished. In less than thirty seconds a tall man in corduroy trousers and a blue shirt appeared in her place. He said respectfully, "Come in, suh. My woman didn't know—" Abashed, he led Jeff into a small side room, fitted up as a parlor, though it gave little sign of ever being used. Scraping a long match on the seat of his trousers, Baker lit a kerosene lamp. Jeff saw him to be as bony as the woman, with high cheek bones, sunken cheeks, and small bright eyes that shifted like a cat's. They sat down and Jeff lit a cigarette, offering one to Baker who refused.

Jeff said, "I just got off the train, Mr. Baker, and I've got very important word for you from the Bishop."

The man cleared his throat without speaking, and his eyes looked from Jeff to the window, to the wall, and to Jeff again.

Jeff felt his forehead grow moist. "I understand there's a man here named Ely John Bagby."

Baker nodded forcefully. "He's er fine man."

Jeff gnawed his under lip. "Well, I understand from the Bishop that that's not entirely the case. Do you know Mary Porter?"

The bright eyes in the emaciated face stopped still. "I reckon I do. She's ther school teacher here."

Jeff leaned forward. "Do you know she's a Roman Catholic?"

Baker's whole body stiffened. "Are you sure of thet?"

"I came down here to tell you that. Of course I'm sure."

The bright eyes darted faster now. "Roman Catholic. Teachin' our children!"

"Yes, and Bagby got her the job. She's his girl!" Jeff fed the information to Baker in a vengeful tone.

"You come from Richmond ter tell me thet Ely John Bagby's got his girl wukkin' in ther school house?"

Jeff nodded.

The man fell silent. He moved uneasily in his chair, and the gleaming eyes passed over Jeff's face several times, hastily.

Jeff finally broke the quiet. "That's not all I came to say."

Baker hitched up in his seat.

"You're the leader of the Klan here, aren't you?" The man nodded. "Bishop Sterling says you are to drive the girl out of town."

"Ely John Bagby's girl?" Baker's voice held a horrified note.

"This Porter girl! Know where she lives? Okay. You're to get her out of there, strip her, give her a beating, tar and feather her and chase her out. Will you do it?"

The man thought again for a long time. Then he muttered, "A Roman Catholic whore teachin' our children! Yes, sir, we'll do it. Now!" He stood up and stared eagerly at Jeff, who said nothing. Then Baker left the room suddenly. Inside of a minute he returned with a white bundle under his arm. He looked out of the window. "It's gittin' right dark now." To Jeff he added, "Come on."

Together they left the house, and walked quickly across the street and back toward the railroad station about a hundred feet. There Baker knocked on the door. A little girl opened the door cautiously. Baker said, "Tell yore pappy there's er meetin', right now." The child stared, big-eyed, until the two men turned away. Then she ran inside the house. Thus Baker led Jeff from house to house, until they had left word in some eleven households. Soon young boys were to be seen scurrying up a side road, carrying the same message to outlying homes. Men, all with bundles under their arms, were making their way to a spot in the woods not far from the decrepit mill. Baker stopped Jeff in the shadow of a wall, and undid the bundle. From it he held something out to Jeff. "Put this on, Mistuh Coates."

Jeff saw he had a white robe. He said, "I don't think I'd better be in on this."

Baker took a step backward. His voice was shocked. "Not come with us! . . . Here!" He offered the robe again.

Jeff took it, opened it up and put it on over his head. He adjusted the eyeholes, and looked out to see his replica that had been Baker. It struck him suddenly that once the whole group had assembled he would have no way of finding Baker again. He swore to himself in a whisper.

Baker led him to the hidden clearing. More than twenty white figures stood about, looking absurd and ghostly in the night light. Ten more, at least, arrived, and suddenly the figure that was Baker said:

"Hit's time ter start."

Silently the Klan group followed the leader, Jeff mingling among them. No one said anything, but he could hear men breathing heavily, their shoes and boots crunching on the ground underfoot. They walked in this way for more than a mile, to a bare knoll. From its top Jeff caught the glimmer, in the opposite direction from Iron Springs, of lights which indicated the next town. From the time table he recalled its name as Green Hills.

Suddenly on the side of the hill there flamed into view the fiery cross. Jeff didn't know where it came from, though he guessed that a foray squad had made it crudely in the nearby forest. Hoarse voices murmured as it flared, the glowing flames tinged with green afterglow. Jeff looked at the white figures around him. They shuffled their feet nervously, a man coughed, incongruously; they milled on each other constantly. They were waiting.

Then a new mass of white figures came over the brow of the hill toward them, this time nearly fifty in number. Someone shouted unexpectedly; for the rest, silence lay on them all. The new and old arrivals mingled. For ten seconds nothing happened. Then a rugged voice, recognizable to Jeff as Baker's, said:

"Men, I'll tell yer why we're called here ternight. We have found out that ther school teacher, Mary Porter, is er Roman Catholic. She's ben a-teachin' our children for near a year, and she's teachin' 'em ter obey the Pope in Rome. We can't hev thet no longer, 'n' thet's why yer here!" Voices muttered surprisedly. The ghostly figures moved nervously.

"Not only thet! Not only is she er Roman Catholic, but she's the whore of Ely John Bagby. He made 'er the school teacher here! He did it ter hev his whore near 'im, 'n he put her ter teachin' our children! We're not goin' ter hev that no more! The Klan won't hev that no more!

We're goin' ter drive her inter the next county! Are yer ready?"

The white figures surged forward. Someone cursed. "Get the God-damn' bitch!" "Whar is she?" "Lead us ter the whore!" In accord, the mass of figures turned back toward Iron Springs. Jeff, sweating under his covering, was shoved and jostled. Voices swore in muffled tones. The crunch on the dirt road of many heavily shod feet sounded steadily, and the speed of the men accelerated. A dim, faint moon began to come up, casting its pale light on the band of hooded men. A dog barked in a farmyard they passed. They were nearing the outskirts of town. A squad of five men broke into a run, cutting across country toward the back of the town.

A voice in the troop cried, "Thet's right! Git ther tar and feathers!" Other voices laughed, cursed, coughed. Jeff's clothes were drenched with sweat. They tramped on, faster and faster. Now and again the burning cross, carried at the rear, flamed up suddenly, throwing sparks, and casting over them all a deep red light.

They came to the head of the street. It could not have been more than eight or eight-thirty, but the town was dark. Every household hid. The men broke into a run, their feet pounding on the hard road. Jeff dropped his hat as he ran.

A voice cried, "Here's the house!" followed by the crash of glass. Jeff heard the click of a revolver barrel under the robe of a man near him.

The door of the house flew open suddenly, and a young boy, not more than twenty, stepped out onto the porch. He was silhouetted against the light indoors. His long hair fell partially over his eyes.

"Git outer ther way, Clem!"

"Git, you young bastard!"

The boy cried, "What do yer want?"

Many voices snarled at once, unintelligibly. A window pane behind the boy splintered at the impact of a small rock. A woman's face appeared at a second-floor window. Shouts broke out: "Thar she is! Git her!" "Roman whore!" "Git her quick!"

The boy on the porch shrieked, "Let her alone, yer cowards!"

White figures surged toward the house. A shot rang out, seemingly muffled. The boy pitched forward, his face down. A woman, somewhere nearby, screamed. The white robed men charged the house.

12.

WHIPS, TAR AND FEATHERS

THE TINY frame building had no room for more than a few of the Klan raiders. Their figures appeared at the lower story windows, then in the upper. Window panes smashed, their glass sprinkling the ground below.

"Git her!"

Harsh cries sounded; the Klansmen outside formed a cordon around the beleaguered house. A woman's voice screamed repeatedly inside the house. Another shot roared. The body of the boy lay half on, half off, the ramshackle porch. Jeff looked at him as he was swept by. No one else seemed to pay any atention. The building shook to the pounding of heavy feet on its little interior staircase. Men laughed, some once, some steadily, though nothing funny was happening. A squad of men charged out of the house, down into the street.

Among them they bore the girl. Her dress was torn across the back. Her skirt had crawled above her knees, revealing, as she struggled, the white of her legs bare above rolled stockings. Her hands clawed at the white robes encircling her. A concerted roar broke from the Klansmen. As a single unit, they turned and surged back toward the clearing where first they had gathered. Jeff ran among them, his breath sobbing in his throat.

In the clearing one group piled broken planks into a bonfire; the rest gathered in a circle. Those holding the girl threw her forward toward the fire. She fell on her hands and knees, then started up again, looking wildly around at the ring of hooded men. Then she caught sight of the tar-and-feather squad, heating a bucket of the black stuff over a smaller fire at one side. Her voice cracked in a high scream.

"Let me go!" She got up to run. Her wild pace took her into the arms of one Klansman taller than the rest. He laughed loudly, seized her arms and shoved her back toward the fire again. She did not fall, but stood suddenly still, one arm covering her chest, her other hand, claw-like, pushing bobbed hair back from her forehead.

Jeff had the chance to look at her more closely. She was not pretty. Two small eyes—he couldn't make out the color—rolled in their sockets with terror. A thin, pointed nose gave her the look of a horror-stricken bird. Her short, plump figure cowered in the flaring fire light. Her voice, when she unexpectedly screamed again, was shrill and irritating in quality.

Three Klansmen, at a signal from the very tall man, started toward her. She ran backward away from them, stumbled over a root and fell, her head almost touching the flames. The three men grabbed her, their hands tore at her clothes. Cheap silk ripped with a scratchy sound. She kicked one of the men in the groin. He staggered back.

He straightened up, yelling, "God-damn yer!" His white arm swung, the fist catching the girl on the side of the head. Other men in the circle growled, stepped forward.

"Thet's it!"

"Git the bitch!"

In less than a minute the girl was naked. Her hands passed over her body trying to cover it. The men who had stripped her threw the tatters of her clothes—bits of blue, of pink, the black of stockings—into the flames. Other men came forward now, one with a short whip in his right hand. The girl sobbed, screamed, whimpered.

"Mary Porter, yer goin' ter git whipped!" the man shouted.

"Mother of Jesus, save me!" The girl suddenly fell on her knees, opened her arms wide, lifted them toward the dark sky. Her small pointed breasts moved to the sobs that shook her body. The whip was in the air behind her; it swished and cracked across her naked back. She jumped up, ran blindly, fell against the outer circle.

Two others drove her back toward the fire. Now three others held her, the whip rose and fell, striking her and leaving long red welts. The blows fell on her back, on her buttocks, legs. Once the tip flicked her breasts. She screamed in sudden agony, her hands flew up for protection and the whip then thudded against her thighs. Her lips babbled insanely.

"Jesus Christ, save me, save me, save me!" The last syllable soared to a crescendo. Her absurd dumpy body doubled and straightened as the whip blows stung her bare flesh. Her plump bulging stomach quivered and jerked spasmodically. The pale red of oozing blood made her body look flayed. She fell suddenly full length, on her back. The whip fell once, across her shins. Her legs jerked up. She rolled over, and slowly her hands came up to cover her face. She lay still.

Jeff felt the sweat running down his whole body. His

hands ached from the pain of steady clenching. The men next to him laughed, cried out, surged forward and back, unreasoning. Bodies crouched forward, intent on the girl.

The tar-and-feather squad left its little side fire. One man bore a bucket and brush, another an old pillow with one end ripped open. Two other men took hold of the girl under the arm pits. Her body stiffened, her short round legs flailed out. The men swore at her, shook her till her hair flew crazily about her staring eyes. Tears streamed down her face, and her lips moved steadily.

The Klansmen strengthened their grasps on her till she was unable to move freely. She writhed. Hastily the man with the tar and brush dabbed blotches of the burning black on her back, legs, stomach, anywhere the brush could hit as she wriggled. At the first touch of tar she screamed sobbingly, then drew in her breath in a great gasp that racked her from head to foot. Her lips spat blood.

Savagely, handfuls of feathers were stuck on the blotches of tar, and then they let go of her. Her legs buckled, she fell down, one arm on a red hot ember. She rolled over jerkily, a great red welt on her underarm.

The tall Klansman ran forward, picked her up, others gathered behind him. They half-ran down a path beyond the clearing, and suddenly broke into a road.

"Ter the next county!"

"Ther hell with 'er!"

"Cripes, look at 'er!"

The girl stood up, her head hanging. The tall man pointed up the road. "Git up thet road. Don't let us never see yer here again! Yer a Roman Catholic whore, thet's whut! Now git!"

The girl didn't move; apparently she heard nothing. A man darted from the crowd and pushed her. She fell headlong, then struggled to her feet. She looked back at them once, terror-stricken, then started a staggering walk up the road. Ten feet, she fell again. Once more she struggled to her feet, then a step, two steps, and she was on her way. In the night dimness, her body looked white, with black and gray blotches of tar and feathers. Unexpectedly her head went up, and she ran, wildly, blindly ahead. She turned with the road and was lost to sight.

Jeff looked round him. The men stood quiet, speechless. Then one gave a high-pitched laugh, tore his white robe off, and ran to a tree. He vomited.

Men slunk away from each other. One or two strode off, business-like. Jeff dropped back, then ran to the other side of the road. Through the bushes he crashed, and after several hundred feet, found himself on the railroad tracks. There he turned right, stopped to take off his robe, and then bundled it roughly under his arm. He broke into a run, stumbling over the ties, cursing steadily to himself. Once he thought he was crying, then discovered it was only perspiration.

He ran about three hundred yards, then cut to his right through the bushes. The moonlight was now a little stronger. He headed in the direction of the road, but only after nearly an hour of struggling, tripping, scratching, did he come out on it. He looked up and down its white stretch, saw nothing. He figured he was about half to three-quarters of a mile from Iron Springs and the Klan clearing.

He began walking back toward town, watching the ditches, and the underbrush on either side. Suddenly he turned and trotted back past the point where he had come on the road. He passed another turn, saw nothing. Then he stopped, stared down at the road vacantly, thinking.

He fumbled in his pocket for his pack of cigarettes, found it crumpled. He extracted a whole cigarette, and lit it, then began walking more slowly, carefully, back toward Iron Springs again. Once he heard the sound of something moving in the bushes. He plunged in, and only startled some small animal away in fear.

Many times he stopped to listen, but heard nothing. He picked up speed in his walking, until he almost fell over the girl. He stopped and bent down to her.

She was lying half in the ditch, her arms and legs sprawled out. She was breathing, but was unconscious. He picked her up and propped her against his knee. Then he spread over her shoulders the white robe he had carried with him. He chafed her wrists, looked around for water. After several minutes, she came to.

He said quickly, "It's all right. Don't worry. I'm your friend."

She struggled, he held her, and she cried out in pain. He said: "Don't get scared. I want to help you. You're all right. Now sit still. Sit still."

She grabbed his hand and tried to pull herself upright. Her lips twitched. She moaned: "Let me go, let me go. Oh, God, I wish I was dead! Mother of Jesus, Holy Mary . . . help me!"

"I'll help you if you'll sit still. Get it in your head, I'm your friend." He held on to her.

Suddenly she relaxed against him, her hands dropped to the ground. "Kill me," she said.

He fumbled again in his pocket for the cigarettes. He

put one between her lips. Immediately she began sucking at it greedily. "Wait'll I get it lit." He held a match to it, she drew in great lungfuls. She smoked rapidly, then threw the cigarette away. She burst into racking sobs, and cried in gasps without covering her face, unconscious of her whipped, naked body. He let her cry.

At last he asked, "How far is it to Green Hills?"

She didn't answer, but the sobs began to quiet down. She said first: "It hurts, it hurts. Oh, Christ, why didn't they kill me?"

He repeated: "How far is it to Green Hills?" He looked up and down the road. There was nothing.

"I don't know. Two miles, three miles. . . . Oh, God!"

"Can you walk?" He looked at her feet.

"Kill me. Let me die here. I don't want to live." Her body shuddered. Her hands began to explore her body. This reminded her of her nakedness. She tried to cover herself.

"Now you're comin' to life. Here." He took off his shoes, and tried to put them on her feet. They were too big. Instead he put his socks on her, first stuffing a handkerchief down into the foot of each one as added protection. Then she was able to stand. She wouldn't look at him.

Then he took the white robe from around her shoulders, and straightened it out for her to put on. He saw the raised red welts on her flesh; dried blood caked on her, bruises and cuts covered her all over. He lifted her lifeless arms and forced her into the robe. She moaned in pain when the cloth rasped her burns and wounds.

"Now you're okay. Just keep it up off the ground. Now, come on."

He took her hand, and started to lead her along. She staggered away from him, retching. Then that quieted down. They walked slowly along. He guessed it was nearly eleven o'clock.

She hobbled, leaning on him for support. Now she said nothing, made no noise, except that once in a while a wordless sound escaped her. Every several hundred feet they stopped. Then she had to sit down for a rest.

During the second rest she asked dully, "Who are you? I don't know you?"

"I'm a stranger in Iron Springs. I happened to find you on the road."

She was silent. Then she said suddenly, "You were in that mob! This robe!" She tried to get up. "Let me go! Let me go!"

He held her down. "For Christ's sake, sit quiet! I'm not goin' to hurt you."

She relaxed.

"I'm helpin' you. Never mind how I got this robe. You're alive and safe. That's all you gotta worry about."

She sudsided into her previous dulled state. Soon they got up and went on.

Several times they smoked, but rarely talked. Fully three hours later they topped a rise. Less than half a mile away were several lights. They stopped.

Jeff asked her, "Got any friends here?"

She started to laugh, and suddenly turned on Jeff hysterically. "Friends! God curse them, I have no friends! Don't let me stay alive! Do you hear me! Kill me right here! For Christ's sake!" He clapped a hand over her mouth. She struggled, then fell into his arms in a faint.

"Hell's bells," he said, and laid her out comfortably,

cushioning her head on his lap. Again he rubbed her wrists, but this time he had to wait more than twenty minutes before she came to. Then she began to cry, silently, until he gave up trying to quiet her.

An hour later she lay on the ground, quivering, trembling, but not crying any more.

"How do you feel?" he said.

She didn't answer.

"How can you get word to Bagby?"

She looked up. "How do you know about him?"

He realized the break. "Oh—everybody knows, I reckon! How can you reach him?"

She sighed, long and gaspingly. "I don't know."

He stopped talking to her. After a few more minutes he helped her to her feet, and they marched on.

She started talking unexpectedly: "I don't know you, but you saved my life. This is punishment for my sins. I deserve it. I'm Ely John Bagby's girl." She shuddered, then went on in a low, miserable voice: "I've been punished and now I see it. Holy God—"

"That's nonsense." Jeff broke in. "You got caught, that's all. Forget it."

They were now on the outskirts of Green Hills. Fifteen minutes more and they were in front of a large house, with a garden before it, and a white picket fence guarding it from the road.

Jeff said, "Come on, we'll go in here." He led her up to the front door, and knocked loudly, over and over again.

After five minutes a man's voice said from a second-floor window: "Who's there?"

Jeff stepped out where he could see a dark shape in the

window. "Please let us in. I've got a girl with me. She's almost killed."

The dark shape hesitated, then vanished. Jeff stood where he was until the front door opened cautiously. The man's head appeared, said, "Jesus Christ," and then the door opened wide.

"Take it easy with her. She's cut to bits."

The man put on lights inside, and said, "Come on in. Shut the door." He allowed Jeff to lead the girl into a front room. Then he roused a Negro servant, and the three of them carried the girl upstairs into an empty bedroom. The house-owner looked at her seriously.

Jeff told him. "The Klan in Iron Springs got her. She was beaten, tarred and feathered, and—"

"God-damned cowards! Where'd she get the white robe?"

"I'll tell you about that later."

Jeff turned to the girl. "You better sleep, or fix yourself up. Hot water maybe'll get that tar off. Got bandages?"

The Negro servant helped the girl into the bathroom; they heard the sound of running water.

They went downstairs. "Got anything to drink?" Jeff asked. "I've been out all night."

The man brought out a gallon of corn liquor. "I'll buy it from you," Jeff said.

"Go ahead, drink it."

"Let me buy it. Here's four dollars."

The man looked at him in silence, then went upstairs.

Jeff looked out of the window. It was barely getting light. He began drinking corn, followed with water chasers. He felt it burn in his empty stomach. Then suddenly he fell asleep, and woke up every few minutes. So passed at least three hours. No sound came from upstairs. He supposed the girl was sleeping.

At length the room became light enough for him to see the clock. Seven-thirty. He began drinking again. His host came downstairs.

"Morning."

"How's the girl?"

"I'm getting the doctor for her soon. Who is she?"

Jeff told him. The man raised his eyebrows. "I'll phone Bagby." He rang the party line, and finally got his man. "Hello, Bagby? This is McKeever in Green Hills. I've got your girl here. The Klan got her last night." He listened, then finished with: "All right." He hung up, and told Jeff, "He's comin' over to fetch her."

Jeff said, "There were Green Springs men in the bunch that did her up."

The man looked at him sideways. "That so?"

Jeff gave himself another drink of corn. Soon the Negro servant announced breakfast. They went into another room and ate ham and eggs, pancakes, and coffee, with muffins and butter. Then they returned to the front room. Jeff started his drinking again.

It was close to nine o'clock when a car tore past the house. The host said, "That's Bagby."

Jeff ran outside. He stumbled, and realized he was drunk. Now in the light he saw that this McKeever's house was almost in the center of the very small village of Green Springs. He breathed in a great lungful of cool hill air, and ran on to where he saw Bagby's car stopped. Several men were congregating around it. Jeff wondered foggily why the politician had gone on when he knew the girl was in McKeever's house.

He came up to the car, and was about to shout to get Bagby's attention, when he heard the man say:

"Well, which of you was in that crowd last night?"

Sullen silence was the only answer. More people, now including women, were attracted to the car. Jeff made out Ely John Bagby to be a tall, well-set-up man, with deeply tanned face of a higher cast than most he had seen around here. He wore riding breeches and a khaki blouse open at the neck. He must have been in his early forties.

The political leader shouted again. "Some of you brave men were in that crowd last night? Which of you?" Silence. Bagby went on. "You men have known me for years. I'm standing up in front of you now, unarmed. I think— I know—that everyone of you was either in that crowd last night, or else knew about it. I call you cowards!"

The men stared at him blankly.

Bagby raged. "A dirty lot of cowards to attack a girl. Do any of you know where she is now? Do you care? God-damn your rotten souls!"

One man said, "Watch your tongue, Bagby!"

The man in riding breeches sat down behind his wheel. "Get back in your pig-styes where you belong!"

He turned the car and drove back toward McKeever's house. The man who had told him to hold his tongue laughed scornfully. Then others joined. They shouted vague, derisive sounds after him. Jeff veered back toward McKeever's house. He found that he was very drunk. He turned to a man standing near him.

"Where c'n I get some corn?"

"I reckon yew c'd git some from the store there." The other pointed across the street.

"I thought Bagby was the big boss in these parts."

"He ain't no' mo'. The Klan found out he was whorin'."

Jeff jerked away and bought a quart of corn liquor, and took a drink.

Then he went to the railroad station and waited half an hour for the train to Asheville, Winston-Salem and Richmond.

In the car he drank steadily until he fell asleep.

13.

"THANK GOD, AMERICA SAVED"

AFTER HIS solitary dinner in Washington on the eve of Election Day, a few weeks later, Jeff returned to the apartment he had lately rented. There he found a telegram from Veryl Vernon.

"ARRIVING WASHINGTON NINE O'CLOCK WILL COME STRAIGHT TO YOUR PLACE LOVE

VERYL."

He read it twice, slowly. Then he went to the phone and called a number.

"Hello, Dixie, this is Jeff. Listen, sweet, I can't come over now. The Bish called me downtown. . . . No, it'll be near midnight before I get through with him. I'll call you then, honey . . . 'Bye."

He sat down to wait. The phone rang twenty minutes later.

He picked up the receiver. "Good evening, Miss Blanton. . . . All right, I'll come right down. 'Bye."

He gnawed his lips, staring at the phone, then wrote a note for Veryl.

"Had to go downtown. Back later. Leave your address

and phone number here and I'll call when I get back or in the morning.

Jeff."

He walked the eight blocks to the Tasker Building and went up to Suite 50. It was in a state of hubbub. Two phones were ringing almost continuously; an extra secretary was taking dictated telegrams from the Bishop.

Jeff threw his hat and light overcoat on the divan in the outside room and sat down. The Bishop was saying to the secretary:

"Send this same wire to Asheville, Roanoke, Tidewater, San Antonio, Atlanta, and others. Miss Blanton will tell you.

"MOLLESON IS SURE TO WIN STOP WHITE CANNOT CARRY SOUTH IF YOU DO YOUR PART STOP DEMOCRATS SURE TO SUSTAIN FIRST LOSS OF SOLID SOUTH IN OVER FIFTY YEARS."

"Sign my name. Hello, Jeff!"

"Evening. How goes it?"

Sterling looked at him worriedly. "Honestly, I don't know, Jeff. I think we may carry Virginia."

Clara Blanton said, "Virginia, Doctor! I know we'll take the entire South!"

Jeff asked, "Anything you want me to do?"

Sterling thought a minute. "I wanted you to do something—oh, yes, read those wires that are coming in. We've fallen 'way behind." He gestured to a heap of telegram envelopes on the desk. Jeff seized a handful and began opening them. They were all messages of congratulation and mutual encouragement from dry leaders throughout the Southern States. Jeff handed them to the Bishop, who sent wires in return.

More telegrams arrived, and an hour or more passed feverishly. Then Prince arrived. In his hand he brandished a still damp page proof of *The American People*. He seemed very glad about something.

"Hi, Doctor! I guess we're all set!"

Sterling scowled at him. "You talk like a fool!"

"What do you mean? Why, the South is smashed to bits. I can feel it in my bones."

"So! Votes'll be much better."

Prince still beamed. He unfolded the paper in his hand. "Take a peek at this, Doctor. We have it all ready for this week's issue. How do you like it?" He held the front page up for them all to see. Across the page, in huge screamer type, appeared the words:

THANK GOD, AMERICA SAVED!

Sterling said, doubtfully, "I hope you get a chance to publish it."

Clara Blanton gurgled: "Oh, Mr. Prince, I think that's wonderful! And it's true, too."

Jeff went on reading telegrams.

Senator Seed came in, with his brother Ben. The Senator shook hands all around, and Prince exhibited again the glaring headline. Seed said:

"It isn't God you've got to thank. Nothing like it."

The Blanton woman flared at him. "It's God's work that keeps Jim White out of Washington!"

Seed grinned maliciously at Sterling. "God, in collaboration with *The American People* and the 'Mollycrats' and the Ku Klux Klan, and—"

Sterling rapped at him, "What did you have for dinner?"

Seed laughed and sat down.

Ben Seed came over to Jeff, and put out his hand awkwardly. They shook. "How are yuh, Jeff?" Seed asked. He laughed nervously. "I haven't seen yuh since—" He looked away.

"I been very busy, Ben. Did a lot of traveling."

Ben shuffled, and finally said, "I—I oughta tell yuh— I'm not sore at you for takin' Dixie."

"I didn't take her, Ben. She—she took me."

The brother of the Senator laughed nervously. "Drop in at the old place any time, now we're back in town."

"Thanks, I will. Can I bring Dixie?"

Prince's loud voice could be heard saying, "Why, Senator, I know we're going to win. The reports we have been getting—"

"Are only the kind you want to hear," Seed dropped.

Prince repeated gravely, "I say the reports we have been getting show that Molleson will carry—" he ticked them off on his fingers— "Virginia, North Carolina, Florida, Alabama, Georgia, and Arkansas."

Seed hooted. "Get out! Molleson couldn't carry Arkansas for the Republicans if it was only the size of a nickel cigar! Better be satisfied with Virginia."

Sterling nodded. "That's what I'm afraid of, Sam. I reckon we ought to take at least Virginia and perhaps one or two other States."

Prince couldn't be downed. "I tell you the Democratic

South is a thing of the past. Molleson will be President just because of that!"

Seed shrugged. "I hope Molleson is President, though I hate to see my old friend Jackson licked."

Sterling became venomous. "He deserves a worse fate than that for allowing himself to run with White! I hope he can never come back."

Seed looked at Sterling solemnly. "You're perhaps right." His expression changed to one of malice. "If anybody beats White in the South, you're the man. But I hope you did it legitimately."

"Legitimately?" Sterling's lips twitched. "What do you mean?"

Seed rose to go. "I mean I hope you didn't stuff any ballot boxes, or bribe anybody, or embezzle any funds, or—you know, those Congressional investigations are hard things to beat."

Sterling stared at him, non-plussed. Then he smiled. "If I didn't know you for what you are, Lycurgus Seed, I'd take you seriously."

Seed laughed, and he and Ben left.

"I don't altogether like that man," Prince said. "He says the funniest things."

The Bishop, bending over a letter he was reading, waved a hand airily. "Pay no attention to him. He's our man every way you look at him."

Clara Blanton moved busily about the room. "Yes, indeed, the Doctor is entirely right. Senator Seed is one of our most sincere workers."

Jeff said, "I've read all the telegrams, Doctor. Anything else?"

The old gray man leaned back in his chair wearily. His

face showed its faint purplish patches very plainly in this light. "No, I reckon we can all go home. The rest is beyond our power."

Jeff went out right away, without waiting. Downstairs, outside the building he stopped to light a cigarette. Some-one came up to him and said:

"Jeff, I've been waiting for you."

He looked up. "What's the matter, Dixie?" He took her arm, and they turned the corner.

"Let's go to your place, Jeff. I've got a lot to tell you." She clung to his arm.

"I don't want to go to my place. Come on, we'll get something to eat in here." He steered her into a chop house where they found a corner table. Dixie smiled fondly at him across the table. He reached over and patted her hand.

"Doesn't my baby look pretty?"

"If you really thought so!"

"There you go," he grinned. "What's on your mind?"

After they had ordered sandwiches and coffee, she said, "To night I got confirmation of some very interesting news."

He leaned forward with interest. "About the old coot?"

She nodded in satisfaction. "I couldn't wait for your call later, so I came down to wait for you. I had it by special delivery just after I talked to you."

"Well, what is it?"

She smiled teasingly at him. "First I want you to tell me something. You got me to dig up dirt on the Bishop for you, but you never told me why."

"Do you have to pull this stunt on me every time?" He punched out his cigarette. "All right, I'll tell you. You remember when I went down to the Great Smokies about two-three weeks ago?"

She nodded, smoking thoughtfully.

"I went down there on orders from Sterling. The orders were to have a certain girl whipped, tarred and feathered by the Klan there. I did it."

Her eyes flew open, leaving the black irises entirely surrounded by white. "What do you mean—you did it?"

"I mean I had it done. I saw the whole business. A young kid got killed, and they took this poor dame out, took her clothes off her, beat hell out of her, stuck tar and feathers on her, and drove her out of town."

Dixie's eyes narrowed. "Why?"

"She was bein' kept or something by a guy named Bagby who wouldn't take orders from Tibbetts or the Bishop. They took it out on this girl, and he didn't have any more pull with these hill-billy roughnecks after they found out he had a Catholic mistress. Anyway, I helped the dame get to the next town. Then I got drunk and came back."

"Why didn't you tell me this before, Jeff?"

He moved his hands. "No point. Anyway, that's why I'm goin' to sink that old guy if it's the last thing I do. I needed a reason and now I've got it."

She was silent for many seconds; then asked, "But why take it out on him?"

He bit savagely into his sandwich. "He figured it all out beforehand, didn't he? He made me do it!"

"You didn't have to do it!"

"Yeah, I know. Anyway, I went, figurin' maybe I could at least save the dame. I did."

"Ever see her again?"

"No." He stared at her somberly, then grinned sourly. "She was a terrible-lookin' mess."

"Go ahead and eat your sandwich. Now I'll tell you what I've got. Any time you want, I can tell you the girls he stays with when he goes to New York."

"Tell me now."

She handed him a special delivery envelope. He drew out the letter inside, and read it over.

"Those names and addresses right?"

She nodded with certainty.

"Thanks, kiddo. Does he give 'em dough?"

Dixie's manner became strangely business-like. "We couldn't find that out, Jeff. You mean a lot of money?"

Through a mouthful of sandwich he said, "Yeah. I know he sends dough up to this Silverman broker I told you about. And he's got a lot of cash salted away in out-of-the-way banks, like the one in Lewes. But maybe he throws more around I don't know about."

"Probably does. Anyway, I got so excited when I got that, I wanted to tell you right away."

"Swell baby."

They finished eating and left the restaurant, heading for Dixie's apartment. At the door he stopped. She looked at him in surprise.

"Aren't you coming in, Jeff?"

He leaned over and kissed her on the lips. "No, baby. I'm tired and I'm goin' home. Call you tomorrow."

She pouted. "Aw, Jeff. Come on in for one drink, anyway."

He shook his head. "Thanks for comin' after me, but I'm sleepy. I'll call you around noon."

She pouted some more, then smiled. "I'll be in. Get a good rest."

"Yes, mamma."

She went into her doorway; he walked to his own place. He let himself in, and, remembering that he had turned off all the lights, wondered that some were on. He hung his hat and coat in the front room, then walked into his bedroom.

The first thing he saw on the chair opposite the door was a small black grip, open, with pink women's underthings heaped loosely in it. He looked at the bed.

"What the hell?"

From the bed Veryl said, "Oh, Jeff!" And then she began to cry.

14.

DIXIE, MY DIXIE

ON GOING to bed, Jeff had forgotten to pull down the window shade. Now the mid-morning sun shot a brilliant ray across the foot of the bed, and the glare roused him. He stared groggily at the wall, then remembered Veryl. He turned over gently, to see her still asleep. He watched her a moment, then turned back again to get a cigarette out of his jacket on the chair beside the bed. He lit it, and then lay on his back, blowing gray whorls of smoke toward the ceiling. His wrist-watch told him it was close to eleven o'clock.

The girl next to him stirred, then awoke. Jeff didn't move, but waited. Nothing happened, and he turned his head. Veryl was watching him steadily with wide-open eyes. He said:

"Hello, hello, hello!"

She half-smiled, and stretched out a hand to him. He took it and kissed it. Quickly then she moved up close to him, one arm about his neck, her body close to his.

"I'm so fond of you, Jeff!"

"I should hope so. How do you feel?"

She made no sound, but lay motionless. After a long still time she said in a whisper: "I haven't told you—" She stopped.

He waited for the rest, but it didn't come. He prodded: "You haven't told me what?"

Again silence, until she said in an unexpectedly loud and clear tone, "I haven't told you why I came here last night."

Again he waited, moved his lips nervously, and had to say:

"No, you haven't." He blew smoke toward the ceiling.

"I couldn't. But now I can." She fell silent.

"Don't keep stopping," he said.

Her body moved, as if in uncertainty. She drew a deep breath. "I came to see you—this way—because it's the last time."

"What's the last time?"

"It—it's the last time I'll see you. . . . Oh, Jeff, I can't stand it!" Her breath grew uneven, heralding tears.

Jeff said with deliberate gentleness: "What can't you stand? Why is it the last time?"

Her voice took on, with the same unexpectedness, its previous strong clear tone. "I'm going to marry Tom Herron."

Jeff made no move, but let his cigarette burn slowly.

"What're you doing here then?"

She moved her body away from him in a quick jerk. Wounded, she told him, "Because it's the last time I'll ever see you! That's why!"

He punched out his cigarette butt, and lit a fresh one. He took his time. "Listen, Veryl. . . ." His thought changed suddenly and he burst out, "What is this anyway? We're goin' to get married—or were, 'n you waltz in here with a story about Tom Herron. Who's crazy here—you or I?" He paused for breath. "I'll be God-damned!"

She said hotly, "Jeff! Don't talk that way! I love you—
I always have—but now—but now I can't see you any
more. This is—this is the end of things for us!" Her
heated manner turned again to the beginning of tears.

He propped himself on one elbow and looked down at
her. Her eyelids were red, and her mouth turned down at
the corners. He leaned down and kissed her hard on the
lips. She made no movement.

"Listen, honey. Let's get this straight. You're goin' to
marry Tom Herron? Says who?"

Her voice came strainedly, "I—I oughtn't to tell you—
but I reckon I must. I *am* going to marry Tom!"

He grimaced in sudden irritation. "All right, all right.
But why? When? Who? He's got a wife in Chicago."

"No longer. They're divorced."

"Jesus, Mary and Joseph, will you explain this business? *Why* are you goin' to marry that yahoo? If you're
nuts enough about me to—"

She flared. "I came to you last night because it was all
I could do—all I could think of to do—to let you know
I love you—"

He sighed wearily. Plaintively his next words came. "I
only wish you'd give me the story. I suppose your old
man is in this some place."

She chuckled quietly. He stared at her in surprise.
"I'm your enemy now. My father has switched from your
Bishop to Randolph Taitt."

He ran a hand through his hair. "What do you mean—
that your old man is ditching the Bish for Taitt? Why, for
God's sake?"

The girl pursed her lips. "Now, Jeff, don't think I'm
stupid. But maybe I haven't got all the political stuff

straight. Now let's see. . . . My father is a little afraid of Bishop Sterling, even though they've always been good friends. But a few weeks ago he found out that Randolph Taitt is going to back Tom Herron, one year from now, for Governor of Virginia."

"Taitt is? Has he gone nuts?"

"Now don't expect me to tell you a lot of things I don't know!" she pouted. "Randolph Taitt is going to back Tom for Governor in the next gubernatorial campaign—a year from now—"

"But—first Herron has to be reelected to Congress today!"

"What? What do you mean, Jeff?"

He said: "Look—Taitt can't very well back your boy friend for the Governorship if he isn't reelected to Congress. In other words, if Herron doesn't go back to Congress—and if he doesn't, it's my fault—Taitt won't pick *him* to back. Not by a long shot. Unless he's gone crazy, 'n I don't reckon he has."

"I didn't know. Anyway, Jeff, my father is going to give his support to Herron and Randolph Taitt."

Jeff stared vacantly at the ceiling. Then he said, "And your old man figures that ape is goin' to be the next Governor of Virginia? And you're goin' to be the Governor's wife! Boy, that's a hot one!" He laughed, quietly at first, then in guffaws.

She watched him, offended. "I think you're rotten. I sure do."

He calmed himself after his laugh. "That is playin' a long shot. More power to you, baby. Mrs. Governor! Maybe so at that!"

She grew defiant. "Well, why not? Mr. Herron's a nice

man. I'm right fond of him. And he's going to be elected today, too."

He became serious. He took one of her hands in his. "You're a sweet kid, Veryl. But listen. If Tom Herron is reelected today, your old man will back him and Taitt—say, what's your old man goin' to get out of it?"

"I don't know, Jeff. After all, it's good for the family to have a Governor in it. Maybe Tom will get him a bigger job."

He nodded. "Must be. Something like that. I'm sorry about us."

That brought her back close to him. He kissed her hair, her eyes, her bare arms.

"I wanted to say good-bye to you, Jeff."

He drew back from her, and then sat up against the headboard of the bed. "I'm glad you did."

Her fingers played with the sleeve of his pajamas. "And Jeff—I've got more to tell you."

"Yeah? What now?"

"About your girl friend—that Dixie whatever-her-name-is."

He grinned. "What do you know about her?"

Her voice fell to a barely audible pitch. "N-nothing, Jeff, except—except Tom Herron's been talking to her. She's got a-a-record—something—"

He sat up straighter. "Go ahead. Herron talked with her about the dictograph record. Yeah. Go ahead!"

" 'N he told daddy that if he was reelected today he could buy the record—or whatever it is—from that girl and have you indicted for intimidation. Do you understand, Jeff?"

He jumped out of bed. "Understand? You bet your lily-white neck I understand! When did all this happen?" He shut the window as he talked and let the curtains fall into place.

From the bed Veryl said, "I—I thought it was serious, Jeff, so I thought—"

He stood over her. "Yeah, yeah! But when did he do this talkin' with Dixie? She goin' to sell him this thing?"

The girl's amber eyes clouded. "All I know, Jeff, is what he told daddy. He said if he was reelected today, he knew he could buy that record and have you indicted for intimidation. That's how I remember the words, but I'm not sure what it means."

He breathed fast and deeply. "I do. Don't worry about that. Why didn't you tell me last night?"

"Oh, Jeff, how could I?"

He watched her steadily for several seconds. Then said, "Yeah," took his clothes from the chair and went into the bathroom.

An hour later they sat opposite each other over the breakfast Veryl had prepared in his kitchenette. He drank three cups of coffee, and smoked cigarettes between bites.

"Jeff," she said softly, "don't spoil our last time together."

He looked at her morosely. Then he stood up. "Sorry. . . . What're you goin' to do? Marry that Turk?"

Her eyes dropped; she nodded. "I told you—"

"Leave me flat?"

She said nothing.

"We were goin' to get married. I'll forget about that."

She raised her eyes to his. "Jeff, I don't want to—"

He began talking fast: "You go ahead and marry him. We can still be friends though, can't we?"

She shook her head violently. "This is the last time we'll ever see each other." She held her head proudly high.

"Talk sense. Listen, just because you marry that gorilla is no reason why we can't see each other once in a while. I'm right fond of you. I am, honey. So why shouldn't we—now and then—"

She got up from her chair. Her head was still high, and her voice strong. "Let me have it my way, Jeff. I came to you last night—the way I did—because of that. We must never meet again."

He went around the table and took her by the shoulders. "Stop talkin' like a movie actress in the last reel! Listen to me. We can get together every so often. That's what I want. Now forget this hooey about the last time and having it your way! What do you say?"

She looked at him soberly. "I—I don't know, Jeff."

He dropped his hands and walked away from her. When he turned around, she had on her hat and short jacket. Her bag stood ready to hand.

"I'm goin' back to the hotel, Jeff. I just came along—"

He went to her, took her in his arms and kissed her. Then he said, "I'll be hearin' from you."

She kissed him again for answer. From the doorway she said, "Maybe it's not the last time, Jeff." The door closed gently behind her.

Jeff went to the phone and called Dixie's number. The repetitive signal sounded in his ear, while he held on for almost two minutes. Then he slammed the receiver on the hook, put on his hat and coat and went out. Walking quickly, he was soon ringing her doorbell, over and over again. No answer. He went away.

It was now almost two o'clock. Stores were closed, the few people out loitered in a dulled holiday way. Jeff started for the Tasker Building, turned the corner, then stopped. For several seconds he hesitated, then went back to a small cafeteria on the corner opposite Dixie's apartment house. He got himself a piece of mince pie and a cup of coffee and sat down to wait, watching the entrance across the way. He went with deliberate slowness through his refreshment, but still no Dixie. He left the cafeteria, bought a newspaper, and then determinedly walked downtown to the Tasker Building. The Bishop let him into Suite 50.

"Mornin', Jeff. I didn't expect to see you so early." The old man had been in the midst of straightening out a mess of papers on his desk. Among them Jeff saw several bank passbooks, sheafs of cancelled checks, deposit slips, bank statements and letters. Sterling sat down wearily.

Jeff said: "Hear anything yet?"

The old man shook his head. "We can only hope now. I think Prince is too optimistic. Claiming all those States for Molleson!"

Jeff sat down. "Yeah. By the way, I wanted to ask—have I got any money with Silverman? I think I left a couple hundred with him last time, and—"

Sterling spun around in his swivel chair and sorted over some papers, turning back with a paper in his hand. "I'm right glad you asked me about that, Jeff. I've just been looking over his last statement. Now—let's see—5,000 General Motors—3,500 Lambert—one thousand Steel—here are some odd lots—maybe yours."

"You ran it up, didn't you?" Jeff said with emphasis. "Or else Silverman's a good guesser."

"Ran it up?" The gray eyes seemed startled. "Oh—oh, yes! Well, you see—" he laughed with faint embarrassment—"I've been able to give him a bit more money. I—er—" He stopped and gnawed his thick underlip. He continued with new energy. "I am the executor for the estate of a woman who was a dear friend of mine. She died several years ago. Yes. And my fee as executor was right handsome. It was indeed. So I sent some of that to Silverman."

Jeff sat silent. Sterling looked at him, cleared his throat, then turned back to his desk and dropped Gunter and Company's statement on a heap of other papers. His back to the younger man, he suggested. "Tell you what I'll do. I'm writing to Silverman, and I'll ask him."

Jeff said, "I'd like to pull out whatever is in there. I figure I'll need a little cash soon."

"I see. Need very much?" Jeff saw only the back of the whitish, semi-bald head.

"I don't know. Probably as much as I can get."

Silence for several seconds. Then Sterling said: "I could perhaps lend you several thousand—I have some cash lying around that I'm not any too anxious to bank, and—"

"No, thanks. My affairs aren't that bad, yet. . . . Very kind of you."

Sterling faced him again. "Any time you feel that—"

"Thanks a lot." Jeff prepared to leave. "I'll call you later in the day."

"All right. Good-bye."

Jeff went out, found a phone booth and called Dixie. No answer. It was a quarter past three. He went back to his rooms, stared out of the window. On the phone again he called a different number.

"Hello, Ben? Jeff Coates. How are ya? . . . Say, is Dixie there? No? . . ." He forced a laugh. "You wish she was? No, no, I just wanted to reach her in a hurry . . . okay. I'll see you soon. 'Bye."

He tried to sleep, without success. Again he went out. He turned into a drug store, and from a booth called Voorhees.

"Dixie there? . . . Know where she is? . . . I'll break her neck when I find her . . . . What? . . . No, this is no gag! . . . See ya soon. 'Bye."

He walked back to Dixie's apartment; she had not yet returned. This time he left a note under the door.

"Wait for me when you come back. Important. J."

Then he went back to his own place, and sat down, staring at the wall. He remained in that chair, except for intervals of calling Dixie, until dinner time. Then he forced himself to go out and eat. He ate rapidly and in small quantity, and was out in the street again shortly after seven. He had a headache. This drove him to another restaurant, in the back room of which he had two straight whiskeys. His headache disappeared. Back he went to Dixie's apartment. He rang the bell. She opened to him.

"Here you are!" he said, and walked in rapidly. He threw his hat and coat on a chair and faced her. "I've been lookin' for you all day. Where the hell have you been?"

She pouted. "Don't yell at me that way. I can go out."

He fumbled for his cigarette pack, discovered he had none, and took one of hers from an ebony box on the center table. "You'n I are having a talk. Sit down."

"You could be polite about it. I'll stand up." She was growing angry.

He took uncertain steps back and forth. Then he barked, "I hear you've been seein' Tom Herron."

"Well?"

"You're goin' to sell him that record back again."

She swallowed, and turned away from him. Her words came quietly. "Only maybe."

"Have you done it yet?" He ran his tongue over dry lips.

"I don't see why I should tell you."

"God-damn it, you'll tell me! I want to know what you're up to. Now come across!"

She sat down and took a long time to fit a cigarette into an imitation ivory holder and light it. "A little suspense will do you good."

He ran angry eyes around the room. "Where d'you keep that thing? Got it here?" He went to the desk, opened it, hardly looked inside, and closed it again.

She smiled at him. "What do you think?"

"I'll tell you. I think you're a dirty doublecrosser. I paid you to get that thing, and you held out on me. Now you're goin' to sell me out. Do you know what that guy'll do?"

She nodded casually. "Certainly I know. If he's elected, he'll get you indicted for intimidating a political candidate."

He breathed hard. "Suppose he isn't elected?"

She raised her eyebrows and shrugged carelessly. "Maybe he'll still want to do that."

"Then you haven't sold it to him yet?"

She merely looked at him.

"Answer me!"

"Why don't you get your Bishop to help you?"

He made an inarticulate sound. "You know very well I'm not goin' to him for help!"

She got up and started to put on her coat. He dragged it away from her. "You're not goin' any place."

"I'm hungry. I haven't had any dinner and I want to eat."

"Hell with that! Make yourself some poached eggs."

She inspected him carefully, then put out her cigarette, and went into the kitchenette. Jeff called a number on the phone.

"Hello! Republicans? This is Bishop Sterling's office. Yeah. I want to know if you've got any returns from Tidewater, Virginia, yet? . . . Oh, all right!" He hung up.

He sat, fidgety, while the noise of food in preparation came from the kitchenette. Once Dixie came to the doorway and asked, "What do you want—toast or fresh bread?"

"I ate."

She vanished. After ten minutes more she came into the room with food on a tray: scrambled eggs, several pieces of toast, a glass of milk, and mixed vegetables warmed over. She sat down and began eating.

Between mouthfuls she said, "I don't see why you're so worried."

He watched her.

"If you were nicer to me, I might tell you something." She ate complacently.

"You'll tell me anyway. Where d'you keep it?"

She waved a fork. "Oh, around!"

He inspected the room with his eyes. She got up and

snapped on the radio. A man was lushly singing a ballad.

Jeff said again, "Where d'you keep it?"

She piled dishes together. "Listen, Jeff, I'm not going to tell you. All I'll tell you now is that if Herron is re-elected to Congress today he's going to make me an offer for the record. He doesn't like you."

"You're a liar. You sold it to him already."

Her cheeks went dark red. "I'm giving you the truth."

"You're a liar."

She stood up, inflamed. Her voice was throaty and the black eyes gleamed. "That's the truth, Jeff. I want to see you—" She put a hand over her mouth.

"You want to see me sweat. I hope you're enjoyin' yourself."

Her tone grew softer. "No, Jeff. If only you'd—" Her voice became strained.

He said with controlled eagerness: "If only I'd what—?"

She let out her breath slowly, picked up the dishes and walked with them out of the room. When she came back she was smiling.

"How about a drink?"

"Scotch."

She made two highballs. When she handed him his she laughed: "Don't worry. I'm not going to try to knock you out the way you did me."

"I should've saved the stunt for this time," he said savagely.

Silence fell between them, broken only by the lush ballad-singing on the radio.

"You could be gayer," she said.

She was sitting on the divan. He crossed and sat down

beside her. "Listen, sweetheart, what're you trying to do?"

She did not look at him. "This'll teach you a lesson."

"Yeah—to stay away from you."

She sat up a little straighter. "I don't mean that. I don't want you to. I mean—to be—oh, forget it!"

"Suppose Herron is beaten today. What then?"

She shrugged. "Ask Herron."

"Yah!"

They fell into silence again. After several minutes Jeff called Republican Headquarters again. Still no word from Tidewater. As little information was obtainable from the Democrats.

Soon Dixie went into the bedroom, returning in her black silk Chinese robe with the dragons. She mixed fresh drinks. Jeff's wrist-watch said it was after nine o'clock. Dixie disposed herself in an easy chair with a book, and read, paying no attention to Jeff. He finally lay back on the divan and watched Dixie's shadow on the wall. He yawned, stretched, fixed himself another drink. He told her, "We'll stay here until you tell me."

She continued to read.

In irritation he dialed a different station, then twirled from one to another.

"How much did that ape offer you?" he asked.

"I'm holding out for two thousand."

"I'm safe. He hasn't got it."

"Maybe he can get it. Don't talk to me. I'm reading."

He lay down on the divan again. He fell asleep, awoke with a start, drowsed and dozed again. The room was warm and stuffy. He must have slept about an hour and a half. Dixie was still reading, a fresh drink in her hand. His watch said eleven-thirty. He got up, went into the bathroom and washed his face with cold water. In the front room again, he twirled the radio dial. Dixie raised her head.

"—and now we have the pleasure of bringing you some of the tabulated returns which, incidentally, indicate a landslide for the Republican Party and its candidates, Gilbert Molleson and Henry Faraday, for President and Vice-President respectively. Though it's not possible at this early hour to give nation-wide figures, it looks as if Governor Jim White is going to take an awful beating, perhaps the worst that any Democratic nominee has ever been given by American voters. The East has gone heavily for Molleson, and even the Southern States are showing a surprising enthusiasm for the Republican Party. Virginia, the Old Dominion, may turn against its traditional party allegiance. Early returns indicate that three Republican Congressman have been elected in Virginia, and this is certainly—"

Jeff jumped away from the radio to the phone. He called Republican Headquarters. "Bishop Sterling's office again. Radio says there are three Republicans goin' to Congress from Virginia. Can you tell me who they are?" He listened. "Yeah . . . yeah . . . in Tidewater . . . yeah. Okay! Thanks!" He hung up and turned to Dixie. "Get that. Herron's licked."

She stood up hastily, her book sliding to the floor. "Don't lie to me."

He mixed a new drink. "Call 'em up yourself."

She did, and got the same result. "That's a break for you, Jeff." She came over to him and put her arms around his neck. For several long seconds she looked at him, her lips softly curved. Then she almost whispered, "I want you to love me, Jeff."

"I—I—don't you think I do?"

"I don't know." One hand stroked his cheek. Then she left him, went into her bedroom and came back with the record in her hand. He watched her. "Where'd you have it?"

"Oh, hidden! What do you care now?" She handed it to him. "Here, break it."

He didn't wait, but stamped in into bits under his foot on the floor. Then he took a long swallow of highball. He looked at her to see that she was crying. She made no attempt to stop the tears that crawled down her face.

"What on earth now?"

"I'd have done that anyway, you fool. Did you think I'd sell you out?"

He went to her and took her in his arms.

"I wanted you to be afraid of me and be nice and not pay any more attention to that Richmond girl and I thought that this way you'd be—"

"Well, don't worry, I am!"

15.

THE BISHOP
ACQUIRES A SECRETARY

THE ROUTINE of his work in the Washington office of the Wesleyan Board of Public Safety held Jeff in a peaceful rut for most of the next two months. Politics fell into its usual post-Presidential election condition of quietude, and the Board spent its entire time in cracking the whip over the heads of Congressmen whenever the Dry laws were discussed. Money was spent freely on propaganda because there was plenty of money. Boom times were on; a bull market led everybody to believe in a continually ascending price index.

The Bishop made a comparative fortune through Gunter and Company.

But meanwhile Clara Blanton wallowed among the odds and ends of the Molleson-White campaign. The Virginia Anti-White Democrats had to report to the Clerk of the House of Representatives how they had spent the money contributed to them for the campaign. Clara Blanton had a big job, and the report went off. Jeff made, for his own use, a copy of it.

The table of figures showed that the Virginia Anti-White Democrats had run into a deficit amounting to three thousand nine hundred dollars. The Bishop, despite his private stores of cash, did not feel like contributing any more. So he had written a letter to all previous contributors, telling them the sad tale. Lo, the noble cause was in danger of having to hold the bag—and would those who had been so noble once, please be noble again? They were, and sufficient contributions came in during the subsequent three weeks to pay outstanding bills, had the Bishop been minded to do so.

One day early in January, the Bishop showed Jeff a letter from the Evangelical Digest Association, publishers of *The Evangelical Digest,* Wesleyan organ, in New York. It requested him to pay them a personal visit at their Fifth Avenue office at the first opportunity.

That was as good an excuse as any, so Sterling took Jeff to New York with him, first folding in his pocket a copy of the balance sheet showing the three-thousand-nine-hundred-dollar deficit. They arrived in Pennsylvania Station at ten-thirty of a cold, clear, blustery morning. The O'Gilpin Hotel became, as usual, their headquarters. Again the Bishop registered as Sidney Brent.

"I'll have to leave you for a while, Jeff," said the Bishop. "I'll meet you here for dinner."

They met at six that evening in the lobby, Jeff coming a few minutes late to find Sterling ahead of him, as usual reading a paper. Jeff sat down beside him without saying anything.

In a low voice Sterling said, "I've been noticing those two girls over there." He chuckled with faint nervousness. "Pretty, ain't they?"

Jeff looked across the lobby, saw two girls—perhaps women—watching them. They were well, though somewhat flashily, dressed. One of them said something to her companion, then smiled at the two men.

Jeff heard Sterling remark, "They're smiling over here. . . ." He chuckled again.

"Well, let's get some dinner. I'm hungry, aren't you?"

Momentary silence. Sterling: "I—I thought—well, we're not doing anything special tonight—and—"

Jeff turned his head to look at him. "Want to have a little party? Maybe we can pick up these dames."

The old man smiled quickly and nodded. His eyes widened and narrowed in quick excitement. Jeff looked across at the two girls; the one smiled again. He jerked his head toward the street; the same one nodded.

Jeff said, "Come on, we'll meet them outside."

The two men got up and strolled through the revolving door, then sheltered themselves from the cold against the corner of the building. Inside of a minute the two girls joined them.

One said, "Hello!"

Sterling and Jeff tipped their hats.

"Feelin' hungry?" Jeff said. "How about some dinner?"

The other girl who had not spoken yet, laughed in a rough, husky voice. "Say, I'm hungry! Good thing we met you." And she laughed again. "Huh, Alice?"

They entered a cab and were driven to a chop house in the West Forties. The head waiter gave them a corner table. Alice was the younger of the two, with straw-colored hair escaping from a blue cloche hat, a cheap diamond ring on the middle finger of her left hand, and a black serge coat with fur collar. Under that she wore a dress of dark blue silk, so tight that her body seemed about to burst from it. One-quarter sleeves revealed smooth bare

arms, and the neck was low cut. She seemed to pair naturally with Jeff, gave him a routine smile and asked for
a cigarette. Jeff held a match for her.

He heard the other one say, "In town for a spree, huh?"
She let out her husky laugh.

Sterling chuckled. "No law against it, I reckon."

The girl giggled. "Ooh, Alice, we got Southern boys!"

Jeff took a good look at her. She had a longish, thinnish
nose that came to a point over a crooked mouth. Her
heavily rouged lips, when parted, let Jeff see a gold tooth
at one side. Her cheeks were beginning to loosen, and her
neck showed lines. She wore a black dress edged with
white lace and it hung loosely on her. Her hands were bare
of ornament, and the fingers were strong and square-
ended.

The waiter, after taking their orders, leaned toward
the Bishop. "Want a little something to drink?"

Alice said, "Yeah. Gimme a Martini."

Jeff nodded, caught the Bishop's eyes and nodded for
him too. The other girl said, "Make it four. And snappy,
big boy!"

"Yes, ma'am."

Alice said, "Seein' as were gonna have chow together,
let's get acquainted. What's your name?"

Jeff told her his. The girl answered, "Mine's Alice—
Alice Salazar. She's Mary Kennedy."

"How've you been? This is my friend, Mr. Brent. Call
him Sid."

The Kennedy girl coyly chucked Sterling under the
chin. "Okay, Siddie. We'll be friends, huh?" She laughed,
picked up her cocktail and tossed it off quickly. "Jees,
that's good all right!"

Another round of cocktails prefaced the soup, and for the rest of the meal the conversation was made mostly by the two women. When they had finished eating, Sterling said, "Well, how about going out somewhere? Maybe we could dance."

Mary made a face. "Aw, the hell with that! Whadda ya wanna run around for? Let's go up to our apartment. Whadda ya say, Alice?"

"Sure. We'll get some liquor on the way—all we got's a little gin left, I guess. Suit you, Jeff?"

Soon they were in another cab, going through Central Park to the Eighty-fifth Street West Side exit. Mary told the driver, "Stop by that house there—under the light. Whoa!" Then she seized the Bishop's arm and dragged him inside with her.

Alice leaned against Jeff. "I'm tired, sort of. But that was good food, all right."

He said, "Yeah," and waited for the others to return. This they did in five minutes, Sterling bearing under his arm a flat, oblong paper package.

"We got Scotch," said Mary, and gave the cab driver an address in West Ninety-third Street. The address was that of a remodeled private house with a sumptuous entrance, an elaborately furnished lower hallway, with a door at its rear. The two girls took them through this, into a small three-room apartment. Alice snapped on the radio and settled the dial on a dance orchestra. Humming, she removed her hat and coat, then disappeared in one of the two bedrooms.

Sterling looked at Jeff and laughed boyishly. "This is better than a cabaret."

Mary flung her arms around his neck and kissed him

noisily on the cheek. Her lips left a red rouge smudge. "You bet your old neck it is, Siddie. We'll have a hell of a little party. Open the Scotch." And she disappeared into the other bedroom.

Jeff opened the bottles and mixed highballs, watching Sterling sip of his. "Not bad," said the old man.

Mary came back. She had changed from her dress into a semi-transparent negligee that let the men see just how much underwear she had, which was little. The black of her stockings made contrast with the general pink tone of the rest of her. She took her glass and swallowed thirstily.

Alice rejoined them, changed from her tight blue silk to a formless blue robe.

Mary flung herself in a chair. "How do you like our town, Siddie? First visit?"

Sterling sipped his drink. "I reckon I'm right fond of it. But it sure isn't my first visit." He chuckled. "It won't be my last."

Mary crossed her legs, letting the negligee slide away enough to show bare white thigh, "I sho' hope it ain't," she mimicked and laughed loudly.

"You girls got jobs, or are you just heiresses?" Jeff asked.

Alice smiled sideways at him. "Don't get fresh. Only thing I ever inherited was a lousy disposition."

He sat on the arm of her chair. "I reckon so."

She looked at him sharply. "Oh, yeah? Well,, I'm most of the time polite, anyway."

He put his hand on her shoulder. "This is a hell of a time to fight."

She made no answer, but got up to make fresh drinks.

The Bishop had not yet finished his, but she replenished it. Then she rejoined Jeff.

"How're ya feelin', sweetheart?"

Her lower lip went out. "I thought you Southern men were supposed to be so gallant, or whatever it is. I guess that's hooey like everything else. Say—" she turned on him— "did you know yet that Lee surrendered at Gettysburg?"

"It was Appomattox Court House, honey. 'N' you look real sweet when you're mad."

She gave him the Bronx cheer, then laughed and patted his cheek with her hand. "You're all right, Southern boy."

Jeff finished his drink.

"Let's dance," said Alice. They stood up, and began moving slowly about the room to the radio music. She pressed her body against his. "Like it?"

"What, the music?"

She slapped his face lightly. Out of the corner of one eye Jeff saw Sterling bending over Mary, letting out a steady stream of low-toned conversation. She laughed twice in her rough, husky voice. Sterling's hand rested on her knee, then crept slowly to the bare thigh. Alice said: "Naughty boy, mustn't look."

Jeff steered her through the nearest door, into a bedroom. "Naughty boy wants to do, too." He put his arms around her, felt the soft flesh above her hips, kissed hard her very red and wet lips. Her mouth parted under his. He drew back.

"Oh, boy!" she whispered.

Through the open door came another of Mary Kennedy's hoarse laughs. Alice freed herself. "Wait'll I get another couple drinks." She went back into the other room. Jeff removed his coat and vest and sat down on the edge of the bed.

In two minutes, Alice returned with new drinks. She said in surprise, "You don't waste any time!" She shut the door behind her.

"What's happening out there?"

She giggled. "Mary's got him in her room."

"I hope you don't have to get up early," Jeff said.

Jeff awoke soon after nine, to find the bed beside him empty and the door closed. He examined his wallet in his trousers hanging across the bottom of the bed. His sixty-five dollars were still there. He took out a ten and put it under Alice's pillow. From the living room he heard sounds of dishes.

He rose, washed and dressed, and went out. He found Alice, again in her mandarin robe, preparing breakfast of toast, eggs and coffee.

"Hello, Southern boy! Have a good sleep?"

"Sure thing." He looked at Mary's closed door. It opened as he looked and Mary, fully dressed, again in the black silk dress, came out, shutting the door again behind her. She leaned back against it and stretched. Alice went into her own room.

Mary stifled a yawn, came close to Jeff and said, "Say, your friend is some guy. How the hell old is he, anyway?"

Jeff grinned. "Bit over sixty, I reckon. More maybe. Why?"

She turned away from him, then looked back over her shoulder and smiled crookedly. "He's a little out of my line, that's all."

"Oh!"

Mary was about to say something further, but changed her mind when Alice came back. Jeff looked at Alice. She said, "Thanks, big boy."

"Let's eat."

They sat down, when Sterling came out of the bedroom. "Good morning, everybody." He smiled, but seemed not very chipper. He sat down and breakfast passed almost in silence. After the second cup of coffee all around, Sterling looked at his watch. "We'd better be getting along, Jeff. I want to go downtown, and then—"

They found hats and coats, Jeff kissed Alice, and started for the door, when Mary's husky voice said sharply, "Haven't you forgotten something, old-timer?"

Silence. Jeff turned. Sterling's face was a furious red. "Oh—er—" The nervous chuckle came in—"Sorry." He fished out his wallet, handed Mary a ten. She looked at it distastefully.

"That all?" she said. He gave her another one. Then Mary laughed and kissed him on the cheek. "There's a good old skate. Come and see me again."

"I will—I will." The Bishop made for the door. "Good-bye."

In the cab on the way to see Silverman at Gunter and Company, Sterling said, "A right nice girl, that. I'm glad we—er—"

"Like her?"

Sterling allowed himself a little enthusiasm. The spectacles made his gray eyes seem to gleam, but the purplish patches of dissipation showed cruelly in the morning light. "I reckon I do."

"She's certainly a prize."

Bishop Sterling looked uncertainly at him, and said nothing more.

They found Silverman in his usual little office apart from the main room of Gunter and Company. He gave them his wolfish smile.

"Well, gentlemen, I'm glad to see you here again. How do you like our market, today?"

"I want some of that Perkins Airways," Sterling said. "It went up five yesterday."

"I wouldn't advise that," Silverman objected. "And I want to give you your monthly statements, gentlemen. Will you excuse me?" He returned a few minutes later with a long envelope for each one. Jeff's statement contained the summary of only a few transactions. He had some shares of an oil stock remaining from the time Sterling had sold almost everything for him some weeks before. Sterling pocketed his statement for later examination. Then he pulled out his wallet, and dumped on the table a packet of bills. "Count that," he told Silverman. The thickish lips of the Bishop twitched, his hands fumbled for envelope and pencil. He figured quickly. "I can let you have most of that cash."

Silverman was counting. "As I make it, thirty-seven hundred. That right? I'll have our cashier count it and give you a receipt."

Sterling nodded. "Put it all on whatever you think best. I don't need that money."

Silverman left them, returned with a receipt for the cash, and bade them good-bye. In the doorway he smiled and said: "I'll try to run that up for you before the market goes to hell."

"It never will!" said Sterling.

From there Sterling led Jeff to an office on Fifth Avenue in the Twenties: publishing headquarters of the Evangelical Digest Association. They were taken into the General Director's office.

He was a short, round man, with a perfectly bald head and steel-rimmed glasses. He bounced out of his seat and literally rushed across his office to shake the Bishop's hand.

"Bishop Sterling, this is indeed a pleasure—an honor, sir! Please sit down. And this is? . . ." He turned the steel-rimmed glasses on Jeff. Sterling introduced him. The Director gave him a little soft hand.

When they were all seated, the Director leaned back in his chair. Jeff noticed it had specially built high legs, so that visitors could see the Director over the top of the desk.

"Bishop," he pronounced solemnly, "you may have wondered why we sent you that letter urging an early visit on your part to our headquarters here in New York. And I am indeed glad that you were able to come so swiftly. Glad indeed."

"I made this visit to you the point of my whole trip, sir."

The General Director nodded his pellet head. "And now let me inform you, sir, of the reason for what may have seemed to you an extraordinary request. But we have what we consider an extraordinary reason, my dear Bishop. Extraordinary!"

Sterling nodded.

"As you know, sir, it is the custom of this organization to reward, in some small way within our limited power, those men of the Wesleyan Church who have distinguished themselves in their work. This year it has been far less difficult than usual to choose the most worthy one from among the multitude of worthy ones. A multitude, my dear Bishop!" After each repetition of a word or phrase he stopped and stared. This time he received no answering comment.

"For we have chosen you, my dear Bishop Sterling, as the most worthy of all Wesleyan churchmen. We have reviewed your record carefully, sir. We have seen what you did in Peru and Morocco. Your organizing work as Missionary Bishop has been truly epoch-making. Truly epoch—"

"That's very kind of you," Sterling broke in.

The General Director inclined his head gravely. "Over and above that, we have given due credit to your influence and leadership on the Church as a whole, and on the Wesleyan Church, South, in particular. And it gives me the greatest pleasure to inform you that this early Spring, within a very few weeks, in fact, the Evangelical Digest Association will award you the prize as the contributor of the most valuable religious work of the past year!"

Sterling stood up, cleared his throat. "I ought to say, sir, that this honor is too great for me. I have tried to do my part and am naturally gratified that it has had some results. Let me thank you with all my heart."

The Director bounced from his seat and became again a little man trying to look important. The two shook hands, and Jeff followed them into the outer office. There the Director declaimed, "Very soon, Bishop, you will receive official notice of the award. I thought it fitting to give you this advance notice in view of the nature of the award."

Sterling fingered his lower lip. "That's right friendly of you, sir. Just what is the prize?"

"A trip to the Holy Land!"

"Wonderful, sir, wonderful!" They shook hands again, and Jeff and the Bishop went down into the street again. They walked along a few steps in silence.

Then Bishop Sterling said, "That's right nice of them."

"Swell vacation."

"That trip will be valuable to me. I ought to have a secretary along."

Jeff said nothing.

Sterling: "I shall take a literary secretary with me."

Jeff suggested, "Clara Blanton."

He heard Sterling snort, then chuckle. "No. Mary Kennedy."

16.

MARY KENNEDY DEPOSETH AND SAITH--

WITHIN SIX weeks the Evangelical Digest Association made announcement of its award to Thomas Henderson Sterling, D.D., Missionary Bishop of the Wesleyan Church, South, for his religious work of the past year. An amount of money to cover a four-months' trip to the Holy Land and Near East was presented to the Bishop, and he went.

Mary Kennedy gave up her apartment with Alice Salazar and took the cabin opposite the Bishop's. But the plump little director of the Evangelical Digest Association didn't know that; nor did Clara L. Blanton know that; only Jeff knew it, because he took her to the dock in a taxi, stayed inside while she got out, received her crooked, red-lipped smile through the cab window, and ran to catch the Washington train.

Jeff went back to Washington, and spent four-and-a-half months producing a stream of Prohibition propaganda stuff from his desk in the Wesleyan Board of Public Safety offices on Pennsylvania Avenue. Dixie had given up her own apartment and had moved in with him. She cooked his breakfasts, and dinners when they grew tired of eating out.

One mid-morning she phoned him at the office. He listened to her attentively, said, "No, I haven't seen it. I'll get one now. . . okay! See you 'bout six. 'Bye."

He went into the street and bought an early edition of an afternoon paper. Then he went into a restaurant. On the front page, as he ate, he read:

GUNTER FAILURE REVEALS PROMINENT CUSTOMERS

Sudden Bankruptcy of Bucket-Shop Involves Possible Millions of Dollars

Bishop Sterling Listed Among Clients

New York, N. Y. (Special to *Washington Gazette*)—An involuntary bankruptcy plea entered this morning in the Supreme Court revealed that Gunter and Company, dealers in securities on margin, had fallen into severe financial difficulties, involving the sum of nearly a million dollars. Assets of the company are given at $243,000 in securities loaned out, and liabilities at $922,000, while the plea, entered by a group of former clients represented by Leo T. Melkenitz, attorney, charges also that the firm has for years plundered widows and orphans by selling doubtful securities through the mail. Jacob K. Gunter, Otto Fleisch and Maurice Silverman are named in the mail accusation.

The action has made public the names of some of the clients of Gunter and Company's bucket-shop methods. Included among these is the name of Bishop Thomas Henderson Sterling, of Richmond and Washington, of the Wesleyan Church, South. It could not be learned how large his speculations were.

It was said by Mr. Melkenitz, counsel for the former Gunter clients, that evidence of the company having used the mails to defraud would be presented to the coming Grand Jury through the District Attorney's office. The individuals named in these charges have been held temporarily under bail until trial date is set.

The list of Gunter clients, as revealed in the company's books turned over to the Court, follows:

And here Jeff read a list of several hundred names, including his own, without further identification.

He finished his luncheon quickly and walked north to the Colorado Building. He found Voorhees reading the same paper.

"I can always tell when you're coming up here—every time your boy friend gets in a jam of some sort." He smiled dapperly.

Jeff sat down. "Yeah. I thought I had a beat on this stuff—and now the outfit has to flop. Cost me about two hundred."

"Plunger," remarked Voorhees.

"I want to know, is this all there is to the yarn? Have you heard anything?"

"What else could there be? Was your boy friend mixed up in the company—I mean, was he just a sucker?"

Jeff shook his head. "As far as I know, he wasn't mixed up in any way at all. And he wasn't altogether a sucker. I reckon he made plenty at one time or another."

Voorhees raised his eyebrows. "Plenty? You have to have *something* before you can make anything."

"Sure. He's been using Anti-White campaign money for months. I saw him drop thirty-seven hundred in cash on this feller's desk—and that was only one time."

Voorhees sighed. "That's big money for him."

Jeff snorted and grinned. "And for you too, big shot. What else do you know, if any? I've got a trade last, so yours had better be good."

The neat newspaperman looked at him sideways. "I met a friend of yours a few days ago on a party. Said she hadn't seen you recently. She's pretty as hell and all, so I figured she wasn't being exactly truthful."

Jeff relaxed in his seat. "Thanks. Who was it?"

"Viola Stane!" Voorhees watched him casually. "Is that hot, or isn't it? I don't know. You probably haven't seen her since last night."

Jeff sat up. "Viola Stane? Sure of the name?"

Voorhees grinned and fished out an address book. "Bet your neck I'm sure. Here it is: 67 Ashton Place, N.W. An apartment house and you can get the number in the phone book. Her private number is Capitol 7638."

Jeff stared at him. "That's hot, all right. What's she doing?"

"This will give you a laugh. She is now in the employ of the Anti-Liquor League of America. File clerk or something. She's attractive as all hell'n' gone. If you aren't—"

Absently Jeff waved his hand. "Go to it. I'm satisfied where I am. Did she tell you anything?"

Voorhees played with a pencil. "No. All she said was she had met you some place—thought maybe it was in Richmond—and hadn't seen you—"

"It was Tidewater. Hell, I have to tell you everything! This is the dame I scared away from Tom Herron—I told you something about it. It was a lousy deal, and soft-hearted me tells her to dig me up in Washington. But I reckon I was most of the time in Richmond and I thought —well, I didn't know. I only saw her once in my life. She was Herron's girl friend."

Voorhees tapped his pencil thoughtfully on the desk. "I'd keep track of her, if I were you. Or else stay away completely."

Jeff stared at the desk. "I always thought I should sort

of give her a steer around this town. But she didn't find me. I blew in there and busted up her life with that ape, and I figured I owed her something. Advice, or maybe see she didn't starve."

"Yeah."

"Oh, hell, I mean on the level! She's a serious kid and I—"

"You're only interested in her talent."

"Nuts to you! Let's talk about something else. Did I ever tell you about Mary Kennedy? No, I didn't. So I will now tell you about Mary Kennedy."

Voorhees sighed lugubriously. "More women—all I can offer are Congressmen and Cabinet officers. If you want to know who's being kept by the Secretary of the Interior, or why fourteen Senators refuse to promise Republican support—"

Jeff was sitting up straight again. "That'll come later. I'm gettin' as weary as the devil writin' this hooey about Prohibition, so I thought I'd ask you—"

The correspondent shrugged. "What the hell d'you hang on for? Quit when your boy friend gets back. When'll he be back?"

"Two weeks. That's not the point. I want to quit, all right, but I want to do myself some good. That's where you come in. The reason I'm waiting is so I can get the dope on Mary Kennedy, see?"

"No."

"Well, this Kennedy dame is what you newspaper hounds call a lady of easy virtue. The Bish met her—with me in New York—and stayed with her. Then he took her on this trip with him as literary secretary. Now, I—"

Voorhees hooted. "A dame like that as literary secretary?" And he began to chuckle. The chuckles grew into guffaws and the guffaws into roars. He had to hold his stomach and his eyes watered. Jeff grinned at him sympathetically. Voorhees at last gurgled: "That's marvelous! God, it's marvelous! You can't hate a guy with nerve enough for that!" And he laughed some more.

Jeff waited till he had calmed down. Then he said, "I don't love him, but—well, anyway, I want to know the rest of that situation, unless he ditched her in Palestine. That's why I'm hanging on."

Voorhees mopped his eyes with a handkerchief. "Oh, God, oh, God! This is the high spot of the year! I wish I could use that story."

"You lay off!" Jeff waited calmly.

Voorhees made a gesture. "We couldn't print that. No paper could. But you can use it." He sobered, and his face grew crafty. "Wait." He lit a cigarette and thought hard.

"I thought you might have an idea."

"What do you want out of it? Dough?" Jeff shook his head vigorously. "A newspaper job here?" Jeff nodded. Then Voorhees became energetic again. "Only the Sloat papers have the guts to use that yarn. Why don't you talk to them?"

"Talk to them!" Jeff mocked. "To who? Sloat and his twenty-six newspapers, and I'm gonna walk in and say—"

"I'll give you a note to Salton—Victor Salton. But you'll have to go to New York."

"I have to go in a couple of weeks to meet the Bish when he gets in, and give him the Gunter and Company dope. Salton's the guy who made the Democratic keynote speech."

Voorhees nodded. "He's got some drag with Slater—

Sloat's right-hand man—anyway, enough to get you in."

Jeff bit his underlip. "And after I'm in, what do I say?"

The correspondent coughed to clear his throat. "You say this: you say you have a very hot yarn—or rather the smell of one—and if you tell them how to get it, will they promise you a Washington job. That's all. That's their language."

Jeff thought it over, then nodded. "I reckon you're right. I can do that easy."

Voorhees said, "Certainly. This is good." He typed a brief note to Salton and gave it to Jeff. "Get hold of Salton and give him this. Get him to take you in to Slater. He'll do it."

"Thanks." Jeff started for the door, and then turned back. "What did you say Viola Stane's address and number were?"

Voorhees told him. Jeff wrote it down, and looked up to see Voorhees grinning. "You have a dirty mind," said Jeff and went out.

Jeff went to New York the day before the ship bringing Bishop Sterling back to the United States was expected. He went to the offices of the Sloat papers on lower Hudson Street, and sent his note to Salton. A secretary then led him to a coop on the third floor of the newspaper plant. Huge windows let daylight into the several floors; the vague rumble of presses vibrated the building. Inside the coop was the tall, ironic man whom Jeff had last seen, though from a distance, in the Houston Convention Hall.

Salton said, "Sit down, Mr. Coates. What can I do for you?"

"I don't exactly know. I'll tell you my story. Perhaps

Mr. Voorhees' note doesn't say so, but for more than a year I've been a kind of right-hand man to Bishop Sterling." He waited for a reaction, but noted none. "Consequently, I have a right good slant on his activities. Better than good. And at this moment I have what I believe is a rip-snorting story on him—if that's what you can use—"

Salton asked quietly, "What is it?"

"We'll get to that," Jeff said. "Point is, I want to know what you'll give me for it."

Salton lifted one corner of his mouth. "You can never sell anything until you exhibit it, Mr. Coates. I'm afraid—"

"In this case, Mr. Salton, you'll have to take my word that it's hot. If you can get it—and I'll help—it's worth plenty. I'd like to tell it to you and Mr. Slater."

Salton pursed his lips. Then he said into a house phone, "Mr. Slater's secretary, please. . . . Hello, Mr. Salton speaking. . . . Is Mr. Slater free? . . . Fine. Will you tell him I'm coming right up?" He hung up. Together they climbed one flight of steel and concrete steps to the next floor. On the way, Salton suggested, "When you talk to Mr. Slater, bear in mind that he's a very busy man."

"Of course."

They entered a large office partitioned off from the floor. At a desk sat a slim man of about forty-five with pince-nez on a nose so long that it overshadowed his upper lip, which was short and firm. He nodded to Salton and switched his gaze to Jeff.

Salton said, "Mr. Slater, this is Mr. Coates, connected with Bishop Sterling—" Slater's eyebrows moved "—and he says he has a good story—"

"What's the story?" Slater asked in a low quick voice.

"I'll tell you," said Jeff, "under one condition."

"What's that?"

"I want a Washington job on one of your papers—later—if the story turns out as I say it will."

Slater snapped, "Can't promise anything like that, but it's not an exorbitant demand. If your story's good, we'll talk that over seriously. What's the story?"

"Sterling took a prostitute with him as literary secretary on his trip to the Holy Land," Jeff said. "I believe she can be induced to talk. They'll be back in town tomorrow."

Slater stared hard at him. "I'll give you two reporters. Good ones. You guide 'em. Will you need cash? Tell the reporters and they'll have it with them. Then come back and we'll talk about the rest of it." He looked down at the papers on his desk. Jeff followed Salton out and back down to Salton's coop.

In fifteen minutes two men came in and one of them said, "This Mr. Coates? Mr. Slater sent us."

They shook hands, Salton introducing. Jeff outlined the story, and arranged to call them up at their office the next morning as soon as he knew certain details. He got their names—Spink and McMurray—and left.

The ship bearing Bishop Sterling docked at ten-forty-five the next morning. Jeff waited on the dock and greeted the Bishop as he stepped away from the gangplank. The gray fox-face lighted up in a smile. They shook hands.

"Jeff! It's right nice of you to meet me here. I didn't expect it. I sure didn't!" The face was plumper, relaxed, but the faint purplish patches were still there. And though the cheeks protruded a bit more, the lines on either side of the thick-lipped mouth were deeper.

Jeff: "Nice trip?"

They were standing by the Customs inspection division. Sterling said to him rapidly, glancing furtively beyond the younger man, "Listen, Jeff, Miss Kennedy is down yonder, and here come some of the brethren to welcome me. I forgot to give her some extra money. She's goin' to the Burlington Hotel, East Fifty-eighth Street, and I want you to take this—" He passed something into Jeff's hand. "—Go down there and talk to her, give her that, take her to the hotel and tell her I'll write her in a day or so. Got it? I'm going right on to Washington before—"

A group of solemn men gathered in a group behind Jeff. They regarded the Bishop with professionally abject joy. Sterling cried out, "If you'll please wait just one minute— just one minute—" And he added hurriedly to Jeff— "You come right on to Washington tonight—after—and give me some information on Gunter." He smiled with sudden cordiality. "Good-bye, young man, and many thanks for welcoming me home."

Jeff left him, wandered down the dock to lose himself in the crowd, until he came to the K section. There he saw Mary Kennedy, wearily watching an Inspector probe her baggage. Jeff went up to her.

"Hello, Miss Kennedy. How are you?"

She started, then smiled. "Hello, Southern boy, you here?" They clasped hands momentarily. She was better dressed than when Jeff had seen her last—Paris clothes bought probably on the Riviera.

"I'm to take you to the hotel. I'll wait outside."

He stood by the taxi stand at the end of the dock and

joined Mary Kennedy when she came out. Baggage placed beside the driver, they started. Jeff said, "The Doctor said to give you this." He handed her the tightly rolled bills. She put them in her purse without counting. "He said he was goin' right on to Washington and will write you to-morrow."

She sighed. "Okay, big boy. How're things with you?"

"Fine."

"Jesus, you're as bad as the old geezer. I wouldn't know a young guy if I saw one. Tell him for me he doesn't ever have to write. I guess he feels the same way." Jeff kept silent. She went on. "No kiddin', it's a strain on a girl to travel with a guy like that. He's crusty as hell. Nothin' softy about him, no, sir!" She whistled with relief.

"I reckon so."

She looked at Jeff sideways, then hooked her arm through his. "Listen, I was only kiddin'. Don't you go runnin' back and tell him what I just said. Will ya?"

Jeff smiled pleasantly at her. "I wouldn't think of it. Forget about it."

She maintained silence, at any rate. He saw her installed in the hotel, shook hands with her, and left. A phone booth at the corner was his next stop. At Sloat's he got McMurray on the wire. "Coates speaking. Listen, the dame is in the Burlington Hotel, East Fifty-eighth Street. Know it? . . . okay. . . . You birds blow in there and hire a room near hers—she's got 816—eight-one-six—and I'll meet you there in an hour. I'll come right up. . . .Yeah. . . . And hey—don't forget to take some baggage. You know —It's not a bad place. . . . Okay, an hour." He hung up, went across the street and spent an hour in eating.

It was one o'clock when he went to the desk, and in-

quired for Mr. McMurray's room number. They told him
819. He went up, saw no one in the corridor, and entered
Room 819. Spink—stocky, muscular, red-headed—and
McMurray—six-foot-six if an inch, with the wiryness of
a lifelong rider—were sitting and smoking. They nodded
to Jeff. He shut the door behind him.

"Her room's across the way." He had seen 816's door
not three feet from 819, at an elbow in the hallway.

"Now what?" said McMurray.

"Ever do anything like this before?" Jeff asked.

"Sure," Spink said. "But you're supposed to have a
special angle on this dame. What's she like?"

Jeff sat down. "She's tough, but not hard. What do you
figure to do?"

McMurray asked dourly, "What're we supposed to get?
You tell us."

"Got cash on you? Good. Then see if she'll sell you
any letters she's got. She ought to be ready to pull a stunt
like this—she's sick of the old bird. Letters first, then a
signed story, affidavit, whatever you want to call it, see?
Get her to spill the story of how she met Sterling, and what
happened afterwards."

Spink nodded. "We'll brace her when she gets back
from lunch. Might keep the door a little open, so we can
see." McMurray hoisted his tall frame up off the bed,
opened the door two inches, giving Spink a narrow view
down the corridor. Jeff moved out of eyesight. They
waited. Jeff grew warm, opened his vest. All three smoked
too much, until the room was gray. An hour dragged by,
a half-hour crept by, another half-hour, and then footsteps falling on thick carpet.

"Who is it?" Jeff whispered.

Spink watched out of the corner of his eye. They heard a key inserted in a lock, a door open, then close. "816 all right," Spink let out. He looked at Jeff and then at the Irishman.

Jeff said, "Go ahead, before she starts takin' a bath or anything. Her name's Mary Kennedy. Don't forget it!"

The two Sloat men rose, sauntered to the door and opened it. McMurray grinned wolfishly at Jeff. "Let's hope she is takin' a bath." They vanished silently, bringing the door again almost shut.

Jeff listened. He heard them knock, and then a door opened.

McMurray: "Is this Miss Kennedy?"

"Yes . . .who're you?" in sudden suspicion.

"We're reporters, Miss Kennedy. We understand you're just returned from Europe, and we'd like to—"

There was an indeterminate sound of movement, then: "I'll holler for help!" More muffled scuffling, then Mary Kennedy's frightened voice: "You're dicks!"

"Oh, no!" Spink protested. The door shut, and then Jeff heard nothing for over an hour.

His palms were damp with nervous sweat, he smoked, walked up and down, tried to listen, but could hear nothing except a vague murmur of voices. Somewhat more than an hour passed; he heard the door of 816 come open. He stood up and watched, alert.

McMurray's voice said with finality, "Good-bye, Miss Kennedy, and thanks."

No answer. The door slammed shut, and a bolt slid into place. McMurray's head appeared in the opened door, he beckoned. Jeff followed them out and downstairs. Both reporters' faces were drawn.

In the street Spink said, "I'm gonna ask for a hundred percent raise after that one!"

Jeff said, "Get it, all right?"

McMurray nodded. They took a cab to the Sloat plant, and went straight up to Slater's office. In the cab, Spink told Jeff, "Boy, you were right enough. What a story!"

"And what a dame!" added McMurray, staring moodily out the taxi window.

In Slater's office, McMurray pulled from his pocket a package of three letters, Spink produced four hand-written pages, they dumped them on the General Manager's desk. He picked up the affidavit, and read it over. Then he handed it to Jeff.

"I am telling these facts in a clear mind and fully aware of what I'm doing. I met Bishop Sterling in the lobby of the O'Gilpin Hotel in the company of a woman friend of mine. He had another man with him and we went to my apartment. There I had my first sexual relations with Dr. Sterling and in the morning he paid me twenty dollars. After that I saw him nearly every time he came to New York—"

Followed a brief outline of the trip to the Holy Land, on which she officiated as "literary secretary."

"How much did you give her?" Slater wanted to know.

"Five hundred," Spink answered.

"She's a damned fool," Slater said. "Take this down to Squire, tell him to get a series out of this." He picked up his house phone. "Miss Belcher, wire all the papers and ask if they want a sensational exposé of Bishop Sterling. Let me know their answers. Phone the Sloat Syndicate, the Weekly and let me know. And come in here when you get finished." He hung up.

To Jeff he said, "You win, young man. "You'll hear from me, but I don't know exactly when." The sharp eyes inspected him.

Jeff said, "That's all I wanted to know. Good-bye."

17.

HEADLINES AND WHITEWASH

MY FRIEND, BISHOP STERLING

By Mary Kennedy

A Series of Articles, Exclusive to the Sloat Papers, by the
Closest Woman Friend of the Wesleyan
Prohibition Leader

The Southern tradition of a gallant gentleman is still lived
up to, millions of American women will be glad to know, even
if the chivalry of Bishop Thomas Henderson Sterling, nationally
known religious personality and leader in the Prohibition movement, is not exactly the kind you might expect.

The Sloat newspapers have come into possession of a sworn
statement by Mary Kennedy, love light of the cleric's declining
years. She was met at the dock by Sloat reporters as she stepped
off the ship that brought her back from a four-months' trip
to the Near East in the company of Bishop Sterling.

Startling facts concerning the private life of one of the most
fiery agitators for "moral reform" in this country are thus
brought to light, and add an interesting and sensational touch
to the picture of the man—a minister of God with millions of
followers—recently revealed as a stock market speculator of the
wildcat type. Herewith is published for Sloat readers the first
installment of the statement given by Mary Kennedy, as she
sobbed over the rupture between herself and the Bishop now
that they have returned to this country where he is so well-

known. Mary will go back to her old life and old friends—if they'll take her back. Or perhaps Mary will always remember fondly the happy days when she was the most intimate female acquaintance of the great Bishop Sterling.

Then appeared about four paragraphs—in bold face— of the affidavit which Jeff had read in scrawly handwriting the afternoon before. Jeff had bought a copy of the New York *Morning Press,* containing the story, as he left the train which brought him to Washington in the morning. He read the story over twice as he had breakfast, then stuffed the paper in his pocket as he taxied to his apartment. He pointed it out to Dixie, who was not yet out of bed, left it with her, and went off to the Wesleyan Board of Public Safety. They told him there that the Bishop had telephoned from the Tasker Building that he was going to New York. Jeff hot-footed it up Pennsylvania Avenue to the Capitol, across Capitol Park and to the red musty building containing Suite 50. He found the Bishop packing a bag.

The gray face was pasty, causing the purplish patches of dissipation to stand out almost like birthmarks. "I'm going to New York, Jeff!"

Jeff had nothing to say. He sat down and put a sympathetic expression on his face.

Sterling grated: "May the Lord God help me—such punishment for sins I have not committed. I will have vengeance on them, I will!"

"Anything I can do for you here? Or there?" Jeff kept his eyes on the floor.

The Bishop snapped shut his bag. "Put me in a taxi— that's all." The gray eyes were craftily narrowed; they glittered. "That woman will take that all back—mark my words. May the Lord God help me!" He stopped in front of Jeff and pointed at him. "For more than thirty-five years I have believed in and preached Christ and Him crucified. That faith has been a staff to me in the wilderness of my soul, and it shall not fail me now." The thick lips worked. "Why did I trust that harlot?" He stared at Jeff without seeing him. Jeff's throat was so dry it hurt. The old man turned and tramped out, leaving his bag for Jeff to carry. In the street below, Jeff assisted Sterling into a taxi.

The Bishop said to him, "I'll be back——" but the taxi started with a grind of gears and Jeff nodded automatically. The machine turned the corner and was gone.

Jeff walked over to the Senate Office Building, and went into Randolph Taitt's office. The secretary took his name in, and admitted him.

Taitt's underjaw seemed not so prominent as usual. He stuck out a well-shaped, hard hand for Jeff to shake. "Sit down, my friend."

"I'm glad to see you, Senator. Lynchburg was the last place, wasn't it?"

"Yes. Have you made up your mind?" The underjaw moved out.

Jeff nodded. Taitt's lips tightened, but Jeff forestalled him. "I've made up my mind, Senator, but not the way we originally talked about. I don't think it would be wise for me ever to——"

The small hands made a gesture of angry impatience. "If you came here to shilly-shally, I'm definitely not——"

"I didn't. I came to tell you that the time for us to start has arrived. I'll work with you, but not for you."

Taitt looked at him, as a man looks when he is revolving

something in his mind. "How much will you want?" he asked.

Jeff felt his face grow dully red. "I don't want anything from you—either money—or—I'm doin' a rotten enough thing without—oh, hell!" He stopped, then started again. "I've got a good reason for doin' what I'm ready to do. Let's let it go at that. Maybe I'll tell you some other time."

Taitt's face lost its expression. "I beg your pardon, suh. I do."

Jeff broke the awkward pause. "You read the story in the Sloat papers this morning?"

Taitt nodded. "Is it true?"

Jeff answered: "As far as I know. But here's the point. From the looks of it—unless he stops them, and he can't —they're goin' to make a big thing of it. That'll damage him publicly, won't it? So that now's the second for you to bring up other matters. The ball's begun to roll."

"What other matters?" the Senator asked.

Jeff waved his cigarette. "I'll tell you lots, but—"

Taitt spoke in a deprecating way. "Of course, we can refer in passing to his early days—his extraordinary way of lobbying—actually calling members of the House of Delegates out of the Virginia Capitol to take his orders— to get the One-Quart Law through; and then that story of the flour speculation when he was President of Gray-gables, but I never thought that was really so. There are such things—"

"You know as well as I do, Senator, that that stuff's not enough. Now, I should think his Church would want to do something about his stock gambling—encourage them—make the point in a speech. But your big point is this—his campaign expenditures' report to the Clerk of the House wasn't on the level."

Taitt leaped in his seat, and stood up over his desk. "Say that again!"

Jeff repeated it. Taitt looked at him in open astonishment. Then: "Are you certain of that? Are you right certain?"

Jeff grew warm behind the ears. "I know that he got almost seventy-five thousand dollars from an insurance man named Johnsbury—Henry L.—in New York. Other contributions amounted to maybe fifty thousand. I know that all the Johnsbury money wasn't reported. Now, unless there's a lot of technicalities—"

Tait sat down again. From a hand manual on his desk, after thumbing over some pages, he read:

" 'Section 305. (a) The Treasurer of a political committee shall file with the Clerk of the House of Representatives . . . on such-and-such dates . . . preceding the date on which a general election is to be held, at which candidates are to be elected in two or more States . . . a statement containing . . ' " Taitt looked up, then back at the page. "Then it gives all the particulars. Names and addresses of those who contribute one hundred dollars or over, the lump total of lesser sums, then the itemization of lesser sums, and so on."

Jeff plucked at his lower lip with the finger of his right hand. "What're the catches in that?"

Taitt lifted his bushy eyebrows. "There aren't many. The whole law covers pages in this. It's right complete."

Jeff nodded satisfiedly. "Then that's all you need. He didn't report all the Johnsbury money received, or spent, by the Virginia Anti-White Democrats. All that's—"

Taitt raised a forefinger. "Was the money spent just in Virginia or throughout the South?"

"All over. He sent literature to every Southern State, he used paid advertisements in newspapers in Virginia *and* North Carolina. Oh—and he travelled all over. So did I."

Taitt nodded. "Splendid. But I'm not the man to start it off. You talk to—to—" his thin-lipped mouth smiled— "—Representative Wallace—Teddy Wallace—He's our man. We discussed him before."

"You talk to him. I don't know him. He'd never do!"

Taitt's smile became a chuckle. "I know better than that. Wallace is soaking Wet, he's liberal, non-sectarian, and he's been dying for a go at our friend for years. Now you tell him what you've—"

"What's he got it in for Ster—"

"Sterling irritates him. Wallace resents Dry leaders of Sterling's type—or any type—even though he and I are good personal friends. Tell him what you've told me. He'll start something." Taitt's deep-sunken eyes held a look of self-satisfaction.

Jeff protested stubbornly. "You'd be better."

Taitt made a wry face. "For one thing, my boy, I am a Wesleyan deacon. I can't attack a member of my own Church."

Jeff stood up, grinning. "I never thought of that. Will you let Wallace know I'm coming to see him?"

Taitt nodded. Jeff left. It was afternoon before he found Wallace—the strange bearded forty-year-old who represented a Boston district—in his office. He turned out to be a six-footer, with the wide powerful shoulders of a man who took good care of himself. Jeff knew he spent between-sessions hunting wild animals in Africa, and created the impression, by the extreme liberality of his Republican-progressive views, that he admitted no ruler either in his home or in his electoral bailiwick.

He said "How do you do?" in a deep polite voice, and extended a vast hand for Jeff to shake. They sat down.

Jeff re-outlined, in short sentences, what he had told Senator Taitt. Wallace's deep-set brown eyes brooded on him, lighting up only when Jeff had nearly reached the end of his tale. When Jeff did finish, Wallace said, "I'll be glad to go ahead as the Senator suggests. Suppose we let it rest there?"

"Anything further you want to know—here's my phone number." Jeff wrote it on a piece of paper and handed it to Wallace, who inclined his head. "And my name, of course, doesn't come in."

"Of course not," the Congressman agreed.

Jeff added as a careful afterthought: "I want to emphasize in your mind that the stock trading in itself doesn't mean anything. The bankruptcy hearings of Gunter found that the Bishop was a customer only. At worst he was only a sucker. The point is that the amount of stock trading is out of proportion to his known income—therefore, he got money somewhere else. The second point is the failure of Clara Blanton, Secretary of the Anti-Whites, to report *all* of Johnsbury's contributions. Put the two inferences side by side. Call 'em facts later, when they're definitely proved. Incidentally, I don't think that this Blanton woman did this on her own hook."

Wallace nodded again, thoughtfully. "I believe I have it all straight. I'll check the Clerk's report file. . . . You leave it to me." He extended the big hand again. "I am glad to have met you."

Jeff left him.

Jeff kept close to his desk in the Wesleyan Building the rest of that day and the next. The day following all the papers carried a new story:

BISHOP STERLING SUES SLOAT

Million Dollar Libel Charged by Cleric in 'Closest-Woman-Friend' Articles in Papers Owned by Walter Rupert Sloat

Bishop Produces Affidavit from Mary Kennedy Denying Trvth of Articles Published—Claims Duress

New York, N. Y.—Bishop Thomas Henderson Sterling, high-placed clergyman of the Wesleyan Church, South, who makes his headquarters in Washington, D. C., and Richmond, Va., today filed suit against Walter Rupert Sloat personally, James Slater, General Manager of the Sloat publications, and two Sloat papers (New York and San Francisco) charging libel in the articles published as confessions of one Mary Kennedy, with damages amounting to one million dollars. The individuals and papers are named jointly.

In the notice of his suit for libel, Bishop Sterling ascribes "malicious, evil and immoral will to harm" to those connected with the articles. He states also that he has in his possession an affidavit from Mary Kennedy denying the truth of the articles appearing under her name and adds that any statements given by her to reporters of the New York *Morning Press* were given under threats of physical violence, and consequently are not to be regarded as truthful.

The suit has been placed on the calendar of the New York Supreme Court, but, court attendants said, may not come up for trial for several years. . . .

Et cetera, et cetera.

For several days thereafter the Bishop did not attend to his official duties, nor would he see anyone. He remained in Suite 50, Tasker Building.

Two days later Representative Theodore Wallace, (R., Mass.) made his statement to the press, which appeared thus:

WALLACE CHARGES STERLING DIVERTED FUNDS

Republican Congressman "Has Reason to Believe" Bishop Used Religious Funds for Political Purposes

Washington, D. C.—In a statement to newspapermen last night, Rep. Theodore Wallace (R., Mass.) said that he had discovered evidence which led him to believe that funds of the Virginia Board of Public Safety had been employed by Bishop Thomas Henderson Sterling, Wesleyan Church, South, during the recent Presidential campaign in his successful attempt to bring about the defeat of Governor White of New York, Democratic Presidential nominee, by breaking the traditional Solid South. Mr. Wallace accused the Wesleyan Church in general, and Bishop Sterling in particular, of using funds contributed to the Church for the foreign purpose of influencing the election of candidates for public office. . . . .

From his secluded office, the Bishop replied in a statement published under the following headlines:

STERLING DENIES WALLACE CHARGE

Hurls Counter-Accusation of "Misinformation and Muddleheadedness" at Massachusetts Representative

The newspapermen took this to Theodore Wallace, and he gave them a broadside that appeared as:

WALLACE CALLS STERLING FINANCIAL MAINSTAY OF VIRGINIA ANTI-WHITES

Congressman Says Bishop Was Direct Source of Greatest Amount of Contributions Made to Mollycrats—

Believes Sterling Used Campaign as Stepping-Stone to Greater Lobby Power

The Bishop's reply was headlined:

STERLING ADMITS PERSONAL CONTRIBUTIONS

Says Defeat of White Was Demanded by God and Was Willing to Sacrifice Personal Funds

This seemingly confounded Representative Wallace, for he remained silent for five days. At the end of the second day, Jeff received a telephone call from the Bishop, announcing a trip to Richmond. Jeff remained in the Capital.

Three days after that, there came from Richmond the following:

BOARD VOTES CONFIDENCE IN STERLING

Virginia Board of Public Safety Last Night Gave Its Chairman an Expression of Its Confidence in Him—Sterling Calls This "Beautiful Vindication"—Says Wallace Animated by Blind Political Greed

At last Jeff saw what he had been awaiting: a speech by Senator Randolph Taitt reprinted under the following heading:

TAITT JOINS STERLING ATTACK

*At Public Dinner Promises "Ample Attention" to Bishop's
Statements—Threat to Sterling Power in Virginia
Seen in Senator's Attitude*

The bearded Bostonian played ball at once:

WALLACE URGES STERLING INVESTIGATION

*Massachusetts Representative Urges Department of Justice
Investigate Source of Loans Made to Anti-White
Democrats by Bishop Sterling*

Doubts Clergyman's Capacity to Loan Much

The Massachusetts Congressman waited for no one
else the next day; he urged that a bill be introduced in
the Senate, authorizing a Senatorial investigation of wide
powers, to delve into the activities of lobbies and of campaign expenditures.

No one doubted that he was aiming it at Sterling when
Taitt again came forward. He promised to introduce such
a bill as soon as possible.

From Richmond, Jeff learned from the Bishop that he
had gone to attend the General Conference of the Wesleyan Church, South, taking place in Knoxville, Tennessee. The papers told briefly what happened there: how
the Alabama delegation, headed by Bishop Blake, had
demanded serious answers to the Wallace accusations, and
had ended by preferring charges against Sterling, naming
"undue political activity" as the chief offence. The charges
were dismissed; Bishop Sterling was acquitted of having
indulged in "political activities at variance with the true

duties of a Wesleyan Bishop and at variance with the historic ideals and principles of the Wesleyan Church, South."

Randolph Taitt, stung to fury by the General Conference happenings, blared out:

TAITT PROMISES STERLING INDICTMENT

Virginia Senator Says He Will Leave No Stone Unturned to Prove Bishop Thomas Sterling Guilty of Violating Federal Corrupt Practices Act—Says Bishop's Private Life May be Scrutinized

Jeff paid more attention to the latter part of the statement, in which Taitt either deliberately planned, or was feinting a threat, to rake up the Kennedy scandal.

The day after that Bishop Sterling telephoned Jeff at breakfast time to meet him within the hour at the Union Station. They were going to New York.

During the five-hour trip from Washington to Pennsylvania Station, the Bishop said little. His overcoat pockets —both of them—were stuffed with newspaper clippings, as usual. He read different newspapers all of the five-hour trip, taking time out only to open the brown paper parcel containing crude sandwiches and consume the three bread-and-hams within.

It was two P. M. when they detrained. A taxi took them to an obscure apartment hotel on East Eleventh Street, and in a room on the third floor they found Mary Kennedy. Her face remained expressionless when the two men walked in.

Sterling said, "Are you all ready?"

The girl hesitated as if to say something, changed her mind and put on her hat and coat. By the door, already packed, were two suitcases plastered with foreign hotel labels. Over her arm she threw another light coat, picked up her bag and faced them.

Sterling said: "Now, this is the plan. Jeff, you take Mary to Wilmington—there's a train at three-fifteen that you can catch. Wait for me in the station there—the main waiting room. I'll take the next train at four-thirty. That leaves you a little over an hour to wait. Here's money—" He handed Jeff some bills apparently counted beforehand, because he pulled them out of his pocket and gave them over at once. Jeff looked at Mary Kennedy, who was watching them. She lowered her eyes quickly.

"Ready, Miss Kennedy?"

The three went downstairs together, the two men waiting near the door while she checked out. There the Bishop said to Jeff, "Keep an eye on her. Be sure to . . ." He stopped when the girl joined them.

She and Jeff used a taxi to the station, leaving the Bishop behind. Mary Kennedy kept her head turned away from him; Jeff was content to be speechless.

He bought tickets for them both, then she accompanied him while he hastily ate a sandwich and drank some coffee in an arcade drug store. A little before train time they occupied their parlor seats, and disposed themselves for the journey. Out of her smaller bag, Mary Kennedy took a confession magazine and began reading at once. Jeff excused himself and went into the men's smoking compartment. There he stayed until Wilmington was nearly reached. He rejoined her, to find the confession magazine still in her hand.

In the station, Jeff found himself hungry again, as she was also. They ate. The silence finally got Jeff.

"How'd you know we were coming?"

She gave him a cryptic inspection. "He phoned."

"Know what this is all about?"

The crooked lips hiding her one gold tooth twisted. She patted his hand with deliberate condescension. "I'm only the old boy's playmate. Don't expect me to know. But you can bet your bridge-plate it's something snappy."

"It always is."

She went back to her fruit salad and her silence.

The Bishop arrived duly, met them, put Mary Kennedy in one hotel, and himself in another with Jeff.

Two days later, after the requisite formalities had been endured, Thomas Henderson Sterling married Mary Kennedy. Jeff paired off as a witness with a Magistrate's attendant.

Returned to Washington, Jeff was willing to rest, but Sterling had other plans for him. A lengthy conference in the Wesleyan Building office gave Jeff the first inkling of a new epoch.

Sterling told him, "This detail won't interest you particularly, but I have taken you off the payroll here and transferred you to my own. You are now my personal representative."

Jeff said, "Oh, yes!"

Sterling's lips were relaxed for the first time in weeks. He rubbed his hands stealthily. "We face an interesting situation in Virginia where you are to work. I have made up my mind that those leaders who remained loyal to White ought not to be retained in power. In other words, they must accept my candidate—a man who stands for the same ideals as the Anti-White Democrats: enforcement of the Prohibition laws!"

"Who's that?"

Sterling nodded decisively; he had more of the air Jeff had first seen in him than ever. "I have chosen a man whom the Democratic leaders must accept as their candidate for Governor. His name is Grant—Professor Roxwell Grant of Richmond and Jefferson College. He has accepted my suggestion that he run in the Democratic primaries next month. Now—"

"You coming to Richmond, or is this all on me?" Jeff asked.

Sterling let him have a side look. "I'm staying here—to arrange certain matters with Mrs. Sterling." His face grew suddenly hard, triumphant. "They can't make a man's wife testify against him! Do you get the point? It's against the law to put a wife on the witness stand and question her to her husband's detriment."

"I don't think Taitt would ever have brought her into it," Jeff said gently.

Sterling merely looked at him, then returned to Professor Grant. "I'll come down later—perhaps in two or three weeks. Anyway, I want you to tell them—Taitt, and the rest—that unless they accept Grant as Democrat nominee for the Governorship, I'll fight them to a finish! Let them know I mean it. Remind them that I—nobody else—smashed the Solid South, and that I'll smash them forever if they don't take heed. I want Grant to be the next Governor, and I want him to win in the primaries. If not, I'll get him endorsed by the Republicans for the election. Make that clear to them!" The gray eyes were narrowed and glittering.

"It will be a pleasure to tell them," Jeff said. "Shall I meet Grant?"

Sterling shrugged. "He'll be no help to you in this work. Oh—be sure to see Senator Beauchamp after you see Taitt—I want all of them to understand this message. See Governor Falconer—every one of them!"

18.

VIRGINIA REDEEMED

IN RICHMOND again, Jeff got his old room in Murphy's Hotel, and found himself glad to see beneath him once more the slow stream of Broad Street traffic. He perspired profusely in the July heat, but didn't mind it.

A little questioning of Clara Blanton, on the job as usual in the office-suite, told him that Randolph Taitt was staying at the John Marshall, that Senator Beauchamp was at the Jefferson. Bishop Sterling had instructed Jeff to see Taitt first. Jeff telephoned Senator Beauchamp his second morning in town.

"This is the representative of Bishop Sterling, Senator. I'd like to have a little talk with you. . . . Eleven-thirty? Fine. I'll be there."

At eleven-twenty-five Jeff went in the Franklin Street entrance of the Jefferson Hotel. He threaded his way among the potted palms surrounding the famous alligator pools, trod the huge flight of steps leading down into the main lobby, and announced himself to the desk clerk. A moment later he was told to go up to Room 521.

The vast lobby, peopled only by ascending gilt columns and a stray guest reading a newspaper, was warm and silent. Jeff took the elevator to the fifth floor, found Room 521 and went in.

Senator Alexander Beauchamp did not rise from his rocking chair—the Jefferson still has rocking chairs—nor did he offer to shake hands. He inclined his white, venerable head and pronounced:

"Good mo'nin,' suh. Please sit down."

"Thank you," Jeff said, and placed himself on the straight-back chair by the writing table. Past Beauchamp, across the courtyard, he could see a very fat lady walking around her room in a very pink slip.

Senator Beauchamp's oratorical tones uttered: "You come here as a representative of Bishop Sterling?"

"Yes, sir. I have a message from him to you."

The white eyebrows moved slightly, the sage head nodded ponderously. "What is it?"

Jeff kept his eyes on the venerable head of Taitt's co-Senator from Virginia and co-political leader of the Commonwealth. "The Bishop wants me to say that unless the Democratic Party of Virginia will support his candidate in the coming primaries, he will fight to a finish—"

Senator Beauchamp's rage was alive in the room before he spoke. Jeff stopped and waited, watching.

Fully ten seconds elapsed before the Senator intoned: "Is this a threat, suh? Does Bishop Sterling dare to issue such orders to the Democratic Party of this State? In all my political experience, suh, I have never had an affront of this nature offered me. I may say—" His rage silenced him in the middle of a sentence.

Jeff watched him closely. "Those are the instructions I was given, Senator. It's not my responsibility. Bishop Sterling believes that those who supported Governor White in the Presidential campaign—" He paused. "He wishes you to support Professor Grant in the primaries and in the election to follow. Otherwise—"

Beauchamp permitted himself to say very loudly, "This is in damned bad taste, suh! An outrageous piece of clerical impudence!" The faded lips under the drooping white moustache worked, the blue-veined hands seized the arms of the rocking chair. The very fat lady across the court noticed Jeff casually looking and pulled down the shade with a haughty glare.

Jeff said, "I am here only to deliver the message as I was instructed. Doubtless—" He rose as if to leave.

One of the blue-veined hands lifted. Jeff stood still. The white head turned and for a long time stared out of the window. Then it returned to Jeff. The sonorous voice said, "I have received the message. Tell the Bishop that there may be something in what he says. At any rate, he will realize that we have no wish to disrupt the Democratic Party in Virginia—"

"Yes, sir. Thank you, and good morning."

Jeff left Senator Alexander Beauchamp to ruminate. His watch told him it was ten minutes to twelve. From a telephone booth in the Jefferson lobby he communicated with Randolph Taitt. They had to page him. At last he came to the phone. Jeff said, "I have an urgent message for you from Bishop Sterling . . . The hell I *haven't!*" Jeff laughed. "When can I see you? . . . . Okay—two o'clock in Room 813. 'Bye."

At two o'clock, after luncheon in the John Marshall Coffee Shop, Jeff went directly to Room 813 without being announced. He found the peppery Taitt in his shirtsleeves. Bottles of ginger ale were on the writing table; Taitt poured out two bubbling glasses.

Facing Jeff, he put his hands on his hips and thrust out his chin. "Your Bishop is sending me a message, eh? The infernal impudence!"

Jeff drank of his ginger ale, laughed and sat down. "Excuse me, Senator, but I'm going to talk right out. I saw Senator Beauchamp this morning. I gave him the message, and he—"

Taitt snapped, "What's this message?"

Jeff repeated to him what he had told the sage in the Jefferson. Taitt watched him, listening carefully.

Jeff finished. "That's not only the sense of it, but almost the wording. You support Professor Grant, or else the Bishop will fight you to a finish in the primaries and in the election. That scared Beauchamp almost to death."

Taitt sat down. "Why wouldn't it? Good God, man, there may not be a Democratic Party in this State any more, for all we know! Look what your Bishop did to it! Why shouldn't old Beauchamp be scared?"

"At the end he said he'd think it over, that maybe the Bishop was right."

"Oh, he did, did he? Well, right now I'll tell you my answer. Tell him to go to hell!" The underjaw was far out.

"Don't take it out on me. I can't tell the Bishop that."

Taitt smiled thinly. "Paraphrase it, then. . . . Why did you go to Beauchamp first, instead of me?" The deep-sunken eyes watched Jeff.

"Because I wanted to see what he'd do, how seriously you people really take this threat." He looked straight at the Senator.

"Did you find out?"

"Didn't I?"

Taitt made no answer for some moments. Then he said uncertainly, "We'll probably have to run Tom Herron."

Jeff said loudly: "What?"

Taitt regarded him steadily. "Tom Herron, I said."

"But he was defeated by the Mollycrats! Besides, he had plans to run for Governor this time, but the licking he took put him out of it."

"I don't see why you're worried by him," Taitt said. "But you're entirely right. That defeat doesn't make him an ideal candidate by any means. . . ."

Jeff added: "Even without the defeat! . . . "

Taitt said ruminatively, "But he's a rip-roaring campaigner. He'll make your college Professor seem anemic."

Jeff remained silent.

Taitt said, "No doubt, though, this needs lots of thought."

"Shirley Vernon kept his seat by a wide majority, didn't he?" Taitt nodded. Jeff went on: "He and Tom Herron have always been friendly. I reckon Herron's strength in Richmond would depend on Vernon's help, wouldn't it? And you've got that?"

"Oh, yes, indeed," Taitt threw out confidently. "Herron wouldn't be at all strong in this part of the State without that mealy-mouthed Vernon."

"I'll be in town steadily now for a while," Jeff said. "I think I'd enjoy seeing this Grant give you a run for your money."

"Would you, now?" Taitt said hurriedly.

Jeff left him.

After dinner Jeff walked out toward Representative Vernon's house. Necessarily, because of approaching primaries and the making of nominations, all the local politicians were in Richmond, whereas otherwise they would have been in cooler spots. Jeff approached the house from the far side and saw that the lights were on in the living room. Past the open window went a female figure: Veryl, probably. Jeff plucked at his lower lip with his fingers, started to walk back whence he had come, then changed his mind again and went to the house. Representative Vernon opened the door for him.

"Jeff, if it isn't Jeff! How are you, my boy! I'm right glad to see you, I am. Come in, come in!" But the joviality wasn't entirely easy; the collie smile struck Jeff as startled and strained. He followed the Congressman into the living room. There was no one else there.

"I'm in Richmond again for a while, sir," Jeff said, "and I thought I'd drop in and see how you were. It's some time since—"

Vernon laughed without mirth. "Yes, it is, Jeff, it sure is. I reckon it must be—well, let's see now—"

Voices sounded in the kitchen, Jeff heard the door to the garden close. Veryl laughed in a low, pleased voice. Vernon stopped talking. He and Jeff watched the door from the kitchen.

Veryl came in, stopped when she saw Jeff, said, "Oh!" Tom Herron almost trod on her heels.

"Here we are," Jeff said.

Vernon said, "Er—Veryl—hadn't you better—will you bring me that pipe I left in my room this morning?"

Veryl still looked at Jeff, then she dropped her eyes as she went past him. "Certainly." That left the three men alone.

Herron wasted no time. "I'm goin' to take advantage

of this opportunity while I've got it." He advanced to the middle of the room. Jeff remained seated on the divan, Vernon reoccupied his high-backed easy chair by the fireplace. Herron stood, poised forward, his hands hanging at his sides. "Let me say you've got no God-damn' business here. *You* haven't."

Jeff said: "Brave lad. Talk first and later—"

Herron sneered heavily, his eyelids lowered. "Later, hell!" He turned his head toward Vernon, whose collie face was pale and masklike. "You know this feller longer than I do, but you don't know what I do. I'll tell you, and he'll stay away from you."

Vernon protested in a low voice. "Tom, I don't think it's fair to Jeff—engaged to Veryl—and—" He flickered out.

Herron barked: "Forget it! You know he works for Sterling, don't you? You know he does all Sterling's dirty work, don't you?" Herron's heavy-lidded eyes inspected Jeff slowly.

"Go on, spill it," Jeff said quickly, leaning forward. He looked toward the door into the hall. No one there.

Herron jerked his head. "I will. When I get through, you won't come round here any more, let me tell—"

"You own this house?" Jeff's lips were back from his teeth.

Vernon sat back in his chair, still.

The Tidewater ex-Congressman talked to Vernon, but watched Jeff. "Did you ever know he tried to blackmail me before my last campaign? No? By threatening me with exposure of a girl he said I was keeping? The Bishop made him do that—*made* him, hell! He loved it! He stole the girl away, and God knows what he did with her. Then, when he was afraid I'd get back at him for threatening me

—that's a criminal offense—he put one of his high-class blackmailers on me—she stole the dictograph record I had. You think that's something?" Herron made an inarticulate sound. "See how you like this, Coates. See how you'd like it known that you had a girl beaten by the Klan in North Carolina—and nearly killed—"

"Talk faster," Jeff said. He found himself breathing hard.

"I will, don't worry." Herron's hand wiped his lips. "Coward that you are—Klan beating of a defenseless girl —that's the Bishop's political method, isn't it? And you're his helper. Get that, Vernon? That's Jeff Coates. Woman-beater—hiding under a white robe."

Vernon said in a low mechanical voice, "Is that the truth?"

Jeff grated: "Where'd you learn all this?"

Herron gloated over him. "Never occurred to you that Ely John Bagby would talk—or that his girl told him who—"

Jeff snarled. "Then why don't you say that I saved her—that I helped her—"

"Yah! You went down there—you helped to—" Herron's rage grew, his voice was unsteady. "And God knows how much else like that you've done. I suppose you're mixed up in all that Bishop's deals—stocks and women and—"

"Shut your lousy mouth!" Jeff stood up. He forgot Vernon, until he heard the Congressman declare very loudly: "All I can say is, that this is horrible—horrible!" Jeff, keeping his eyes on Herron, saw Vernon get up, cross the room hurriedly and call up the stairs in the hall, "Veryl, Veryl, come here!"

All three men stood still. Jeff heard Veryl's voice in the room. "Yes?"

Vernon was babbling to her. "Tom, Tom, you tell her, tell her. To think that—"

Herron's mouth was open to talk when Jeff said, without taking his eyes off the politician's, "This friend of yours has dug up things about me. A lot of it is true. But—"

Herron said: "Stop defending yourself!"

Jeff: "Shut up, you!"

Vernon: "Jeff, I must say that you and Veryl—"

Jeff flexed his hands. "Yeah, me and Veryl! That's off a long time, isn't it, Veryl?"

"Jeff!" she cried in a wounded tone.

A strange silence gripped them; Jeff broke it. "I'm better off outside. I'm not going very far, Herron."

Herron watched him go out. Veryl was standing against the jamb of the door between the living room and the foyer, one hand over her mouth. Her eyes were widely pleading; Jeff passed her, ignoring Vernon. Outside, he crossed the street and waited under a tree where the shadow was thick. He had just lit a cigarette, found his fingers shaking, when he saw Herron come out of the Vernon house. Over his shoulder appeared the frightened faces of Veryl and her father. Then the door shut them from view. Herron's head swung from side to side.

Jeff called out softly, "Go around the corner."

Herron stopped, stared uncertainly toward Jeff, then walked around the corner. This took them out of sight of the Vernon house. Jeff stripped off his jacket, held his hat in his hand. Herron turned to face him on the sidewalk. They were on the pavement in front of a school building. A high wire fence separated the walk from the school yard, trees were spaced between the pavement and the street itself. The thoroughfare was as deserted as Richmond's residential section always is after dark.

"Well?" Herron said.

Jeff threw his jacket across the wire fence and dropped his hat against its foot. He said nothing, but charged suddenly at the big man. His swinging fist grazed Herron's shoulder and bounced off harmlessly. His left went into action, but met Herron's blocking movement of a forearm. He attempted to dodge a coming blow, miscalculated, the impact rang his ear and jarred his teeth. He heard himself grunt. Herron circled for advantage, leapt forward fast. Jeff slipped to one side, let go from below Herron's defense and put one on the big man's chin. Jeff's hand cracked; Herron swore. His return caught Jeff again in the same place and he stumbled.

Herron had begun a swing as Jeff's foot turned under him—Jeff was inside the punch; in turn the younger man sprang forward and up, letting go a one-two that rocked Herron and dazed him. For a fractional moment the other's arms loosened; Jeff gave him another one-two, and caught Herron's return flush on the chest. Nausea gripped his stomach, he gulped noisily.

Herron, moving his feet clumsily, swung hard with his left. Jeff went inside it, caught the big man's wrist against his ear, and brought his right fist upward, hard from close in. Herron let out a sigh, his right catching Jeff against the ribs. A sudden pain racked Jeff's midriff, he almost doubled up. Herron's fist smashed against his forehead, a wild one, to which Jeff answered with a left to the eye.

Blood started on Herron's face, ran over one eye. Jeff felt his shin kicked.

"Yow!"

His right, a feeble blow, raked the side of Herron's face, and he felt the same ear take another scraping. He tasted something hot and salty. He went forward again, not seeing the politician's left coming toward his chin; only luck made the blow rasp his cheek. He put all he had into a right aimed at Herron's unprotected flank. It jarred a grunt of pain from the big barrel body. The force spun Herron slightly away, Jeff hit the same place again. Herron covered that spot, brought his right toward Jeff's face, leaving his own chin open. Jeff dove for it, smacked it full, sending a racking agony up his own arm. Herron staggered away against the fence, rallied and charged, bearing Jeff down over the curb into the street. Jeff twisted, jumped, failed to evade Herron's left that knocked him blindly against a tree. He clung, gasping for a second, then propelled himself forward from it. His left, swinging wide, knocked down Herron's defense and crashed against the back part of the jaw. Herron's nose was bleeding badly, he rushed at Jeff but couldn't see well. Jeff backed, sent a weak left to the man's jaw, stopped him in his tracks.

Jeff forced words between his lips. "You can't see."

Herron swayed, peering. "No."

Jeff let all the breath out of his lungs, then filled them deeply. He didn't know from the taste in his mouth if he were sweating or bleeding. Herron lurched suddenly backward, but caught himself and didn't fall. He fumbled for a handkerchief, drew it out and wiped blood from his face. Then he turned and started to walk away, leaving

Jeff standing there. Too surprised to move, Jeff watched until the big figure went slowly, uncertainly, around the far corner.

Jeff looked around; no one seemingly had heard them; they had fought unnoticed. He wiped his face with a handkerchief, found some blood, but mostly perspiration upon his handkerchief. He was drenched to the skin, and tried to straighten his clothes. He donned his jacket, and, carrying his hat, began to walk downtown, taking a different street than Herron had turned into.

Six blocks farther on, walking as rapidly as his shaking legs would take him, Jeff found a drug store. Pulling his hat low over his face, he ducked into the phone booth and called the office of the *Globe-Bulletin* and asked for the night city desk.

"Hello—listen—here's a tip for you—yeah, never mind who this is—listen, send a man down to Murphy's right away—tell him to watch for Tom Herron—Herron—yeah. Got it? He's been in a fight, and there's a good story for you." He hung up and went out. A cigarette soothed him somewhat, though his head ached throbbingly.

But he could still grin, and he did.

Before going down to breakfast in the morning he inspected his face thoroughly in his bathroom mirror. His left ear was swollen and reddened; his chin had a big lump on the right side, his cheeks were raked and bruised. He stared at himself, whistling in a minor key. Then he rinsed his face very briskly with icy water from the tap, finishing by powdering with talcum. He stepped back and surveyed himself again. If he kept out of strong light, he might get by. He went down to breakfast.

At the table he read his morning copy of the *Globe-Bulletin*. Second column, front page, he saw:

HERRON IN MYSTERIOUS BRAWL

Tidewater Ex-Congressman Refuses to Explain Battered Condition—Robber Theory Scorned—Hints at Personal Enemies But Will Give No Facts

At eleven o'clock last night, ex-Congressman Tom Herron of Tidewater was seen returning to his hotel with strong evidences about him of having been seriously attacked and beaten. Sympathetic friends sought an explanation, but Mr. Herron, suffering from a badly cut eye and other bruises about the face and body, was reluctant to offer any hint of an explanation. Asked if thieves had assaulted him, he said: "No. This is my own business. It has no significance of any kind."

Followers of recent Virginia political history are familiar with Mr. Herron's reputation as a pugnacious campaigner, and the theory has been advanced that this is the opening gun of his next political campaign, since those who know him cannot believe that Commonwealth politics would be complete without the stormy petrel of Tidewater. Facetious individuals have even suggested that Tom Herron had just come from a meeting of Democratic State leaders, though it is doubtful if there is one fist in that group capable of inflicting such damage on the doughty ex-Representative. . . . .

Jeff grinned; his face hurt, and he stopped. Stuffing the paper in his pocket, he went over to the John Marshall, and had himself announced to Taitt. He went up to Room 813, and was admitted by the Senator, again in shirt-sleeves.

"Good morning. Come in, come in."

Jeff went to the window and turned to face the room to keep his face out of the light.

"What's on your mind at this hour?" Taitt asked.

Jeff said, "Nothing special. I thought you might have a different message for me to send to the Bishop."

Taitt glared. "Oh, did you?"

"I thought you might have changed your mind—about Herron."

The fiery Senator took short steps to and fro. "Damn this heat! What's this fight Herron got into? Doesn't he know what a fool he'll be made by the papers? Do you know anything about it?"

"I read the story."

Taitt inspected him, squinting. "So did I. I miss my guess if anybody would support Herron—acting like a schoolboy—I never—"

Jeff said: "You don't think he's still available?"

The underjaw came forward. "Not while I have anything to say! That fool, Governor of Virginia!"

"Better than Grant, perhaps." Jeff grinned and his face hurt again.

Taitt snorted. "God send me a good man! Of all silly laws I ever heard, Virginia has the prize. Imagine not permitting a Governor to serve successive terms. What poppycock! Falconer could be reelected without—what's the matter with your face?"

"Nothing."

Taitt forgot his first topic and stared carefully at Jeff. He said quickly, "Did you fight with Herron? I'll bet you did it purposely."

"I did not. And even if I had, I couldn't have planned it. That fight of Herron's is a Godsend to me. And besides, if I *had* been his mysterious enemy, I couldn't admit it to *you*."

Taitt said: "Hmmm!" He inspected Jeff. "Where were you last night?"

"I was in a little argument with some reporters."

"Hmmm!" Then the thin lips parted in a smile. "If it *was* you—" And he smiled, gently, for a few seconds. Jeff said nothing.

Taitt whistled tunelessly. Jeff said suddenly, "What's the matter with Vernon?"

"Vernon? Matter with him? You mean for Governor?" Taitt was openly astonished.

Jeff gestured. "Why not? Ever think of him?"

"Of course. I've thought of everybody. Don't be a lunatic."

"Well, Vernon's your man. Look at him. He's Dry, he's a good Wesleyan, respectable, held his seat by a big majority, and besides," Jeff added slowly, "he'd be lots easier to manage than Herron."

"He's such a pinhead. You're insane." But Taitt watched him with interest.

"Of course he's a pinhead. But he's the only really available man you could defeat Sterling with—or Sterling's candidate. After all, you don't know if you've got a party any more, and you've got to play sure things."

Taitt renewed his tuneless whistling. At last he said, "Well, it's a thought, anyway. You'll excuse me—"

"Oh, I'm sorry to have delayed you!" Jeff said hurriedly. "I'll be in touch with you."

Taitt held the door open for him, and said suddenly as Jeff stepped into the corridor, "Vernon might not be bad!"

A week later it was publicly announced that Shirley D.

Vernon would be designated by the organization to run in the Democratic primaries for the selection of a gubernatorial candidate. He would be opposed by Professor Roxwell Grant, supported by Bishop Sterling and those who resented the forces that had stuck to White the year before.

Vernon came to see Jeff at the hotel late the next afternoon. Abashed, he waited for Jeff to invite him in. Jeff waited for the opening words. Vernon prefaced them with a collie grin, more assured than when Jeff had last seen it.

"Jeff, my boy, I reckon I have to apologize to you. I reckon I do! Er—" He wet his lips. "Er—I reckon I made a terrible mistake the other night. I did, I'm sure, and I feel I ought to apologize." His close-set eyes inspected Jeff with anxiety.

Jeff lounged on the bed. "Sit down. We can forget all about the other night."

Vernon was immediately relieved. "My boy, you have heaped coals of fire on my head. You have. I almost believed the worst, and if it hadn't been for my little girl Veryl—she's right fond of you, Jeff—" He wagged his narrow head knowingly. "If it hadn't been for her, I don't know—" Then he added another sentence in a rush of words. "And I want to thank you for mentioning my name to Senator Taitt."

Jeff was startled. "Did he tell you that?"

The collie smile appeared again. "He did, and there isn't anything I won't do for you. If I'm elected Governor, Jeff, you'll be a Colonel on my staff. My house is open to you, my boy. It is, indeed!"

"That's right kind of you. I'm glad I could do you a favor."

"I'm going to defeat the candidate of Bishop Sterling!
I shall redeem Virginia!"

"You're just the man I thought could do it."

Shirley D. Vernon beamed with simple pleasure.

The election confirmed Vernon's own prediction. He
swept into office with a commanding lead over Professor
Grant, whom the Bishop had backed after the primaries
as the Republican nominee. Also Governor-elect Vernon's
victory reestablished the Democratic Party in Virginia
and Bishop Sterling, shorn of political might, decided to
take a trip.

About the middle of November Bishop and Mrs. Sterling sailed for Peru, where, the Bishop told the world via
the press, he had "important missionary work to do." He
added, like the sting in a dying scorpion's tail, that he
was "convinced that Democratic Virginia had perjured
itself by electing to the Governorship a man of Shirley D.
Vernon's stamp—a convinced personal and political Pro-
hibitionist, who had besmirched his conscience by lending
his support the year before to the rum and Romanism
of Governor Jim White of New York."

Jeff, returned to the payroll of the National Wesleyan
Board of Public Safety, again subsided into a peaceful
existence, and devoted himself to writing Dry propaganda,
now and again interviewing the people's representatives
to remind them that the Wesleyan Board expected them
to remain Dry.

The opening weeks of the session of Congress were
enlivened by the introduction of a Senate resolution calling for the appointment of a committee with wide powers
to investigate charges of corrupt practices in campaign

expenditures during the recent Presidential campaign. The resolution was introduced by Senator Randolph Taitt and adopted by a record vote.

"Your friend Lycurgus Seed will be chairman," Taitt told Jeff one night in the Senator's four-room apartment where first they had met.

Jeff was openly astonished. "Seed? He's very buddy with the Bishop."

Taitt's compressed lips smiled a thin, satisfied smile. "He's the best possible man. He's entitled to it by seniority and—understand this—his sharp tongue is worth it to us. But here's the real point—as chairman he won't be politically able to obstruct the Committee." He raised his eyebrows at Jeff.

19.

BUT FOR THE GRACE OF GOD!

NOT A month before the expected return of the Bishop, his old enemies of Alabama attacked him again, this time at the quarterly Conference of the Wesleyan Church, South, taking place in Dallas. They revived the charges formerly brought against the Bishop in the General Conference nine months before, on the ground that they had been too hastily disposed of by the big meeting. Again Sterling was accused of introducing political activities into the pulpit—a practice contrary to Wesleyan Church, South, ideals. Again he was accused of conduct unbecoming a Bishop in speculating on the stock market. The quarterly Conference, however, encouraged by renewed votes of confidence from the Virginia and National Boards of Public Safety, decided not to reverse the verdict of the General Conference. The Bishop was again handsomely whitewashed.

Late in April, the Bishop and Mrs. Sterling took up their residence in Washington again, leasing an apartment near the Tasker Building, while the old gentleman himself kept Suite 50 in order, as his private and political office.

On May fourth, the Committee brought into being by the Senate resolution held its first session under the chairmanship of Senator Lycurgus Seed. The Committee became known as the Seed Committee. Its first step was to read into the record the complete file of campaign expenditures, as made to the House clerk by Clara Blanton, of the Anti-White Democrats. This led them to the name of Henry L. Johnsbury, who appeared as a contributor of some $40,000. A subpoena was issued for him and on May 7th he appeared before the Seed Committee, was duly sworn, gave his name and occupation.

Seed: "Mr. Johnsbury, we are interested in learning certain details connected with your contributions of money to the Anti-White Democrats. Have you any objection, on any grounds whatever, to our interest?"

Johnsbury: "Oh, none at all, Senator!"

Seed: "That's really very kind of you. We find here that you are listed as a contributor to the Anti-White Democrats. Did you contribute to any other political groups during the recent Presidential campaign?"

Johnsbury: "Oh, yes! To the Republican National Committee, to the Anti-Liquor League, to the—"

Seed: "I beg your pardon for interrupting. The Anti-Liquor League is not a political group."

Johnsbury: "I beg your pardon. I contributed, as I say, to the Republican National Committee and to local Republican organizations. On the sheet I am handing you the others are listed."

Seed: "You hand me a list of all your campaign expenditures. I give it to the reporter to be inserted in the record, first striking out any reference to the Anti-Liquor League as a political body. I take it, Mr. Johnsbury, you are interested in the Eighteenth Amendment."

Johnsbury: "I am a great believer in the Eighteenth Amendment."

Seed: "Oh, you had no political strings out, no hope that—"

Johnsbury: "Not at all, Senator."

Seed: "That is a relief to me, Mr. Johnsbury. It simplifies matters."

Johnsbury: "My only interest in seeing Mr. Molleson elected was the enforcement of the Eighteenth Amendment and the laws enacted under it."

Seed: "That is very praiseworthy, Mr. Johnsbury. Now, I note here that you list some forty thousand dollars contributed—broken up into smaller amounts—to the Virginia Anti-White Democrats."

Johnsbury: "That is correct."

Seed: "And here, further down, I notice another series of contributions to the Anti-White Democrats—this time to the Headquarters Committee. Will you explain that, please?"

Johnsbury: "Bishop Sterling—among the correspondence I have brought in response to your subpoena is a letter from Bishop Sterling which will explain that."

Seed: "Will you leave this correspondence with the Committee long enough for it to be photostated? Thank you. Now, what does that letter say?"

Johnsbury: "I will read it to you."

Seed: "You are really most kind, Mr. Johnsbury. It isn't every day that we have such cooperative witnesses."

Johnsbury: "The letter says: 'Dear Mr. Johnsbury, I suggest you report contributions as follows in order to tally exactly with our report: Virginia Committee, $41,-200; Headquarters Committee, $33,200.' "

Seed: "Is that the way you made the contributions, Mr. Johnsbury?"

Johnsbury: "That was two or three years ago, Senator. It's hard to recall exactly—"

Seed: "My dear Mr. Johnsbury, it will be difficult for this Committee to understand how you fail to recollect the disposition of sums like this. Over seventy thousand dollars, isn't it?"

Johnsbury: "The checking records will show, Senator, that I paid the money all to Bishop Sterling, as he requested—in the form he requested. I had no reason to—"

Seed: "You took his word, eh? Now this Committee finds that there is no report of your contribution to the 'Headquarters Committee' of the Anti-White Democrats. Can you account for that?"

Johnsbury: "I contributed that money to help the cause of Gilbert Molleson. I contributed in good faith, as I contributed in good faith to the Republican National Committee. I cannot be held responsible—"

Seed: "This Committee has no wish to hold you responsible. We are merely seeking explanation of some strange and suggestive facts, and appreciate your helpful attitude. Were you to receive any reward for your contributions?"

Johnsbury: "Reward? I don't know what you mean?"

Seed: "I think that will be all, Mr. Johnsbury. Thank you for your kindness. We may have to call upon you again."

Mr. Johnsbury stepped down.

There was read into the record a letter to Senator Seed from Bishop Sterling, protesting that the Committee had no right to examine into the affairs of the Virginia Anti-White Committee, since that did not fall within the scope of the Federal Corrupt Practices Act, which required money to be reported that had been spent in two or more

States. Succeeding days' testimony developed that Wint had brought Sterling and Johnsbury and Oberwasser together; that no report was available on the detailed expenditures of the so-called Headquarters Committee. Witnesses were called to discover just how the Anti-Whites had been organized. It was established that money had been spent by the Virginia committee in many States, but that it had failed to assist independent Anti-White groups. There was no evidence to show that the "Headquarters Committee" had been more than a name.

This led to an examination by the Committee of the exact relationship between a Bishop of an established Church and a political organization.

At this point another letter of protest from Bishop Sterling was read into the record, stating that no Senatorial committee had the right to question a man's political convictions or his activities in that regard. The letter contained a challenge to the Seed Committee to do so. It also defended his failure to report all expenditures on the ground that the Federal Corrupt Practices Act did not cover that contingency.

Approached on this point for an opinion, Senator Seed admitted sententiously his personal belief that no Government inquiry had a moral right to question a man's political work.

The next day the Bishop appeared of his own accord, permitting many letters, telegrams and other data to be inserted in the record as having a bearing on his relationship to campaign contributors. Extended questioning established his religious work, but when asked if there were any relationship between his religious and political work, he declined to answer. Asked further, if there were any connection between the money paid him for his work as Bishop and as head of the Virginia Board of Public Safety, he also declined to answer. His other testimony confirmed what Henry L. Johnsbury had admitted, as to the $74,400.

His reason for refusing to answer any questions relating to his strictly political work was the one he had given before: that the political activities of any American citizen were free from question of any kind. Senator Seed pushed the point far, but gained nothing. The Senators forming the rest of the Committee attacked the Bishop strongly, but he firmly maintained his position.

The next morning when the Committee met again, the Bishop requested permission to read into the record a statement he had to make. This permission was granted him.

He read: "I urgently request that this Committee, appointed for the purpose of investigating campaign expenditures, give careful consideration to the fact that thus far I have appeared here as a voluntary witness. I have willingly produced all available records, and have gladly corroborated the statements of other witnesses which may have a bearing on myself.

"However, inasmuch as the questions directed at me thus far in the inquiry have been aimed at my work in calling the Corinth Conference, at my position as leader, if not actual head, of the Virginia and general Anti-White Democrats, and as to the manner in which I supervised the expenditure of funds contributed to assist in the defeat of White for President, I feel that this inquiry has chosen gratuitously to hit upon me, out of all the organizations which took part on one side or the other, in the recent campaign. No attempt has been made by this Committee to investigate other organizations. I have been centered on, and I wish to state, without disrespect to the Senate of which this Committee is a part, that I deeply resent the inferences which may be publicly drawn from this attitude.

"Furthermore, let me remind this Committee that I have thus far appeared as a voluntary witness, but now I must withdraw from that capacity. The Committee has the right to call me by subpoena. Otherwise I must respectfully decline to continue as a witness."

Cullop of Montana: "Let me say to the Bishop that he is allowed to make this statement because of this Committee's desire to be fair—"

Sterling: "That is very kind."

Cullop: "But let me add that this Committee cannot see the incident in the same light as the Bishop at all."

Sterling: "I see."

Cullop: "This Committee was brought into being to investigate all known examples of political lobbying and campaigning that can be called to its attention. If it is within your power to elucidate any such cases—as seems to be your desire—we shall be only too glad to promise full and complete investigation after we have finished with the Anti-White activities in Virginia and the South. At the worst, this Committee can fulfill its duty in that regard. Furthermore, I believe this Committee understands your intent—in making your statement at this time—and that is to obstruct the Committee."

Sterling: "I beg your pardon. I felt called upon to defend myself in my capacity as a voluntary witness, which I no longer am. As I pointed out, the right to issue a subpoena for me—"

Cullop: "That is not the point now. You have this morning, and previously, been duly sworn as a witness. If you persist in refusing—"

Sterling: "I must say that unless I am subpoenaed I shall withdraw."

Cullop: "We cannot hold you by force, but please note that you are a sworn witness and you have not been dismissed. I see that Senator Baker wishes to question you."

Baker of New York: "I consider it appropriate that we place in the record at this point the telegrams which passed between you and Senator Seed—chairman of this Committee unfortunately not present today—which resulted in your appearing as witness. I believe they will show that you voluntarily placed yourself within the jurisdiction of this Committee, and consequently cannot refuse to answer its question without risking serious dangers."

Sterling: "That is already in the record, I believe."

Baker: "Also I wish it to appear in the record that I heartily concur in what my colleague, Senator Cullop, has said."

Sterling: "My address is known to the Committee. A subpoena—"

Baker: "This Committee must investigate lobbying and campaign activities, and—"

The Committee reporter wrote in his notebook: "The witness went out of the Committee room."

Jeff heard nothing from the Bishop until the following Monday evening just after dinner. The Bishop asked him to come to Suite 50, Tasker Building, at once.

"He's got a nerve," Dixie said. "Why don't you tell him to go to hell?"

"And lose out just when this is getting hot? I'll be home early, honey."

There was no one else except the Bishop in Suite 50. The old man was tired. He sat down slowly, wearily. The lids of his eyes drooped, his fingers moved uncertainly. He said, in a worn voice, "I asked you here for a special purpose. Senator Seed is coming—and I want a witness."

"All right. Want me to take down anything?"

"No. Just remember what he says, so that he can't change his mind later." The Bishop passed a hand over his mouth.

A few minutes later Jeff let the Senator in. He scowled at the young man, but went inside, did not shake hands, but sat down on the edge of a chair.

"Good evening, Senator," said the Bishop.

Seed was in no mood for politeness. "Before we start, or before you tell me why you asked me to come over here, I wish to protest against the presence of this young man."

Sterling grinned maliciously. "We're not in a Committee room now. This young man is here because he is my personal representative in certain matters, that's all. Now, first I want to thank you for coming here."

"Never mind that. Let me tell you I've had a devil of a time eluding reporters. They want to know why I don't order you subpoenaed."

Sterling, suavely: "Why, we agreed you were to stay away from that meeting of the Committee. That's your—"

Seed snarled, "That doesn't let me out by any means. Now, look here, Sterling—"

The Bishop sat up straighter in his chair. Jeff saw him make the physical effort to bring energy back into his nerves and muscles. "I'm not worried about your situa-

tion. Don't forget that we—the moral forces of this country—put men like you in the Senate. Yes, and keep you
there! Don't think you can turn around and dictate to us.
We spent millions of dollars to put Dry-voting men in the
Senate, but where do you think you'd be otherwise—you
and the several hundred others of second-rate politicians?"

"Now, I don't see why—"

The Bishop pointed a finger at him: "You'll see before
I'm finished. I'm an old man, and I've got to spend a lot
of time explaining perfectly obvious things to you Senators, who think that because—now, here's what I wanted
to tell you, and I'm glad you brought it up. I don't want
to stand for this investigation. I won't be a witness any
more. And if you don't see the situation my way, you may
believe it that this is your last term as a Senator!"

"What—the Wesleyan Board will do me in? They're
backing out from behind you!"

Sterling's lips twitched. "The Anti-Liquor League can
unseat you easily. Don't forget it."

Seed found courage to laugh. His mouth twisted. "I'm
sorry, Bishop, but that sort of threat won't impress me
now. You're too far gone in this investigation to expect—"

"You call off the whole investigation!"

The Senator from Arkansas merely inspected the
Bishop. Then: "Nothing doing. Besides, it couldn't be
done even if I wanted to—"

Sterling said: "I defy your Committee to subpoena
me."

Seed's lower lip came out in a placating expression.
"There's no use our fighting about this. I doubt if we will
subpoena you."

The Bishop leaned back in his chair. "That's better!"

"But you'll have to help me out of my position."

The Bishop brooded over him for several seconds. "Help you—?"

Seed leaned forward eagerly: "Of course. We've got to help each other out of this. I'll make a bargain with you—"

Sterling laughed, but Seed cut him short with, "Yes, we'll make a bargain! I'll see that you're not subpoenaed, but you've got to apologize to the Committee."

Sterling was straight up in his chair again. "Apologize? What for?"

"For embarrassing its chairman," Seed said smoothly.

The Bishop looked at him sideways. Seed added: "It's the only way out. I believe then they'll excuse you as a witness—"

"I'll apologize—but let it be clear that I do so to purge myself of contempt of the Senate—not because I'll answer political questions—"

Seed stood up, anxious to go. "All right. The Committee meets day after tomorrow. Will you appear?"

The Bishop nodded. Seed left without further words. Once he was gone, Jeff helped the Bishop into his light coat—June was warm outdoors—and they left together, the Bishop to go home to Mrs. Sterling. He said nothing in the elevator going downstairs, nor on the street till they came to the corner where they parted.

"Good night, Jeff," he said. "Don't forget—"

"No. Good night."

The next morning Seed told the papers that the Committee would not subpœna Bishop Sterling—editorials accused Seed of taking the Bishop's side—because the Committee did not find it necessary. Jeff read the hint there that other witnesses would serve as well, perhaps better.

The afternoon editions of the papers carried a story which interested Jeff more. He picked up a copy about four-thirty, and found a dispatch from Tidewater:

EX-CONGRESSMAN ACCUSES STERLING

*Tom Herron Hurls Serious Charges at Richmond Cleric
—Alleges Underhandedness*

Special from Tidewater, Va.—Ex-Representative Tom Herron, it was learned this afternoon, believes that his personal life, and perhaps political career also, were ruined by certain activities of Bishop Thomas Henderson Sterling in connection with a young girl whom, Herron said, he had at one time intended to marry. Speaking to a group of Tidewater Democratic Committeemen, he said that he would never have mentioned this tragic incident had he not found it imperative to allay a "whispering campaign" which was seriously damaging his political standing in his home city.

Though he was reluctant to give details, Mr. Herron declared that there had been a young lady who had won his affections and whom he had planned to marry some time in the future. However, by means of promises of a lucrative position in Washington made her by one Jeffries Coates, whom Herron described as a "Sterling henchman," the girl was lured to Washington, where she fell into the hands of Bishop Sterling. Herron intimated that the girl was now no better than an underworld character.

Herron said he deeply regretted this step, but that he hoped it would in some measure account for the unpleasant rumors which had persisted in coupling his name with that of the girl in question in a nasty way. This "whispering campaign" was begun during the Herron-Dellenbaugh primaries.

———

Bishop Sterling, who three days ago defied a Senate Commitee concerning his political activities during the Presidential campaign, could not be reached.

Jeff was outside the office when he read this. He fished papers out of his pocket, read the backs of envelopes till he found what he wanted. Then he located a phone booth and a directory. He looked up Viola Stane, at 67 Ashton Place, N.W., the address Voorhees had given him previously. He heard the phone ring, but there was no answer.

He consulted the directory again, found the number he wanted and called the switchboard of the apartment house. The elevator boy said he had not seen Miss Stane since she had left that morning.

Warmer than the weather, Jeff went to the Anti-Liquor League headquarters where Viola Stane was working. The reception clerk stared haughtily at him till he explained that he came from the Wesleyan Board. She said that Miss Stane had complained of a headache a half-hour before and had gone home.

"How long does it take her to get out to Ashton Place?"

The girl shrugged. "Sorry, sir. I don't know for sure. About thirty minutes, I suppose. It's pretty far."

"All right. Thanks."

Outside once more, Jeff used the phone again, calling Viola Stane's number. Again it rang endlessly without reply. Again Jeff called the switchboard.

"Miss Stane come in yet? . . . She did—when? . . . Half an hour—" He hung up without waiting for more, inserted another nickel in the slot and called his own place.

"H'lo, Dixie—Jeff. Listen, meet me in the lobby of 67 Ashton Place, N.W., as soon as you can get there. . . .I'm out of the way. I'll meet you there. . . . Oh, hell, take a cab! I may need you out there—Make it snappy."

He hailed a cab, directed the driver to 67 Ashton Place. Even at a swift pace, it was more than twenty minutes before they were there. He found himself before a painfully new ten-story apartment building opposite a children's playground and school. He went into the lobby.

It was another ten minutes before Dixie arrived in another taxi. She came in fast.

"What is it, Jeff? Cocktail party here?"

He said in a lowered voice, "I think a girl is in a jam. I'll—here, read this." He thrust the Herron story under her nose. She read rapidly.

"Is that on the level?"

"I split Herron and the girl all right, but not that way. I haven't seen her but once in my life, and Sterling never saw her. I don't know what the hell—let's go upstairs."

In the elevator, Jeff said to the operator, "Got the time, buddy?"

The man consulted a turnip. "Five-forty-two, sir, I make it."

"Just what I have. Thanks. Miss Stane go out again?"

"No, sir!" The man pointed to the farthest door in the hall. He went down again, leaving Jeff and Dixie.

"What're you trying to do?" she asked.

"I don't know. This dame is funny. I want to talk to her, and—" He rang the doorbell, once, twice, then loud and long. No answer. He listened at the panel. No sound.

"Maybe she's out," Dixie said.

Jeff shook his head. "She came in an hour ago, and you just heard the guy. He said she's in."

They stood in silence before the closed door. Jeff stared at Dixie. She waited.

Jeff said, "I'm gonna bust in."

"Get the Superintendent and a key."

"Good idea. Find that elevator guy. Tell him—" Dixie ran back to the elevator, rang, and fortunately the elevator man himself had a master key. He came and said:

"I ain't got no right to go in tenants' apartments—"

"Listen. Something's wrong here—" Jeff seized the key out of the man's hand, opened the door and went in.

In the door of the bedroom he stopped, Dixie and the elevator man behind him. On the bed lay Viola Stane, bare shoulders above the counterpane, her dark hair spread on the very white pillow, her hands and all her body covered.

Jeff said, "Hey!" He approached the bed, looked at the girl. He said again: "Hey!"

Dixie was beside him. "She's dead or something, you fool!"

"Holy Jesus!" And again, louder, "Hey!"

They waited. Then Viola Stane's eyelids flickered. She moaned and said, "Leave me alone."

Jeff and Dixie stared at one another. The elevator man was watching, his mouth open. Then Jeff said: "You— call police and a doctor. Hurry!" The man used the phone right in the apartment.

Dixie dropped on one knee. "What's the matter, honey? Sick?"

Viola Stane's voice came very faintly: "I'm dying. I did it myself. That's all. Tom didn't want me—I did it—"

Carefully Dixie drew down the counterpane as far as the girl's waist. A thin brassiere was her only covering above the waist. The lower curve of her left breast was torn by a bullet; wet blood still oozed from the wound over her flat stomach and down her flank, soaking the bed under her. In the blood lay a nickel-plated .38 revolver.

The girl moaned again; her breasts jerked in a spasm of agonized breathing.

Jeff kneeled beside Dixie. His voice was very low. "Why —why did you do it—?"

The pasty eyelids flickered, the head rolled toward him as if detached from the trunk. "I know you. Tom came—to get me back—I—I love him—I love him—but I wouldn't—go—back—."

Dixie turned to the elevator man. "Where's the doctor?"

The scared operator gulped. "Coming."

Jeff said, "But this—" His hand plucked the edge of the bed.

Viola Stane's voice grew dry in her throat. "I'm ashamed to live—I want to—God—I want to—" From between her barely open lids came tears, slowly like blood from the wound in her side. "Ashamed—I couldn't after he said—"

"That was a lie!"

The head rolled again with that ghastly looseness. "I'll die now—I know you—you said I could do—well—in Washington." The lips that Jeff remembered as warmly red moved in the beginning of a smile. "I love him—tell him—somebody—" Her diaphragm jerked again, her voice moaned faintly.

Heavy footsteps came behind them, a man's voice said: "Let me at that."

More footsteps. Jeff and Dixie stood aside to let two plainclothesmen look at the dying girl. One turned to Jeff. "Who're you?"

Jeff told him, also accounted for Dixie. The detective told them both to wait until they had the doctor's verdict. The police surgeon was working busily with bandages. After nearly fifteen minutes, he turned around and shook his head in professional distaste.

Three minutes later, with a clean white bandage encircling her body, Viola Stane died without making a sound.

The plainclothesmen took Jeff, Dixie and the operator to the station house for questioning. The operator told how Jeff had phoned previously, how Miss Stane had come in nearly an hour before the young man had arrived, how they had checked their watches in the elevator on the way to the apartment. They were released, promising to remain available for further questioning if needed.

Forgetting hunger, Jeff said to Dixie outside the police station, "Well?"

Dixie's face was pale, her lips taut. "Poor kid. Trying to be something—"

"I told her maybe she could."

Dixie grimaced. "If God hadn't given me a little more brains, that would be me lying in that bed that way."

Jeff said absently, "Yeah." Then: "Come on while I see Sterling. He'll want to fire me after this—"

They taxied from the police station to the Tasker Building. While Jeff went upstairs, Dixie awaited him in the lobby of the Dempsey Hotel, next door. Mrs. Sterling admitted Jeff, and he found the Bishop in bed.

"What's the matter?"

The Bishop had deeper lines than ever on each side of his mouth. The woman said, "He's gettin' sick and tired, that's all." She sat down and lit a cigarette, puffing at it copiously.

"You saw the Herron story?" Jeff asked.

The Bishop nodded. "That's our old friend. I'm sorry he had to mix you up in it. Pure lie, that's all."

"Know who the girl was?"

"I suppose he meant the girl we learned about. I never saw her in my life."

"I did," Jeff said. "She's dead."

Sterling's face tightened in expression. "What do you mean?"

"Just that." Jeff took a deep breath. "When I broke her away from Herron, she came to Washington on my suggestion. She was a beautiful kid and I thought with a little help she could—get somewhere. But when Herron tried to get her back, she wouldn't go. God knows why, I don't. She said she was ashamed to live after—well, what he said, or implied. Shot herself about an hour ago."

"What a break," Mary Kennedy Sterling said compassionately.

Sterling said, "Tragic." Then he added, "I'm sorry for you. Though it wasn't your fault. That's Herron for you."

Jeff made no answer.

Sterling said: "We've got to come back at him. Take this down, and give it out either tonight or in the morning." Jeff prepared paper and pencil. The Bishop stated: "In reply to the outrageous and completely unfounded accusations made yesterday by Tom Herron, I do not hesitate to call him a liar. The ex-Representative has chosen to distort and to fabricate, and to sully the reputations of innocent people without regard for truth. I never saw or met the young lady he refers to, and I understand that Mr. Jeffries Coates saw her but once in his life. On this slim basis, Herron has built a foul piece of misrepresentation. I challenge Tom Herron to produce any facts whatever to substantiate his accusations, and if he fails, he may expect that I shall have recourse to the processes of law and libel, for his slanderous remarks have done me an incalculable damage."

"I'm going to eat now," Jeff said.

He left the Bishop in bed, reading newspapers as always, and attended by the slightly sulky Mrs. Sterling.

In the lobby of the Dempsey Hotel he found Dixie.

"You took a long time," she said. "I'd like a drink."

They left the hotel. "Well, he was sorry for me. But he was a whole lot sorer at Herron for libeling him."

"Did he fire you?"

"Hell, no! He said he was sorry for me, knowing the girl and all. Libel! Says he'll sue Herron. He talks libel and suing like nobody's business."

"Let's get a drink some place."

"Okay."

"You look like you've seen a ghost. Poor Jeff."

20.

FOUR TRAVELLING ELDERS

APPARENTLY SHOCKED by the suicide of Viola Stane, Herron made a feeble retraction through the press within a week after the event, and the matter ended. No connection between Herron's accusations and Viola Stane's death was established publicly.

The summer passed tranquilly, with the Bishop's health remaining precarious. He did not appear before the Seed Committee again, which contented itself, and that efficiently enough, by establishing the uses of the money contributed to the Anti-White Democratic organizations headed by the Bishop. They even established, to some extent, the ins and outs of his bank accounts.

The Bishop continued to greet Jeff in friendly fashion, and voiced the hope freely that he himself would be well enough to attend the impending gathering of the Wesleyan College of Bishops. Two weeks before this meeting of the thirteen bishops of the Wesleyan Church, South, word of a new attack on Sterling arrived.

A letter to the Bishop from a Wilmington preacher friendly to Sterling set forth the facts.

Four travelling elders of the Wesleyan Church had assembled all the available records of the stock gambling, and the personal and political charges against the Bishop, and intended to present them to the College of Bishops.

The travelling elders were Pepper, Dean, Curtin, and were headed by one Younghusband, of Wilmington, Delaware.

This procedure necessitated that the charges be examined before the presiding Bishop—Bingham of Tennessee—and the remaining twelve as a special committee.

The meeting of the episcopal college was to take place in Montgomery, Alabama.

On receipt of the letter the Bishop allowed himself a chuckle.

Fortunately his health improved, so that four days before the opening of the meeting, he was preparing for the journey. He did not plan to take Mrs. Sterling with him.

That same day Jeff received a wire from Slater, General Manager of the Sloat papers.

"CAN NOW FULFILL PROMISE TO YOU STOP PLEASE TAKE OVER DESK IN OUR WASHINGTON BUREAU STOP FIRST ASSIGNMENT MONTGOMERY ALABAMA COVER TRIAL OF BISHOP STERLING STOP DISCUSS SALARY WITH SALTON NOW IN WASHINGTON STOP ADVISE OF ACCEPTANCE SLATER"

Jeff went to the Colorado Building, arranged the terms of his salary with Victor Salton whom he found there, now more friendly than before. On the way out he stopped in to tell Voorhees.

"I'm a Sloat man now."

"Good boy!" The dapper correspondent pumped his arm.

From there Jeff went to the Wesleyan Building and gave notice of immediate departure. Craig, official secretary to Sterling, was not displeased. Then Jeff went to Suite 50, Tasker Building. He found Mrs. Sterling helping the Bishop to pack papers in a briefcase.

Jeff said, "I'm just in time to say good-bye."

"Yes. I'll be back within a week, I believe. When I get this off my mind, I think we'll go to work—"

Jeff stood up very straight. "I've come up to resign, Doctor."

Sterling stopped what he was doing and looked at Jeff. "Resign? Why, I can't spare you now, Jeff."

"I'm right sorry about that. I just gave my resignation to Craig. He was glad."

Sterling sat down and looked at Jeff. "What are you going to do?"

Jeff told him. "I'm going back to a paper."

"Is that so? What paper?"

"Detroit *Reporter*."

Sterling's eyebrows came together. "That belongs to Sloat, doesn't it?"

"That's right."

"Hmmm! They offer you the job?"

"In a manner of speaking."

Sterling stood up again. "I'd rather you didn't do that."

Jeff stood back on his heels. "It's best for me."

"Walking out from behind me, eh?" Sterling grew suddenly nasty. "What are you going to do for them?"

"My first job is to cover your trial at Montgomery."

"For Sloat, eh?" Sterling's face seemed to bloat. His lips worked with coming rage. "You're double-crossing me! I won't stand for it. Why, you dirty little—"

"Let's not go into that." Jeff felt the hair at the back of his head prickle.

"We'll go into it. I took you on when you were out of a job. I've paid you a good salary—I've treated you like a son—"

His voice controlled, Jeff said, "I don't see why we have to fight about it."

"Don't you?" Sterling bit his underlip, his eyes watched Jeff warily. "You're double-crossing me with Sloat—that's what?"

Jeff lost his temper. "All right then, I am. But don't forget there's something on my side, too. I did lots of dirty work for you. Plenty of it. I've been wanting to say this for a long time, and now I'm going to say it. I went down to the Smokies and had a girl stripped and beaten because you ordered it. You didn't give a damn about anybody in that deal except your lousy politics. You didn't give a damn if that girl was killed—or what the hell happened—"

Sterling said with deliberate craft, "But you did it."

Jeff kept his hands behind his back. "Sure I did. And now we're through. I don't have to feel bad about double-crossing a man who—"

"You talk like a sixteen-year-old!"

Jeff stormed, "Because I worked for you, I got mixed up in that Klan deal and a girl shooting herself—do you think she'd have done that if I hadn't gone down to Tide-water. Who had me do that?"

"But you did it!" The Bishop's lips only smiled.

Jeff was suddenly silent. He had a vague impression of Mrs. Sterling watching him with interest. The Bishop waited. Jeff turned and walked out.

Jeff vented his feelings in a speech to Dixie, who listened patiently. He marched up and down the room, waving his arms, yelling at her as he had yelled at the Bishop.

She said, "You are pretty lousy. You've double crossed him all the way."

"Double cross is double cross, but every once in a while I think of those God-damn' girls and—" his face worked.

She stood up and came to him. Her arms went around his neck. "You're not so hard-boiled."

He laughed nervously, then suddenly took her in his arms. When he looked at her again, her eye rims were red.

"What's the matter?"

She shook her head. "Nothing. You make me laugh, that's all."

George Voorhees and Jeff went down to Montgomery together, for most of the Eastern and Middle Western papers had ordered this new trial of Bishop Sterling by his own Church covered by first string men. They took quarters in the Napier Hotel, only two blocks from the old State House where Jefferson Davis took the oath as President of the Confederacy. The weather was mild and sluggish.

Bishop Sterling, they learned, had made his headquarters in the Yancey House, three blocks away. Voorhees went up there, and returned with the news that Sterling had resigned his position as chairman of the board of trustees of Graygables College. Jeff told him of

Sterling's early presidency of the institution. Both dispatched the item to their papers.

They received a setback when they found that they could not possibly be present at the episcopal meeting. All sessions were to be private. They fell back on the usual correspondent's recourse of picking up news from the outside. Their first try was an interview with Gordon Pepper, one of the four travelling elders who were preferring the charges. They found him at breakfast, for he was also staying in their hotel.

He regarded them solemnly. "Gentlemen, I am sure you realize how impossible it is for me to tell you anything. Only this I can say, that though these charges were so lightly dismissed by the general and other Conferences of our Church, Brother Younghusband does not intend to let such a thing happen again without a pretty stiff fight!"

"That's very interesting, Mr. Pepper." Voorhees looked disappointed. They left Brother Pepper to finish his breakfast.

The Bishops' College met that morning and remained nearly all day in session. At dinner that evening, Brother Pepper was still unable to say anything.

The next morning the College met again, and at twelve-ten handed down a decision that Bishop Sterling could not legally be punished for his sins. He had done nothing, in the opinion of the Bishops, to merit their censure. They commended him to prayer.

This time Brother Pepper was furious. Voorhees suggested that they go up to his room. Once there, Voorhees said:

"I hope there's something you can tell us now, Mr. Pepper."

Jeff did not talk.

Pepper protested. "There's nothing I can tell you. It would be violating the code of our Church. I'm sure—"

Voorhees pushed on. "Oh, we wouldn't want to use your name, but if we could get an idea of why the College refused to listen to your evidence—it seems most unfair, Mr. Pepper."

This got the elder. "Unfair! I'll tell you it is atrocious. Why, Bishop Sterling was not even asked any questions!"

"Is that so?"

The mouse-like Pepper nodded vigorously. "We presented our charges. They are based on well-reasoned principles, and we have the information. We accused him of speculating in stocks in a way no Bishop of our Church should permit himself. We accused him of personal behavior with women that tends to degrade him as a moral leader. We accused him of undue political activity—using his religious position to influence our members."

"What about his apparent violation of the Federal Corrupt Practices Act?"

"That is none of our concern, sir. That belongs to our Government. But the most outrageous thing of all—the Bishop was acquitted after no investigation at all. He was allowed to read a paper—it took him all yesterday afternoon, sir. Three hours or more. And do you know what it was? It was nothing but a categorical denial of everything! Amazing."

Voorhees shifted in his seat. "You mean he presented no proof of his statements, or disproof of yours?"

"That is it, precisely," Pepper said. "He merely denied.

And on that alone our arguments were coolly dismissed. That is an insult to us, sir, as travelling elders of the Wesleyan Church, South!"

Jeff spoke for the first time, "How did he deny?"

"By denying, sir. We were able to introduce an affidavit made out by this Kennedy woman and later published in the Sloat papers. He answered that by another affidavit, also from her—she is now his wife—simply denying the truth of the first. Let me tell you gentlemen that Brother Younghusband will never allow this to pass uncontested."

"This is most interesting, Mr. Pepper. We will make no reference to your name or position."

Pepper stood up. "I believe I can depend on you as to that. In my experience as a Church leader I have always found you newspapermen to be highly honorable." His face clouded again. "And here is something else—though this should not even be mentioned in whatever you write —Brother Younghusband plans to place this matter before certain lay friends—in an open letter outlining the facts of our case."

"Brother Younghusband is from Wilmington, Delaware, isn't he?" Jeff wanted to know.

Pepper nodded. "We will win yet!" He stalked out, to leave Jeff and Voorhees grinning at each other.

"Pretty hot, Brother Coates!"

"Right-o, Brother Voorhees! I'd like to see that Younghusband letter—if he ever writes it."

They sent off their stories about two hours later.

As they were walking around town just before dinner, they passed the Yancey House. Out of it, almost bumping into them, came Bishop Sterling with a briefcase in his hand. He stood still when he saw Jeff.

"Well, young man?"

"Congratulations, Bishop."

Voorhees watched with interest.

Sterling's eyes narrowed. "You've had a trip for nothing, young man. How do you like it?"

"I'm getting along."

Clara Blanton came out of the hotel and joined them. "Oh, so it's you? I always told the Bishop not to trust you!"

Jeff said with elaborate courtesy, "I'm very glad to know you don't like me."

"The impudence!"

Sterling said: "Here's another little item for you, young man. The Wesleyan Virginia Board of Public Safety has just given me its vote of confidence. I trust you will enjoy reporting that to your paper." The Bishop laughed.

21.

THE SEED Committee recessed until shortly before the opening of the next Congressional session. Early in November, many Senators and Representatives began filtering into the Capital, and resumed their lurking in the corridors of the Congressional Office Building, preparing for the coming gathering.

One of the first to return was Senator Lycurgus Seed of Arkansas, a few days in advance of the next meetings of the committee of which he was chairman. Jeff went to interview him. In the outer office he found Ben.

"How are ya, Jeff?" The brother of the Senator was sincerely cordial, and faintly subservient. "Say, I'm glad to see ya. I hear ya've come up in the world." He winked with broad solemnity.

"Somewhat. Is your brother here? I want to talk to him."

"Sure. Go right in. You know him all right, doncha? Say, I'll wait for ya and we'll have maybe a glass of beer, huh?"

"Okay!" Jeff went into the Senator's inner office and found the ironic Seed leaning his head on one hand, the elbow propped on the desk. He looked up, then knitted his brows.

"May I interrupt you, Senator?" Jeff asked. "You may remember me—I was Bishop Sterling's—er—assistant."

Seed nodded, satisfied. "You looked familiar—I ought to remember you. I always saw you when I didn't want to."

Jeff grinned. "I hope it's different now. I'm not with the Bishop any more—not for about six or eight weeks."

"Congratulations."

"Thanks. These days I'm correspondent for the Detroit *Reporter*. I want to interview you."

Seed's eyelids drooped heavily. "What about?"

"Your Committee."

Seed gave him a wearily amused glance. "Of course I can't be quoted. But I'll tell you a few things. What do you want to know?"

Jeff sat down. "I'd like to get some idea of what you think the Committee will do. Will you call the Bishop before you?"

Seed leaned back in his chair, wiped his lips with a handkerchief. "You'll excuse me, I hope. I'm not feeling at all well today. Er—will we call the Bishop? I don't know. Before we go further—bear in mind I'm giving you this information as information only, to which you're entitled as a newspaperman. You mustn't use it under my name. Better not use it at all."

"That's agreeable to me."

Seed nodded slowly. "Of course, what I say doesn't hold for the rest of the Committee. It's just what I believe will happen." He laughed. "In a way this is amusing— *you* asking me about Bishop Sterling."

"I know about Bishop Sterling—All I want to know is what you're going to do to him."

Seed laughed again. "It's funny, though. Well, of course it's no secret to you that we have to proceed carefully; there aren't many of us in the Senate can afford to offend certain groups—like the Anti-Liquor League, the Wesleyan Board, and that lot. You know they're powerful."

Jeff, surprised, said, "I never heard it admitted before, even in private."

Seed let his breath out in a loud sigh. "I suppose not. Well, when I feel this way, it doesn't seem so damned important after all." He went on after that with a strange desperate energy. "However, look at us—myself, Blair of Texas, Gough of Georgia, dozens of others—how long do you think we'd stay here if we offended that lot? That's the way it goes. It may be only my personal bitterness, but I don't believe there was ever such lobbying—such control over legislators—as there is today. Mind you, I agree with them most of the time, but that's not the point.

"I'm just telling you this to explain my attitude toward this Committee. As long as his own Church stands back of him, it's going to be very hard to rid ourselves of Bishop Sterling. Religion can't be laughed out of the picture. But I think we'll succeed in nailing him. I really do. If this were merely a case of lobbying—it would be hopeless. But it is the first time that actual crookedness has been discovered in such a man. At any rate, I never heard of it, and I don't think his Church will stand back of him in that. There are too many fine men in it."

"Crookedness? Have you proved it?"

"Apparently," Seed admitted. "We've had an expert accountant working on all Sterling's bank accounts—he's been at it all summer. Good Lord, I never saw such a mess. He had some nine or ten—perhaps more—bank accounts in his own name, in the name of this famous 'Headquarters Committee' of the Anti-White Democrats, another for the Virginia Anti-Whites. He even brought to life a bank account he had had as an executor of a woman's will some ten years ago, and put money in that. Extraordinary!" Seed's eyes inspected Jeff quizzically. "You knew all this, didn't you?"

Jeff kept his face blank. "I knew he had several bank accounts."

"Of course. But you didn't know he pumped money from one to the other to mix the records up, did you? Of course not." Seed's mouth twisted ironically.

"Of course not."

Seed went on after a pause. "The Committee will introduce all this evidence during its early meetings. We shall see how the Bishop explains that."

"He will, somehow."

"Oh, of course! But I mean with some regard for the truth."

"To sum up," Jeff said, "your Committee has learned that he mixed up his political and personal accounts in such a way that it's hard to tell whether he did it for himself or not. And that, plus the failure to report adequately some thirty thousand dollars—"

"That's it," Seed said. "That's about all I can tell you."

Jeff rose to leave. "Thanks very much. I hope you'll be feeling better."

"Thanks."

In the outer office Ben was waiting. He and Jeff left the building together and had lunch in a speakeasy.

During the dinner hour a call from the office took Jeff in great haste to the New Willard Hotel. Senator Seed had collapsed of a weak heart at seven o'clock and his condition was critical. In the lobby of the hotel Jeff found most of the other correspondents. Voorhees came in.

They greeted each other. Jeff told him, "I was talking to him just this morning."

Voorhees showed interest. "Really? Have you sent out the story?"

Jeff shook his head. "I just collected some information."

The newspapermen scattered themselves throughout the lobby, waiting for word from upstairs. A discreet canvass of them revealed that Jeff had been the last Washington correspondent to see Seed.

At eight-thirty the Senator's physicians issued their final bulletin:

"At eight-eleven P. M. Senator Lycurgus Seed died of heart failure. After his collapse earlier this evening, he did not regain consciousness, and died without experiencing any pain.

DR. LEOPOLD SCHAFFNER.
DR. GILROY M. SPLITSTONE."

The newspapermen returned to their offices and sent out the story.

After completion of his own yarn Jeff again consulted Voorhees. "I don't want to go wrong on this—I told you I got confidential dope from Seed this morning. Now he's dead—"

Voorhees nodded quickly. "It's okay to use now. You've got a hell of a good story—if he told you anything."

"He did. . . . Thanks."

Jeff followed his story of the Senator's death with another, detailing his interview with Seed, giving an outline of their talk. He referred to the coming introduction of damaging evidence against Bishop Sterling at the Senatorial Committee hearings.

The entire Sloat chain used the story next morning, giving it front page, right hand corner.

SLOAT REPORTER HAS LAST INTERVIEW WITH SEED

Staff Correspondent Saw Seed Yesterday Morning—Predicted Sterling Investigation Will Bring Startling Results

Later that day Jeff had a terse wire from Slater, commending him.

Also that day, Senate leaders announced that Senator Albert P. Ward of North Dakota, next ranking seniority member of the Seed Committee, was taking over the chairmanship. Senator Charles Blair of Texas was appointed to fill the vacancy on the Committee created by Seed's death.

A week later Senator Ward, Dry Republican of progressively liberal tendencies, called the first session. Clara L. Blanton was the first witness called.

Senator Ward swore the witness.

Ward: "Please give the reporter your full name and address."

Miss Blanton: "Before proceeding, I have a statement which I wish to have inserted in the record."

Ward: "You hand me a statement. Do you wish it inserted without being read?"

Miss Blanton: "I wish it read."

Ward: "Does the reporter have your name and address?"

Miss Blanton: "No."

Ward: "Please give it to him."

Miss Blanton: "I think the statement should be read."

Ward: "We will have to know whose statement it is."

Miss Blanton: "My name is on it."

Ward: "What name is that?"

(No reply.)

Cullop: "I think the Committee will have to know who this lady is."

Miss Blanton: "I'll tell you. Clara L. Blanton."

Ward: "What is the address?"

Miss Blanton: "Richmond, Virginia."

Ward: "Shall I read this statement?"

Miss Blanton: "I'll read it."

Ward: "I hand her statement to Miss Blanton."

To the Chairman and Members of the Committee on Campaign Expenditures, Washington, D. C.

Gentlemen: Inasmuch as I am appearing before this Committee in response to a subpoena, and inasmuch as I have no desire to seem guilty of contempt of the United States, I feel that I must make this statement in full.

I make this statement in order to lodge a well-reasoned protest against the actions of this Committee and against the aims of the Senate Resolution under which it is sitting.

Having consulted proper authorities, and also the dictates of my own conscience in this matter, I now believe that the Federal

Corrupt Practices Act is unconstitutional, inasmuch as it infringes on States' Rights and the liberty and freedom guaranteed American citizens by the instrument which gives this Government its being: namely, the Constitution.

Further, the Federal Corrupt Practices Act, even if constitutional, does not apply to activities within the boundaries of one State, as were the activities of the Virginia Anti-White Democrats. It is a matter of record that I was identified with this State organization.

Further, I must say without fear of successful contradiction, that .no violation of any statute on the books of the Federal or State Governments has been deliberately violated by me.

Further, and therefore, this Committee has no right to intervene in what must be a matter of State, not Federal, investigation.

I thus believe that this Committee has no jurisdiction and any investigation of me by it is an infringement of my constitutional rights.

Therefore, I cannot bring myself to furnish this Committee with any testimony whatever.

CLARA L. BLANTON"

Ward: "The statement is contained in your letter that you were connected with the Virginia Anti-White Democrats, which clearly implies your connection with the 'Headquarters Committee'."

Miss Blanton: "I cannot testify."

Ward: "I assume you have sought legal advice, and are therefore aware of the consequences of defying this Committee?"

Miss Blanton: "That is so."

Ward: "There are on record several reports of contributions and expenditures during the recent Presidential campaign by the Anti-White Democratic organization. Did you make and file these reports?"

Miss Blanton: "I cannot testify."

Ward: "Will you tell us how the money was spent by your organizations? Only in Virginia, or all over the South?"

Miss Blanton: "I cannot testify."

Ward: "You persist in your refusal to answer the questions of this Committee?"

Miss Blanton: "I believe I am justified in so doing."

Miss Blanton was dismissed.

The next important witness was the accountant referred to by Seed in his last interview with Jeff.

Senator Ward swore the witness.

Ward: "Please give your name to the reporter. And profession."

Burton: "Emanuel Burton, accountant."

Ward: "Your residence?"

Burton: "Washington, D. C."

Ward: "I believe it will be best for you to proceed in your own way, Mr. Burton, in outlining the results of your investigation."

Burton: "I first hand to the chairman for insertion in the record a list of contributions to the political organizations headed by Bishop Thomas Henderson Sterling by Mr. Henry L. Johnsbury of New York City and Newark, New Jersey."

Ward: "Do you find that all these contributions are so reported by the Virginia Anti-White Democrats or the so-called 'Headquarters Committee?'"

Burton: "I find that they have not all been so reported."

Ward: "In a general way, Mr. Burton, have you been able to ascertain whether there was any financial distinction between the two organizations I just mentioned?"

Burton: "I have been unable to find any financial distinction in bank accounts of that kind. I have, however, found distinctions of an entirely different sort."

Ward: "And what are they, Mr. Burton?"

Burton: "I hand to the chairman, for insertion in the record, a chart of the bank accounts kept from March of the Presidential year until the first of the following January. I wish to point out several particulars before the Committee studies it.

"Bishop Sterling has employed several different methods of endorsing and making out checks and notes. He has used the following differentiations between the various accounts: Thomas Sterling, Chairman—"

Ward: "Pardon me for interrupting. Chairman of what?"

Burton: "Presumably of the Anti-White Democratic organization."

Ward: "Proceed, please."

Burton: "Thomas Sterling, Chairman; Thomas Sterling, Anti-White Democrats; Clara L. Blanton; Thomas Sterling, executor—"

Ward: "For whom?"

Burton: "This is a curious case. Court records show that some ten years ago Bishop Sterling was appointed executor for a woman. I will later ask you to question witnesses who will show that the estate was closed over five years ago, and that most of the money retained by the Bishop as executor was paid out or otherwise disposed of. It would appear that the Bishop brought this account to life again in order to account for certain new and considerable funds in his possession."

Ward: "Thank you, Mr. Burton. The Committee will

call on you again when it has had an opportunity to study your testimony."

Under the chairmanship of Senator Ward, the Committee brought its investigation to a close some three weeks later. Burton's testimony was confirmed in every detail by officers of the eleven banks, in all, which the Bishop had used. Checks were identified, different moneys traced from one account to another, amounts followed from their deposit in the Anti-White Democrats account to one of the Bishop's personal accounts. In this way, all of Johnsbury's money was traced, including the money order to the broker Silverman for three thousand, and also the final payment by Johnsbury of thirty-nine hundred dollars. It was shown that this thirty-nine hundred dollars, to meet the Anti-Whites' deficit, was collected twice: once from Johnsbury and again by letters of solicitation to earlier small contributors.

Ex-Senator Oberwasser was found to have contributed ten thousand dollars, but this was reported. Furthermore, the ex-Senator was travelling in Europe and did not return in time to testify. At the suggestion of Senator Ward, the record was held open for the inclusion of a letter from Oberwasser, which stated his willingness to cooperate with the Committee, and pointed out he was in sympathy with its aims, had met Bishop Sterling only once, through K. Cuthbert Wint. He thanked Senator Ward for his consideration.

With these and a horde of substantiating facts, the record was closed. The report was sent to the Government Printing Office for final preparation and submission to the entire Senate.

A week later the Senate accepted the report in a *viva voce* vote, and officially turned the evidence over to the District Prosecutor with a recommendation for the indictment of Bishop Sterling for violation of the Federal Corrupt Practices Act.

This was greeted by the Bishop in a statement as follows:

"After the grossly unfair and bigoted way in which the Senate Committee has conducted its hearings, and has recklessly violated the constitutional rights of certain American citizens, I am not surprised at its conclusions. It has been more interested in blackening my reputation than in a fair, honest and just presentation of the facts.

"The Committee has deliberately ignored certain easily available evidence, and has merely given concrete expression to the ill-will of many politicians toward the moral forces of this country.

"It has never failed to distort facts, to withhold vital information, or to give vent to its primitive prejudices. I fully expect to be indicted by the Grand Jury of the District of Columbia. The District Prosecutor and two of his assistants are Roman Catholics, and will not hesitate to strike back at the forces in this country which brought about the ignominious defeat of their Presidential candidate and co-religionist.

"Nothing done by irresponsible and bigoted officials will cause me the least astonishment."

When, the next morning, Jeff was working desultorily in his office, Mr. Herron was announced. Jeff looked at the secretary.

"Tom Herron? Big guy, beefy?"

"Yes. He said he was very anxious to see you."

Jeff lit a cigarette. "Show him in."

Herron strode in ten seconds later. He was extravagantly friendly. He did not, however, put out his hand. "How are you, Coates? I'm right glad to find you in. I suppose you saw I got my old seat back."

"Yeah." Jeff remembered very well the high spots, so far as his interests were concerned, of the country-wide elections the preceding month. Senator Randolph Taitt triumphantly returned in Virginia, carrying along with him such small fry as Tom Herron of Tidewater. Bradford Day, ex-ambassador to Cuba, was the victor in New Jersey, after having swamped Oberwasser for the Republican nomination in the primaries. Tibbetts had been routed in North Carolina by a regular Democrat, a blunt chastisement for the old Senator's Party treason as a Mollycrat two years before. Florida and Texas, too, were back in the fold. The last vestiges of Bishop Sterling's political dictatorship in the Deep South were gone, perhaps forever.

Herron sat down, lit a cigar, and continued booming in his loud voice.

"I'm not going to make a secret of why I'm here, in spite of what's happened. I came here to make peace with you."

"What do you care about peace with me? I don't."

Herron smiled broadly. "Why, hell, you're on a big paper now, and—you know, I've been thinking it over, and I reckon the score between us is about even."

"Outside of the girl that shot herself, I reckon you're right."

Herron's heavy face clouded, then brightened quickly.

"Anyway, I think that the time has come for us to bury the hatchet. You can do a lot for me—" He laughed with exaggerated cordiality. "Boy, I'd hate to keep you as an enemy!"

"I don't see why we have to worry about each other at all."

Herron blew a great cloud of cigar smoke toward the ceiling. Then he got up.

"Mind if I shut the door?"

Jeff shifted in his chair. The Tidewater man closed the door into the outer office. Then he sat down and, lowering his voice, continued.

"My opinion is we can do a lot for each other, and that's why I want to make peace. Think I am satisfied to be a Virginia Congressman all my life?"

Jeff said nothing.

"I want to be a Senator from Virginia—and I can. When old Beauchamp or Taitt dies—hell, they can't live forever!—old Vernon and I—get my idea?"

Jeff merely compressed his lips.

"After that—why shouldn't I have an ambassadorship? Why not, eh? Why not?" Herron's face grew crafty. "I've got the temperament, and with the right backing—Gerard was made ambassador to Germany just because the Hearst papers backed him for the job. Now, you're in with Sloat—"

"What do I care what you want to do?"

Herron smiled cagily. "Maybe there's something I can do for you."

Jeff scratched himself behind one ear. "There isn't anything you can do for me."

Herron considered him carefully. "Suppose I made you the best-informed newspaperman in Washington?"

Jeff looked at him.

"I'll make a deal with you. You give me a boost now and then, and in return I'll give you all the dope you want on every House Committee I'm on—or anything else I get. How's that?"

Jeff said, "You're on the short end in this deal—if I say so."

Herron frowned. "Well, I always figured you were a smart feller—reasonable. Say, I'll go a step further. I'll stay away from Veryl Vernon."

Jeff told him, "Don't make me laugh! That doesn't interest me right now. Look here—you give me all the information I want—I'll use it without getting you in any trouble. In return, I'll help you once in a while."

Herron stood up, broadly smiling again. This time he put out his hand. "That's fine, Jeff, old boy. That's a bargain. It'll do us both a lot of good."

"I hope."

22.

THE VERDICT OF THE JURY

AFTER RECEIVING the evidence from the Senate, the Grand Jury soon returned an indictment of Bishop Sterling, and the trial began almost at once. For over three weeks it dragged along, going over again, in the stricter form demanded by a court of law, all that had been studied by the Seed-Ward Committee in its many sessions. Jeff spent at least an hour in court every day, turning in his report of the trial systematically.

After three weeks the day for summing up by the prosecution and defense arrived; then the case would go to the jury. Jeff was up early that morning. Dixie had prepared breakfast for him. He came to the table and beside his plate was a letter with the Commonwealth of Virginia seal on the envelope. He tore it open, read it, then said:

"Listen to this, honey:

" 'My dear Mr. Coates,

"This is to advise you that you have been appointed a Colonel on my staff, effective as of January first.

"Please let me know the date of your next visit to Richmond, so that the short ceremony may be arranged.

"Trusting that you will consider me your friend as always,

"I remain,

> Shirley D. Vernon,
> Governor, Commonwealth of Virginia.' "

"Now you'll have to be nice to me."

Dixie asked, "What does that mean?"

Jeff tossed the letter on the table. "That is what you get when you help a feller to be Governor. It means I'll have to buy a uniform to keep in the closet. Honorary Colonel. Colonel Coates. Not bad, huh?"

Dixie sipped her coffee. "I'm glad for you, Jeff."

"Oh, that don't mean a damn' thing. Except I'm buddies with Governor Vernon. The old hound. He was ready to kill me one night—and now this. Great guy!"

Dixie picked up the letter and read it carefully. "I—I really think it's fine, Jeff. I mean—you'll be somebody."

He finished his poached eggs and picked up his coffee. "What's the matter with you? That's a lot of hooey. I'll go down to Richmond, go through the ceremony, or whatever, and come back here. That's all there is to it."

"I don't know. You're still engaged to his daughter, aren't you?" She didn't look at him.

"How do I know? Was once, but what with this and what with that—"

"Jeff! You've got to get some sense sooner or later. It had better be sooner." She picked up her coffee cup again, then put it down without drinking, and twined her hands together in her lap.

"Do you have to uplift me at breakfast? Gimme a break!"

She looked straight at him, tossing her bobbed hair back from her forehead. "I have to say this, Jeff. You've got a good start—you ought to think a little about it."

He lit a cigarette, tilted his chair back on its hind legs, and surveyed her. After several seconds, he asked, "What's got into you?"

She didn't answer that, but began talking rapidly: "I saw Ben Seed last night. He called and I went over there while you were at the office late. He's inheriting his brother's money. A hundred and twenty-two thousand dollars —cash. Cash, Jeff. He wants me to marry him."

"Where'd Seed get all that money?"

Dixie shrugged. "Investments, or land he owned in Arkansas. That was it, he sold some farm land he had. Ben's getting it all. He wants me to marry him."

"That's what's got you this way? Want to?" He watched her, the cigarette hanging from his lips.

She straightened up, her nostrils distended. "That's not the point. I don't care for anyone but you, Jeff. You know that."

He shook his head, as if to clear it. "What's this all about?"

She looked down at her hands in her lap, took a deep breath. "I—I was glad at first—the colonelcy—not only for you—for *us*. But now I'm glad just for—you. That's what. Oh, I know that doesn't mean anything in itself— Colonel on his staff—but it does mean that you're going to be an important man—you can be, Jeff—I've always told you, and you laughed."

"I'd like to be a big shot, but hell, that's a long way—"

She looked up at him again; her eyes, black-irised, glittered as he had never seen them before. Her lips seemed drawn tight. "You have to plan, Jeff—that's what I want you to do—make yourself big—you can't hang on the outskirts all your life—"

"I've got a good job—what is all this, anyhow?" He let the chair down on the floor again with a bang, and leaned both elbows on the table. "Come on, out with it? Is this a build-up so you can go and marry Ben Seed?"

She flared up. "That's rotten, Jeff. If I *wanted* to do that, I'd tell you right out. I just told you *he* wanted me to. But—but—" She moved her hands helplessly. "Oh, I don't know—"

"What is it, honey?" He tried to take her hands, but she wouldn't surrender them. "We've been pretty good friends, baby. What's the matter? Think we ought to get married, or something?"

She stared at him very hard, searchingly. "I think you ought to go down to Richmond and marry that girl—the Governor's daughter."

He sat up, letting the air out of his lungs suddenly. "Oh, that's it? Why?"

"I told you why, can't you get it in your head? You can't expect to get anywhere—living—this way."

"We'll get married then." He put out his cigarette.

She passed a hand over her eyes. "I—I love you, Jeff. I do. I have from the start." She got up unexpectedly, walked away from the table, then turned to face him. "Maybe I'm getting soft or something, but this is the way I've got it figured out. This is the way it'll be, too. You're going down to marry that girl. That'll make you somebody. The paper will pay some real attention to you. Don't you see, Jeff? You've got a start—if you play it smart you can be one of the biggest—"

He said harshly, "I don't see why I have to marry that girl, I—you and I get on pretty well."

She gestured impatiently. Her voice came raw and strained from her throat. "You fool—what good will it do you to marry me? I've got no reputation—you couldn't get away with taking me around—when you get on and get invited out a lot. They all know me in Washington—we're living together—" Her voice caught, she stopped.

"We could get married," he said.

"Ben Seed has money—that's what I want. He wants to go to Arkansas and live." She laughed slowly, then faster—louder. Jeff jumped from his chair, caught her by the shoulders.

"Cut it out!"

She looked up at him, her eyes tear-filled. "Jeff, will you do that? Don't make me argue." She put her arms around him, held him desperately tight.

He stared over her head out of the window. "I think you're crazy," he said.

Her voice came through sobs. "I'm not, Jeff. You don't really love me—you never have—with her—she can help you—oh—I love you, Jeff!"

"Dixie, baby!" He stroked her head, still staring out of the window. "Why don't you stay in Washington—you and I could still—"

She straightened up and stood away from him. "No. You and I are through. I'll be the wife of the Senator's brother. Maybe they'll appoint him to fill his brother's place—I'll be back. No, that won't happen." Her face was unashamedly tear-stained.

He looked at her intently: "I don't see why I have to

throw over what I want—I want you to stay here—right here—I'll—"

For a second her face lit up, flickeringly, then the dull pain returned. "You know I'm the one that's right. Now go out."

He started. "What time is it?" He consulted his wristwatch, jumped for his hat and coat. "Listen, we'll talk this over tonight. Don't do anyth—"

She watched him, miserably. "Jeff! . . ."

He turned in the doorway. "Wait till I get back, will you?"

"Don't go, Jeff!" Her arms were stretched out toward him.

He hesitated. "Blast it!" He started toward her, then turned back to go out. "Wait here for me! Please! I'm late!"

The door slammed behind him.

When he arrived in the District Court and took his place in the space reserved for reporters, Voorhees yawned at him.

The District Prosecutor was just finishing his summing up to the jury: "—and I call upon you, on the basis of the evidence presented to the Court, to find the defendant guilty as charged!"

Sweating, mopping himself with a handkerchief, the attorney sat down. The Court recessed for lunch. The reporters went out together. In a chop house across the street from the court, six of them found a corner table.

"Did you see the old boy's face! Can't scare him," one of them said.

"He's a tough bird. No?" Voorhees said, turning to Jeff.

"Tough is right."

"You sick or something? You look absent-minded."

Jeff shook his head; they all ordered.

The man next to Jeff said, "Listen, I don't care how guilty he is, they'll never convict him."

"What do you mean?" asked a tall, thin man. "He's guilty as all hell."

Jeff stopped listening, but ate in silence. When they had finished, he left them outside the restaurant and went into the telegraph office next door. There he sent two wires:

One to Governor Vernon of Virginia said:

"THANKS AND APPRECIATION FOR HONOR BESTOWED ON ME STOP WILL BE IN RICHMOND THIS FRIDAY."

Another, to Veryl Vernon, said:

"KEEP YOUR WEEK-END FREE AM COMING DOWN FOR VISIT LOVE."

He went into Court again, took his place at the press table. Counsel for the defense began his summing up. The points made were much the same as those made by the Bishop during his defiance of the Senate Committee:

That the evidence presented by the prosecution ignored several outstanding facts, including the religious nature of the work;

That religious hatred of Roman Catholics against Wesleyans had prompted the inquisitorial methods pursued by the Senate Committee;

That the Federal Corrupt Practices Act did not apply in the case of the Bishop and the Virginia Anti-Whites;

That the funds ascribed by the prosecution to political work were in reality religious funds;

That the prosecution had based its case largely on hearsay evidence, and had been influenced by the desires of envious Wesleyan preachers to expel the Bishop from his position;

That the constitutional rights of the Bishop had been violated;

And a great many legal points and roundabout explanations of the diverted funds.

He drew near his close: "—clearly the duty of this jury of free, unprejudiced and intelligent American jurors is to agree with public opinion in finding this defendant not guilty of the absurd offense with which he is charged. To believe that this man—of forty years' religious and church background—could have stooped to such folly is unthinkable." He had his mouth open for the next sentence, when Bishop Sterling got to his feet.

He said: "Your Honor, I ask permission to finish the summing up begun by my attorney."

The defense lawyer looked around in astonishment; the Judge gravely inclined his head.

Sterling, his face gray and lean, but his voice full of its characteristic dominating quality, began to talk. Jeff heard the familiar guttural rasp.

"Your Honor, gentlemen of the jury. I have heard the summing up by the Prosecuting Attorney. He has done as well as he is able. I have heard also the eloquent defense by my own counsel. But I feel impelled to speak a few words in my own defense.

"I have been pilloried in the stocks of religious prejudice!" His eyes glittered; the jury was leaning forward in its seats. "I led a movement to defeat the political aspirations of a servant of the Pope, and now I am martyred by their envy and malice. That is all. For forty years I have been the shepherd of my flock, with the support of my Church. The moral forces of this country, outraged that a man representing the evil which we have fought for years should have aspired to lead the American people, punished him properly. I am proud that I had a part in that punishment, and if, through my own eagerness, I transgressed somewhat on the laws of my own Church, that is between me and my conscience. From God in his Heaven above I shall beg forgiveness for that sin, if sin it be, but that malicious persons, seeking to bow my head under an attack of bigotry and prejudice, should bring about my downfall is more than any American citizen could bear!

"Find me guilty of all the technical offenses you will— find me guilty of overzeal—of the crusading spirit of a Christian man—but do not find me guilty because I dared to oppose the forces of sin, of debauchery, of medieval intolerance!"

He sat down, breathing hard. Several persons in the audience applauded; others hissed. The gavel rapped.

The Court said: "Gentlemen of the jury, you have heard the evidence. I charge you to consider the evidence as presented and as established, and I must warn you to disregard any statements of opinion which cannot be allowed to have true bearing on the matter in hand. You must see whether the defendant is guilty of the offense with which he is charged within the bounds of the evidence presented. . . ."

The Court gave another twenty minutes to a brief exposition of the law involved, and its implications. He outlined what could and what could not be considered admissible evidence and ended by requesting the jury to go to its deliberations. With suitable ceremony the jury filed out.

The reporters retired in a body to the press room, where tables, packs of cards, telephones and cuspidors had been provided for their use.

The defendant was taken in the custody of court attendants to a separate room.

Four of the reporters began a bridge game. Others lounged, smoked, spat, or merely sat.

The tall, thin man said, "We're likely to be here for days."

Another said, "Forget it. How much will you bet they never convict him?"

"Five to one," said a man in the corner.

"Listen," urged the tall, thin man, "remember the case of the Secretary of the Interior, or assistant—"

"Denton."

"Yeah, Denton. Know what happened? His lawyers let a bank cashier get on the jury—didn't challenge him, or they'd used up their challenges—I don't know. Anyway, this bird knew enough about banks and money and so on to know that no guy carries a lot of money in a suitcase unless he's up to something. But the other eleven eggs didn't know. He held out for guilty, and by God, he talked everyone over to him. If it hadn't been for that bird, Denton would be free today instead of in Leavenworth."

Voorhees asked: "What's that got to do with—"

The tall, thin man explained patiently. "Look, all there has to be on that dumb jury downstairs is one guy who thinks the way the Bishop does—that Catholics are a bunch of bums, and all that hooey. If he has guts enough to hold out, he can talk the other guys over. That's what they'll fight about—not whether he made off with political contributions and violated the Federal Corrupt Practices Act or not."

The man in the corner scoffed. "Say, he's guilty as hell, but my dough is on you. He musta pinched about fifty grand."

Jeff said, "He lost some in the bucket shop deal."

The tall, thin man: "Yah, who cares? I think he's a swell guy, I admire him."

Voorhees asked, "What for?"

"He's a hell-raiser, isn't he? Gay with the gals, and still got plenty of steam. Look at the way he stood up and stormed. Boy, you have to have something—"

Voorhees laughed. "Sure, he's all right. Besides, he's old."

The man in the corner grinned. "Say, old Taitt'll be sore as a pup. That gives me an idea—" He jumped to a phone; the others heard him call the Senate Office Building, to see if Senator Taitt were available for an interview later on. "He's out some place."

Jeff said, "Anyway, Sterling is through. He's sick, and—"

The tall, thin man said, "Don't kid yourself, feller. There's plenty doughheads'll still vote the way he says. He's still on all these Boards of Public Safety—"

Jeff: "The last elections gave him a body-punch polit-ically. But maybe you're right."

"Sure I'm right. I hope he gets off. He's got guts."

The man in the corner wanted to know: "Who spilled all this stuff on him in the first place?"

Silence. Voorhees said casually, "He's got some sleuth-ing enemies in his Church. They dug up the stuff. Didn't you ever see the pamphlet a preacher named Younghus-band wrote—gives plenty of dirt about Sterling. Know Congressman Wallace very well?"

"Certainly."

"Well, he'll give you a copy of the pamphlet any time —for your own information."

Conversation subsided; men read or dozed in their chairs. Others telephoned or chatted. The bridge game went on. Two hours passed. A buzzer called them back into the court room; the jury had reached a decision. Somebody said:

"Hey, that's pretty quick."

A fat correspondent from Milwaukee, who had ex-pressed no opinion before, said:

"On the evidence, they *must* have given him thumbs down."

"I'll bet—well—" the tall, thin man began, and let his voice trail off.

It took some ten minutes for all the necessary individ-uals to get to their places. Bishop Sterling walked slowly to his seat at the table reserved for the defense. The at-torneys on both sides took their positions; all stood up when the Judge came from his chambers. Jeff found the Bishop looking at him. The gray eyes narrowed, the hands clenched the table.

At a nod from the Judge, the door of the jury room was opened and the twelve men filed in, the foreman a few steps in advance of the rest.

The Court: "Gentlemen of the jury, have you reached a verdict?"

Foreman: "We have, Your Honor."

The Court: "What is the verdict?"

Foreman: "Your Honor, we find the defendant not guilty as charged."